MASSACRE
MOUNTAIN

D0020143

P9- BWD- 089

MASSACRE MOUNTAIN

WILLIAM W. JOHNSTONE

with J. A. Johnstone

PINNACLE BOOKS
Kensington Publishing Corp.

www.kensingtonbooks.com

PINNACLE BOOKS are published by

Kensington Publishing Corp.
119 West 40th Street
New York, NY 10018

Copyright © 2011 William W. Johnstone

All rights reserved. No part of this book may be reproduced in any form or by any means without the prior written consent of the publisher, excepting brief quotes used in reviews.

PUBLISHER'S NOTE
Following the death of William W. Johnstone, the Johnstone family is working with a carefully selected writer to organize and complete Mr. Johnstone's outlines and many unfinished manuscripts to create additional novels in all of his series like The Last Gunfighter, Mountain Man, and Eagles, among others. This novel was inspired by Mr. Johnstone's superb storytelling.

If you purchased this book without a cover, you should be aware that this book is stolen property. It was reported as "unsold and destroyed" to the publisher, and neither the author nor the publisher has received any payment for this "stripped book."

All Kensington titles, imprints, and distributed lines are available at special quantity discounts for bulk purchases for sales promotions, premiums, fund-raising, educational, or institutional use. Special book excerpts or customized printings can also be created to fit specific needs. For details, write or phone the office of the Kensington special sales manager: Kensington Publishing Corp., 119 West 40th Street, New York, NY 10018, attn: Special Sales Department; phone 1-800-221-2647.

PINNACLE BOOKS and the Pinnacle logo are Reg. U.S. Pat. & TM Off. The WWJ steer head logo is a trademark of Kensington Publishing Corp.

ISBN-13: 978-0-7860-2346-2
ISBN-10: 0-7860-2346-5

First printing: October 2011

10 9 8 7 6 5 4 3 2 1

Printed in the United States of America

CHAPTER ONE

They were fixing to fire me. That's what this was all about. There was no escaping it, neither. I'd messed up, and pretty quick now the job of sheriff in the county seat of Doubtful, in Puma County, Wyoming, would go to someone else.

All them politicos in their starchy shirts had collected at the log courthouse to have at me. Even my old friend George Waller, mayor of Doubtful, was in there sharpening his hunting knife.

Well, I'd get it over with, saddle up Critter, and go somewhere else and do something else. I ain't one to cry in my beer.

I walked into that courtroom, which was thick with the blue smoke of cheroots. A man could hardly be a politico in Wyoming without puffing away on five-cent cigars the color of a dog turd.

"Ah, there you are, Pickens," said Reggie Thimble, who was the big honcho in these parts. "Have a seat and we'll land on you directly."

He and Waller and Ziggy Camp were all parked in oak swivel chairs behind a big table. They'd brought in Lawyer Stokes, who was whetting his blades before he started carving on me. They were gonna make me stand. That's how it worked. They would sit and I would stand until my feet howled.

"All right, Sheriff, you just tell it in your own words," Lawyer Stokes said, a cheerful if slightly wolfish grin on his pasty face. I guessed he was going to be the prosecutor in this here inquisition.

"I got held up," I said.

"You, Sheriff Pickens, got held up?" asked Stokes, sounding like a funeral oration. "How could this be?"

"Yep. I was doing my rounds, like usual, and the night was plenty dark, no moon anywhere in sight. I peered into store windows looking for crooks, and I rattled doors making sure the places were locked up good and tight, and I checked out the saloons, them two that were still lamplit that late, and checked out the drunks. It was just what I always do. And then it happened."

Lawyer Stokes squinted ominously. "Would you care to elaborate?"

"Feller jumped out from between Barney's Beanery and Maxwell's Funeral Parlor, and waved a six-gun at me. He was wearing a black bandana and yelled at me to stop right there. I glanced around, looking for an accomplice, but this here bandit was alone, and he had a big old iron aimed at my heart. . . .

"So I stopped. 'Your money or your life,' he says. And that sure got me to thinking some.

"I couldn't quite make up my mind. My money or my life? So I thought to humor the skunk for a little, and I said, 'You know, my pa always told me, Cotton, you ain't worth two cents. So I figure that's what I'm worth. You figure it'd be fine with you if I gave you two cents?'

"That bandit got plumb mad at me. 'Your money right now, toss it down right there in the dirt in front of me, or your life.'

"Well, I figured it was a fifty-fifty proposition. My life's worth about what I had in my purse, which was about a dollar and six bits. So I said to him, 'Your choice.'

"That only made him madder. He said he'd blow my brains out. I said I didn't have any, least that's what my ma was always telling me."

"And then what happened, Sheriff?" Lawyer Stokes asked me, kind of oily.

"I told that feller, come and get it, or shoot me, whichever came first."

"And what did he do?"

"He shot my hat off. So I decided right smartly I'd give him the dollar and six bits, even though it meant going without breakfast for a while at two bits for pancakes, so I dug into my britches, found my bull-balls purse, and tossed it at him, real hard. It just bounced off his chest.

"Then he made me pull my pockets out, so I done it, and he got my Barlow knife.

"He says, 'Take off your boots,' so I done that, too.

"'Your feet stink,' he said, and I nodded. Wasn't no arguing with him there.

"He said for me to turn around and start walking away, which I did, and after a bit I looked behind me and he was gone. I'd been robbed."

There was a real quiet in that room. They were all blotting up what I'd said. It came down to this: Doubtful, Wyoming, had itself a sheriff who'd allowed himself to be robbed right on the main street of town.

"And do you know who he was?"

"Nobody I ever seen before. Sort of blocky-looking."

"You're the sheriff and you don't know every lowlife in Doubtful?"

"Not this one."

"And he got away?"

"I sure didn't lasso him."

"And now word is out that the sheriff of Doubtful is, will we say, a pushover for the criminal element? That there's no good man keeping Doubtful safe? That the good citizens of Doubtful are in peril? That there's no one defending the worthy housewife in her kitchen, or the blacksmith at his forge, or the lawyer in his chambers?"

"Well, if you were to give me a raise, I'd be worth more," I said. "Make her forty-five a month and you'd fool my pa and my ma."

Lawyer Stokes peered at me sadly. Then he turned to the others. "See how the man answers my questions. See where his deprived brain has led him. We are naked here in Doubtful."

Then it was Reggie Thimble's turn. "How come you didn't just draw iron and blast him? You chicken or something?"

"Well, I don't guess it'd get much done, not with a bullet through my gizzard while I'm clearing leather."

"We hired you for your speed with a shooting iron, Cotton Pickens, and we expect you to make use of your speed."

"Well, you got a point there, Mr. Supervisor, but I just didn't see that as anything that'd do anything but get me dead."

"You could have been a hero, Pickens. You could've sent a varmint straight to hell, even as you croaked. We'd have put up a statue of you in front of the courthouse."

"Well, you got a point there," I said.

Then it was Ziggy Camp's turn. "How come you didn't know this yahoo?" he asked.

"It was pretty dark," I said.

"You're supposed to know every lowlife in Doubtful."

"Well, I do, but this feller, he come out of the night."

"You's supposed to know them all by their voice. You mean to tell me you didn't even recognize his voice?"

"Can't say as I ever heard it before."

"What kind of voice was it? High and squeaky? Low and mean? What if it was a woman robbing you?"

"I don't rightly remember, Supervisor."

"Well, what kind of sheriff are you, anyway? How tall was this crook?"

"Neither high nor low, sir."

"What kind of answer's that, Pickens?"

"There wasn't much unusual about him, that's all I can say. Just an ordinary bandit."

Camp glanced at Thimble and sighed.

Then my friend the mayor, George Waller, came up to bat. He sort of smiled, to let me know that we'd still be friends after they fired me. "So what have you done about it, Cotton?"

He was using my first name, deliberately, too. He knew how I felt about that name that got hung on me by my ma and pa.

"I told every bartender in town to let me know if someone was on a drinking spree, spending like hell don't have it. I told my friend Studs, over at the poker palace, to snitch on anyone spending big-time."

"One dollar and six bits is big-time?"

"Is for me," I said. "That's why I want a raise."

"You want a raise? Now?"

"It's not every sheriff gets robbed and lives to tell about it."

They stared at me like I was a leper. I don't know what a leper is but I heard it's real bad and fingers and toes melt off. I still have all of mine, last I counted, but I sometimes have trouble getting past eight or seven, but they were all there last I took my boots off.

Lawyer Stokes intervened, flashing his fish-oil smile. "Well, gentlemen, you've heard the case in the sheriff's own colorful words. Right 'out of the mouth of babes,' as the saying goes. So we know where we stand. Doubtful, Wyoming, lies naked to the world. Our young maidens live in peril of being ravished. Our sturdy storekeeps shake with terror that they will be robbed. Our yeomen fear being assailed in the night. Our wives and children are helpless against the malign forces of evil. Unless the town is swiftly protected by a competent man who knows how to ferret out crime and bring the world's meanest dregs to justice, then we are all at grave risk. I, for one, shall not sleep soundly in my humble bed as long as I know that there is nothing betwixt and between me and the thugs who prowl our streets as soon as the sun has set. Where will it stop? Who will stop the crime wave? Is our bank next? Will our citizens lie dead in the streets?"

He paused suddenly, turned toward me, and jabbed an ancient, arthritic finger into my chest. "Fire him," he said.

Then he quietly returned to his swivel chair, and swiveled clear around until he, too, was facing me, like the rest.

"You can take Doubtful and stuff it," I said, fixing to walk out.

"Whoa up, Cotton," Waller said. "We ain't fired you yet."

"Well, I'm quitting!" I yelled.

"We got no replacement yet," Waller said. "So we can't accept your resignation."

"What do you mean by that?"

"You can't quit because we don't accept it."

Now that was mighty strange logic in my book, but who am I to say? My ma always said I was a little slow.

"You got a couple of deputies over there, Burtell and De Graff, but they ain't sheriff material. They're better at taking orders than giving them. If anything, they're even less smart than you. They don't have your native cunning. You were smart enough not to argue with that stickup man, except a little, but if it was De Graff, he'd be plumb dead."

"Oh, George, you give Cotton Pickens too much credit," Reggie Thimble said. "I think we should just let Pickens here saddle up and find someone else."

"Like who?"

"Like Belle," Thimble said.

"Boardinghouse Belle?" Waller was aghast.

"Purse snatchers would be too busy looking at Belle's unforgettable chest to see her level her little revolver," Thimble continued. "She's got two aces and four kings."

There wasn't much anyone was saying about then. Me, I thought Belle might be a good sheriff, but there would be the little matter of persuading her to take the job. She had all she could manage running the boardinghouse for a dozen or so of us unattached males. She made good money, a lot more than she would hanging six-guns on her lush hips and patrolling Doubtful.

"Well, we could ask her," Ziggy Camp said.

Again, Lawyer Stokes intervencd. "We're not going to hire that pneumatic female for our sheriff," he said.

"Then all we got is Pickens here, at least for now."

"We've been through this before," Supervisor Thimble said. "We had sheriffs by the cartload and they all croaked. Doubtful was on the ropes until we got Pickens here. He may not be the smartest man in town, but he's kept the lid on for some while. Fire him, and next thing you know, the Democrats will be taking over again."

I got to remembering that all them county people were anything but Democrats.

"I think I know where to go on this," said Lawyer Stokes. "It's time for us to have a little talk with Cyrus Ralston."

"Ah, there's a thought."

"Cyrus Ralston is a man of some sophistication. He'll know where to go to find a new sheriff."

"Why yes, my impression is that he's well connected throughout the West, with ties reaching into the great cities of the East as well."

"Ralston will give us the skinny," Waller said.

Lawyer Stokes smiled. "We're agreed then?" He turned to me. "We're going to have Ralston find us a new man, Pickens. Until then, you're still sheriff. After that, you won't be."

"Well, I quit."

"Sorry, Pickens, that's quite impossible. We don't accept it."

I sure couldn't figure that one out. If I quit, I quit, but they was saying I didn't and can't.

Cyrus Ralston, the man in black pinstriped suits and homburg hats who was finishing up the new three-hundred-seat opera house on the main drag of Doubtful, would decide my fate. Durned if I could figure that out.

"Ralston will know how to deal with this crime wave," Lawyer Stokes said.

CHAPTER TWO

So there I was, still sheriff until they could get another. That sure was a mess. I'd just as soon have pinned my badge on Lawyer Stokes and let him do the rounds every night, making sure Doubtful was locked up tight.

I didn't quite know how to spend my last days as sheriff, but I'd think of something. That whole business gave me a good excuse to visit the new opera house. That's what they were calling the place, but it looked like a theater to me. It had been going up pretty fast, three or four months, with a swarm of carpenters banging it together.

The front of the place was pretty fancy, with fieldstone facing the street, but the rest was just another frame structure. The stage was pretty small, but it'd do in a little town like Doubtful. They'd gotten a wine-red velvet curtain hung up, and the carpenters were bolting down a mess of seats that came in on the freight wagons. I'd never been inside a theater before, so I was taking a real gander at the whole outfit. Now, take the way the floor rose so that people sitting in the back were higher than people in front, and everyone could see real fine. That sure was a marvel.

Sure enough, there was Cyrus Ralston overseeing the whole deal, wandering around in a black pinstripe suit. I'd never seen one before, and it sort of reminded me of a barber pole.

"Ah, it's you, Sheriff," Ralston said.

"Just poking around," I said. "This place is as foreign to me as California."

"Well, glad to have you. We're close now. I've booked the first show for next week."

"Going to be an opera, is it?"

"Opera? An opera? Oh, no, not at all. It's a variety show. This is an opera house but that's a figure of speech."

"I've never seen a show, opera or other," I said. "What's the deal?"

"Lots of different shows around. Some come with music. Singers like Jenny Lind. Or Lotta Crabtree. Or dancers like Lola Montez."

"I never heard of any of them."

"Actresses, dancers, some of them quite, ah, bold."

"I'd sure come and look," I said.

"We'll have some fine entertainers coming, Sheriff. They're on the circuit."

"What's that?"

"Troupes go from one town to another, more or less prearranged by booking companies. That way they've got work ahead, and know where they're going."

"They'll start rolling in, will they?"

"I'm working on it. Nothing's easy, Sheriff. You've got to persuade the booking companies that they can make some money coming here."

"Mess of fellers roll in and put on a show, is that it?"

"Gals, too, Sheriff."

"Where do they stay?"

"Well, that's a question. Some companies got their own little travel wagons with bunks. Most just book rooms in the town."

"We hardly got any rooms here in Doubtful."

"Yes, I'm working on that. It's hard to book a show here because of it. I've told Belle to put a wing on her boardinghouse."

I talked some with this Ralston, who seemed a lot smarter than anyone else in Doubtful, maybe because he was out of some big city somewheres. And I ended up with a pretty good idea of how this deal worked. Every couple of weeks a new troupe would arrive, and the old one would pack up and go to the next town.

"It sure took some figuring out," I said.

He smiled and nodded. He actually had a kind of cold gaze that missed nothing, and I think he was sort of humoring me when he wanted to be doing something else. But I was still wearing a badge, and people usually will palaver with me when I'm looking to know something. So I got around to the question that was on my mind.

"Mr. Ralston, the county supervisors are saying you know a lot about crime waves."

That sure got his attention. "They say that?"

"I mean, they're going to get in touch with you about finding a new sheriff. They're replacing me."

"Why should I know anything about that? Ralston's whole demeanor had changed, and he was suddenly wary. "And why are they replacing you?"

"I got robbed couple of nights ago, and they can't stand it. Sheriff of Doubtful getting stole from."

"And they're going to consult me? About your replacement?"

"That's what they were saying when they took the axe to me."

Ralston laughed suddenly. "Sheriff, there's some in the world, especially out here in the sticks, who think that show people are crooks and thieves and jailbirds. And that it takes someone like me, with some experience, to keep them toeing the line. That's hardly true. There's a lot of good troupes that cause no trouble; once in a while an outfit rolls in that's looking for ways to fatten their purses and aren't very careful how they do it. I can spot 'em, and I can usually keep the lid on. Time or two, I've cancelled the show and sent them out of town."

"Where was that?"

"Oh, Cheyenne, Deadwood, Miles City, Golden, Laramie. . . ."

"Yeah, but why did you come to Doubtful? We ain't half as big."

"Doubtful's future drew me. Some of the richest ranches in the state. Some mining in the Medicine Bow range. And the town's a stageline hub, coaches going off in three directions. And I'm not forgetting the hot springs, either. Pretty soon now you'll have the resort trade. So, naturally, all these good folks have some coin in their pockets and no place to spend it—at least not until I open up in a few days."

Ralston seemed almost amused, and I didn't much care for him. He seemed always to be talking down his nose, like I was a dummy. Well, maybe he was right. I'm slow. They all say it, starting with my ma.

"Well, the politicians are going to come talk to you about a new sheriff," I said. "Why is that?"

"You're all the sheriff I need, Pickens. I think you and I'll get along fine. Anyone running a show house needs an accommodating sheriff around."

"What's that word mean?"

"Means, you just stay relaxed, and I'll keep Doubtful happy. You look to be just the man I want, and if they come asking, I'll tell 'em so."

He was sort of smiling, but with cold eyes, and I figured I'd have to think about all this.

"You're going to tell them to stick with me?"

"I'll insist on it. You may not be aware of it, but I looked you over pretty closely even before I started business here. Having the right man wearing the star's important to a business like mine. I sell good times, Sheriff. There's lawmen that just don't like anyone having a good time in their towns, and then there's trouble. I wouldn't want to lay out a small fortune to build an opera house in some town where the sheriff hasn't got a happy bone in his body and doesn't want anyone else to be happy either."

"Yeah, well what's that got to do with enforcing the law?"

"Everything, Sheriff."

"I think I get it. If some actress wants to show a little leg you don't want me pinching her."

"Ah, you're mastering it just fine, Pickens."

"There's something you said about some of these outfits causing trouble. What kind of trouble?"

"You're a good man, Pickens. Asking the right questions. Every once in a while, there's a confidence man, or woman, traveling in a troupe. They usually work in saloons, getting suckers to bite on some fake deal or other. Once a pickpocket blew into town with a troupe, working the standup bars. You can do me a favor, and the town a favor, keeping an eye on the saloons when a troupe's playing."

"You put up with it?"

Ralston shrugged. "I don't control the acts. I book companies. If one's coming this way, I'll probably book it. That's why I'm glad to have this little talk with you. Company comes in, and you'll know what to look for, and you can collar the troublemakers. At the same time, you'll see that all the good citizens of Doubtful will be enjoying life at these shows, getting some belly laughs, and that's what I want. I want to sell tickets. Lots of tickets. I want to fill up the place every night. Sell out. SRO—that's standing room only. SRO every single night. You keep the lid on, but let the show go on, too. You treat the performers and artists right, and I'll, say, make it worth your while."

Well, he was talking that subtle stuff I never did figure out, but it sounded a little like a bribe to me. "Worth my while." What did he mean? And "treating the artists right"? What did he mean? And telling the county supervisors I'm the right man for the job, what would he do that for? I couldn't see he was doing anything wrong or causing trouble, but it sure got me to wondering some. I decided I'd keep an eye on the place, and the man. At least until the county supervisors pitched me to the dogs.

He got busy with the workmen, and I watched a while and headed into the sunlight, where it was a lot warmer than in that cold place. Doubtful was busy. There were carriages and wagons on the road. It hadn't rained, so the road kicked up dust, which was better than mud. It was still a raw town, but it was growing, and it seemed like I was seeing new faces every day. The ranches were some of the finest in Wyoming, and all a rancher had to do was push some skinny cows out, and pretty soon they fattened up and grew, and without much help from anyone, either.

Maybe it was a good time for an entertainment palace to come in. There were even a few ladies in Doubtful, but not many. Women were scarce around this place. Maybe a show with a few sweethearts in it would be good business. All them cowboys, living in bunkhouses with lots of other cowboys, most of them with smelly feet, would take to the opera house. That would be fine with me, long as they didn't shoot holes in the roof or scare the performers—Ralston was calling them artists—off that little stage.

I sure had learned a lot this day. I'd never heard of variety shows, and I still didn't know what went on, but I'd find out soon enough. It amazed me that there were regular companies wheeling around in coaches and wagons, setting up their acts in town after town, and then pulling up stakes and heading for the next one. It'd be strange folks, traveling like that, not ever putting down roots, never settling in any place. They'd be a lonely bunch, traveling like that. It all made me wonder how anyone would become a player in a variety show. That would be a hard life, too, moving in all kinds of weather, getting bogged down in mud, or stuck without shelter somewhere. But I guess some people liked it, or they wouldn't be doing it. Maybe a few even got rich, but I sort of doubted it.

So Doubtful was about to get a theater. I'd never met an actress in my life, and I decided I'd meet a few when they rolled in. What did they do for a living? I'd knowed a few female gamblers, slick with cards, and I'd met a few ladies of the night. I had a good idea of how them women got through life. But an actress, now that was a new side of beef for me. If they sang, if they danced, if they did little scenes, they must have gotten the practice of it somewheres.

All in all, I thought, Doubtful was about to get much better.

CHAPTER THREE

Things were pretty quiet in Doubtful for a few days. I talked with a few barkeeps to see if anyone was spending that dollar and six bits, but no one was. I kept an eye out for thick, medium-high bandits with black bandanas, but there weren't any walking around town.

My deputies, De Graff and Burtell, they must have got wind of what was about to befall me, because they quit being my pals and stared away from me whenever we gabbed in the office. Maybe the supervisors had been asking if I done good work.

The one thing that did change was the color of Doubtful. All of a sudden there was these big red and blue and green sheets plastered to the side of buildings. I didn't know what to call them: playbills, or broadsides, or whatever, but Ralston was promoting his opera house and the opening show any way he could, and that meant posting these advertisements from one end of the county to the other.

He'd hung a sign on his new building, calling it "The Ralston." I guess that was better than calling it the Doubtful Opera House. And he'd had some kind of get-together in there, with all the town's bigwigs having a mint julep on stage. I wasn't invited, not being a bigwig.

I don't read so good, but I made out what was on them broadsheets. There was a lot of gorgeous women in that show, all dressed up in feathers. At least that's what the pictures looked like. That would sure draw a crowd in woman-starved Puma County, where there were about ten men for every gal, and the gals were all married. This outfit on its way to Doubtful was called the Gildersleeve Variety Company, run by Madame Magenta Gildersleeve, of the Slovakian Royal Ballet. There would be twenty beauties, along with the well-known comedian and tap dancer Horace Van Der Platz, the maestro of the top hat, cane, and white spats. And there would be a breathtaking *tableau*, featuring the famed women in the paintings of Rubens, displayed exactly as they appeared in his art.

I didn't know what a *tableau* was, but anything that displayed famous women would be worth a gander. I wondered if my badge would let me in free. Down there in the fine print it said the company traveled in thirty-six coaches, and had been the sensation of Prague, London, Cheyenne, Deadwood, and Denver.

Well, I had to hand it to that Ralston. He was going to fill his opera house, and maybe I'd even see this bevy of beauties a second time. Puma County was shy of beauties, although if Belle, who ran the boardinghouse, would lose a little flesh, she might qualify on a night when the light wasn't too bright.

Then one fine day I spotted Ike Berg meandering along our main drag. He was the sheriff over in Medicine Bow County, and I didn't need any help figuring out what he was doing in Doubtful. The supervisors were looking him over for my job. But there he was, dressed in his usual black suit and starched white shirt and string tie. He was the skinniest man I'd ever seen, almost skeletal, and his face was nothing but parchment over skull. He didn't have no flesh on him, just that parchment covering bone. But he was reputed to be as good as they ever got with his Peacemaker Colt. And there he was, grinning at me as we approached each other in front of the smithy.

"I guess I know what you're here for, Ice," I said. No one called him Ike. He was Iceberg to the world.

"I hear you got a crime wave," Iceberg said.

"Stickup man cleaned my purse," I said.

"Town fathers aren't happy with it. They're embarrassed. The sheriff got himself robbed."

Berg smiled, baring even, white teeth. I wonder whether teeth like that came with skinny.

"That was careless of you."

"You applying for my job?"

"The town's foremost citizens sent for me, Pickens. I'm here to oblige them."

He smiled again, like he knew things I didn't know.

"They offering you the job?"

"We're dickering about pay. I'm asking eighty a month and they won't budge from seventy-five."

"Seventy-five! I earn forty."

"We're usually worth what we're paid, Pickens."

His bony hand was actually hovering just over his piece, which sure made me wonder. Did he think I'd shoot him? Or was he just precautionary by nature? Shooting wouldn't be a bad idea, but my ma always said, don't shoot anyone unless it's a good idea.

He was standing there in the sunlight, chewing a toothpick, looking kind of smirky, and I thought that shooting him might improve the peace on Main Street. But I didn't, even though I knew I was faster than he'd ever be.

"When'll you hear?" I asked, since it bore on my future.

"They said there's a mess of petty crooks heading for town, theater riffraff, and they're going to see which of us keeps the lid on."

"You mean you're a lawman around here for a while?"

"Unofficially."

"I think I got the badge, Berg. No one's took it from me yet."

Berg, he just smiled and chewed on that toothpick.

I had to admit Berg would be a good man to have around if things got tough again. He'd come to Medicine City when it was a lawless mining camp, infested with every sort of crook and con man and bitch that ever set out to skin miners out of their metal. They all underestimated Iceberg because he was so skinny, almost frail-looking. But he was quick and ruthless, and he slowly and almost secretly began locking up the worst, banging heads together, and causing a few funerals.

I'd done nothing like that, so maybe that's why I didn't get any more than some ranch cowboy was getting, but I got to live in town. But here he was, and I knew that Reggie Thimble and Ziggie Camp were studying on him. I don't think he weighed ninety pounds, but a lot of lawman came in that skinny package.

And here he was, my rival. I felt kind of low about that. I'd always thought Iceberg was as good as they get, and he had always been sort of an idol of mine. Time or two, I'd found myself wishing I could be good as him. But here he was, walking the streets of my town like he already owned it. I sure had mixed feelings about that.

"You know anything about this variety show, Cotton?" he asked.

"I'll make a deal with you. You don't call me Cotton and I won't call you Ice."

"But I like my name. You don't like yours?"

"It got hung on me by my ma and pa, and I've always been a little tetched since they named me that. I've thought maybe I should get my name changed to Fat. Like Fat Pickens."

"Just call me Iceberg," he said. "It makes barflies shiver."

"I never seed a variety show in my life, but Ralston, he owns the joint, says there's gonna be pretty girls in it. To my mind, any girl's pretty. And there's so few women around that I can't tell pretty from plain."

"I don't like women," Iceberg said. "I can live without 'em."

"Can't get born without 'em," I said.

"Pickens, ain't that real bright," he said. He was smirking at me.

"Guess I'll see you around," I said.

"Maybe not," he replied.

He drifted off, studying our metropolis like it was dead meat.

My ritual is to patrol Doubtful at odd hours, never on a set schedule, because that's a good way to keep the peace. So that's what I did next. I started down Main Street, but I only got as far as the Puma County Merchant Bank before Hubert Sanders waved at me from his front stoop. He was the banker. He'd started it up two years earlier because Doubtful needed a bank, and now he operated with one teller and one bookkeeper, and his bank was thriving along with Doubtful. Hubert was a doleful man and his wife was even more doleful. They both wore wire-rimmed spectacles and their lips looked like they had just eaten pickles. They had gotten in a preacher and started up a Methodist Church, the first house of worship in Doubtful, which I suppose I should have appreciated because it meant Doubtful was getting more civilized and less wild, but somehow, whenever I looked at that whitewashed wooden church I had an itch to get onto Critter and ride until I was about five counties away.

But there was Sanders, wiggling his skinny finger at me, as if he owned the plantation. I walked up the two stone steps into the red brick bank, eyed Willis the teller and Wally the bookkeeper with the green eyeshade and sleeve garters, and headed through a gate to the corner where Sanders had his desk and where he watched the world go by from his big glass window.

"Have a seat, Sheriff. I've been meaning to talk to you for some while now," he said, waving me to a hard oak chair. That was how Sanders operated. The harder the chair, the faster his visitors would get through their business and retreat before their tailbone howled at them.

"Perdition is arriving in Doubtful," he said. "Ruin. Sodom and Gomorrah. We'll all be fleeced."

"Ralston?" I said.

"Of course, Ralston. Do you know how these traveling companies work? They come into a small town like ours, run a few shows, clean out every spare dime the town has, and then head to the next town that is foolish enough to let them in." He eyed me with those owlish eyes. "The Ralston is a poverty machine. It is going to ruin our good ranchers and merchants. It is going to cause wealth to flee. It will empty my bank. My depositors will withdraw their funds and squander their cash on those theater hussies and vixens and worse. I tell you, Sheriff, this is a catastrophe in the making. And it gets worse. There never was a moral person treading the boards of a theater stage. We will have a Gomorrah here. There'll be no one attending church, and no one putting money in the collection plate. The sulfurous smell of Hades will waft through Doubtful, stinking up our fair, clean, lawful city."

I was getting the drift, so I just nodded.

"It all depends on you, Cotton Pickens. It'll be up to you to rescue Doubtful from sin and poverty and madness. It'll be up to you not only to enforce the law in all respects, but to enforce the moral law. If those hussies on that stage bare anything more than an ankle, arrest them for violating public decency. If they dance, pinch them. Good people don't dance. It's against everything that proper people stand for."

"I just enforce the law, such as the legislature gives us," I said. "I got a book of it that I study sometimes."

"You're going to do more than that, Pickens. I'll insist on it. If you don't do what's required, I'll see about finding a man who will. You are going to find the means to shut down Ralston. That fellow is the devil incarnate. I didn't realize at first what he was up to, building that sin palace right on the main street of Doubtful. He didn't borrow a cent from me, and I don't know where his cash came from, but find out. It's probably tainted money."

He stared straight at me through those wire-rimmed spectacles. "Shut him down. You'll find reasons enough. A dozen reasons a night. Shut down any company that comes in. Shut them down for any reason you can think of. Arrest them. Charge them. Tell them to get out of town or they'll face worse."

So that was where Sanders was heading.

Me, I was feeling some heat from all sides. Ralston as much as said he'd welcome an open town, so people could have some fun. The supervisors were convinced a crime wave was cranking up. And now Sanders wanted me to shut the place down before it even got feet under it and started running. And there were a few vultures out there, or at least one anyway, looking to snatch my badge from me.

It sure was getting interesting.

"As long as they're lawful, I don't have any way to shut 'em down," I said.

"You'll find a way. Or a new sheriff will."

I was starting to feel some heat. "Here's what you do, sir," I said. "You tell the supervisors what laws you want, and if they enact them, then I'll enforce them. It's that simple. You want some new laws, you go get the elected officials to put them on the books. Meanwhile, I'll do my best to keep this town as peaceful as I know how."

Sanders arose abruptly. "You are dismissed," he said.

So I was dismissed. I headed out into the sunlight and took a good look at them green-clad mountains off to the west, poking up into a bright blue heaven.

CHAPTER FOUR

The Gildersleeve Variety Company pulled into Doubtful one rainy June afternoon when there was hardly anyone not under a roof. June's about the only month the rain really cuts loose in Puma County, and usually wagons are up to their hubs in gumbo. But the company made it up there from the railroad in Laramie.

There sure wasn't any thirty-six wagons, like it said on the playbills posted around town. There were three muddy coaches drawn by weary horses, and three freight wagons following. I guess this here variety outfit was a lot smaller than it was billed to be. The wagons lumbered in, spitting mud off the iron tires, and the maroon coaches came to a halt at the Ralston Opera House, where Ralston himself was standing in the door, just out of the cold drizzle.

Them draft horses sure looked tired after dragging the outfit through yellow mud for two days.

There wasn't no one on the street, given the lightning and rain, but I did see Hubert Sanders standing in the door of his bank down the street, watching. And sure enough, my rival Ike Berg was watching from the door of McGiver's saloon up a way. And then I spotted the county supervisors studying the company from the window of the log courthouse. Other than that, there was nothing but a wet dog lifting a leg at the corner of the opera house. Well, the theater company was being watched real close after all, even if a cold rain had driven off the crowds. It sure wasn't a circus parade, with a band playing, trapeze artists standing on gilded wagons, and a string of elephants. No, this company looked worn, weary, and maybe broke too.

I knew pretty well where this bunch would be housed. Belle could take four males at her boardinghouse but didn't want any women. The local hotel, a four-room place called The Puma, could handle six more of the troupe, and I heard that Madame Gildersleeve herself would be there. Ralston had found room for the rest at Rosie's House of Heaven, which was upstairs from Mrs. Gladstone's Sampling Room. None of them women in the company seemed to mind; at least that's what I'd heard. Maybe that was because the line between women of the night and women of the theater is real thin.

But now, as I watched from the gallery of the Sampling Room across the street, the coaches disgorged their cargo. If there was anything flashy about these people I sure didn't see it. Them women wore baggy gray dresses, and had shawls wrapped around their shoulders, and looked plumb worn. I couldn't see if they was pretty, but they didn't look it. They looked like a bunch of females that couldn't find anything better to do with their lives. Of course, the way things were in Doubtful, any female was real pretty.

Anyway, there was Ralston in his pinstripes, welcoming that bunch, the actors and actresses, the roustabouts, and Mrs. Gildersleeve herself, dressed in taffeta. They all vanished inside the opera house where I suppose Ralston would get them settled and tell them what's what.

I braved the drizzle to talk to some of them teamsters who were lighting up cheroots under the theater gallery.

"This the whole company?" I asked one, who had handlebar moustaches and carried a fine bullwhip.

"Far as I know, Sheriff," he said.

"You gonna come and get them when they leave?"

"We're staying. We're booked to take them to Casper after this here's done. Then up to Sheridan. Then into Montana Territory. They're here one week, starting tomorrow. They were going to open tonight, but mud slowed us."

"Tough road?"

"Oh, hell, I've seen worse. And we got so many

passengers we can get ourselves out of any mudhole. There's about six roustabouts and a dozen entertainers. That's a lot of spare horse-power."

"What'll you do during the week?"

"Look after the stock, down some red-eye, and tomcat around. Most of the teamsters lay out a bedroll in the livery barn."

"You travel with this show regular?" I asked.

"Yeah, off and on. Sometimes they book a railroad tour and don't need me."

Pretty quick the troupe drifted out of the opera house and the teamsters got them settled in their various quarters. That's about the last I saw of any of them. It was as if Doubtful had swallowed the whole company. I watched rain slide down windows, and silvery puddles form in the clay streets and water blacken the backs of the draft horses, and the miserable travelers with soaked hair and wet shawls and muddied shoes slip into their rooms.

I sure would have liked to follow them into Rosie's House of Heaven. I don't know what Rosie did with her regular girls, but now there were twice as many females up there. Maybe she'd be getting some stage-door johnnies knocking at the door as well as her regular johns.

Wasn't a very flashy life, this traveling with a variety company, I thought. Pretty much misery and weariness. I sure was glad I wasn't stage-struck. I waited for the drizzle to slacken and then drifted over to the Puma County lockup and sheriff's office back around the courthouse. My deputy Rusty was there, looking itchy.

"Well?" he asked.

"Wasn't worth seeing. Few miserable mud-spattered roustabouts, a fancy lady in taffeta who owns the outfit, a dude with her, and some rank-looking performers. One or two play music, and the rest—who knows?"

"Better than what we've got around here," Rusty said. "That Iceberg came in and looked around. He gonna be my next boss?"

"He thinks he is, but not if I can help it. He's hanging around, waiting for the supervisors to make up their minds."

"They ain't happy with you?"

"I got robbed. They call it a crime wave."

Rusty was smiling real mean. "Only crime wave I know of here is them politicians," he said. "Anyway, Sheriff Berg from Medicine Bow County was poking around here, eyeing the jail, studying the place like he was fixing to own it."

"Maybe he will own it, the way things are going."

"What's got him sniffing around?"

"He's asking eighty a month."

Rusty whistled. "Jaysas," he said.

"I think he plans to catch a crook just to show off, and there's nothing like a variety show for that, I gather. I got that from Ralston himself. He said some of them outfits got real sticky fingers.

Iceberg knows it and I'm guessing he's gonna show off, make some pinches just to impress the supervisors."

"Can he arrest? He's not a peace officer in Puma County."

"He's got a star, and that's all he needs."

"Want me to stick around tonight?"

"Nah, we got more law than we need. There's strangers in town, so I'll be working the saloons. De Graff comes in at midnight, so we're set."

I headed over to the Lizard Lounge looking for a bite to eat. Most people avoided the Lizard, because the rumor was they served horsemeat stew, but they were the cheapest joint in Doubtful, and I didn't mind eating horse anyway. Some said they served mule when they were short of horse. I'd eat Critter if I had to. I set down in my usual spot beside a real glass window where I could keep an eye on Doubtful, and Mrs. Studebaker served me up a bowl without asking, just as always.

This was just a regular night, nothing much happening, so I added some salt and spooned the gray stew into me and watched the puddles outside glimmer in lamplight. The streets of Doubtful could still turn into quagmires if it rained hard. Rumor was that a teamster had once vanished in a puddle right across from the Emporium. I doubted it, but I'd been up to my ankles a few times.

There were some suspicious items in the stew this night, but I refused to believe they were horse apples. Boiled groundhog, maybe. Doubtful had better eateries, but none cheaper, and I had to stretch my forty a month as far as it'd go. The town sure was growing. When I'd arrived a couple of years earlier, it was still a wild place, with six-gun law and a string of expired lawmen. Which is why they fetched me. I was the town's last resort. But all that was the past. Now we had people settling the basin country and starting up businesses in town. We were up to seven saloons, one church, fourteen businesses, and an opera house. A town was hardly on the map until it got an opera house. And there had to be some cash around, and people willing to spend it, before anyone would put up an opera house. Down in Colorado, there was a mess of them. Denver, Leadville, Telluride, places like that.

My work had switched around, too. Now I was policing gamblers and crooks and cutpurses. Before, I'd had to settle the troubles of warring ranches and rival cowboy gangs who brought in traveling shootists with big reputations. I don't know how I whipped some of them. My ma, she just thought I was nuts to try.

I knew just what I'd do this night. I was going to tour the saloons. If this variety company brought in any trouble, it would be in the saloons. Them roustabouts would cause any kind of ruckus they could start. I'd busted up a few brawls in my day, and I expected I'd add to the list this night.

I scooped up the last of the stew, paid Mrs. Studebaker her fifteen cents, and headed into the drizzle. My first stop would be the Last Chance, and I'd say hello to Sammy Upward, the barkeep there. He and I went back a way. None of the barkeeps liked me hanging around their watering-holes, but Sammy didn't mind so much. I was pretty quiet about it, just slipping in, studying the drinking fraternity, looking for someone's fingers in someone else's rear pocket, and then tipping my hat to Sammy.

I wandered in there and was hit by the smoke from the lamps, but it looked like business as usual there. I was noticed at once; I always am, even if I look like someone's wash hung out to dry. It's the star. Talk quieted. But Sammy, he just nodded.

"What'll you have, Sheriff?" he asked.

"Sarsaparilla," I said.

He poured it and refused the nickel. I studied the painting of the naked lady over the bar, and eyed the crowd now and then. They were all familiar faces. I've spent the last couple of years getting a handle on everyone in Doubtful. If there were any of those show people or roustabouts around, they weren't in here. But the roustabouts would still be busy unloading, and the show people would be pretty tired and not primed to step out in the rain and celebrate.

There sure wasn't anything entertaining going on there, so I headed down the street to Mrs.

Gladstone's Sampling Room. The rain just wouldn't quit, and it dampened me pretty hard by the time I got there. I pushed through the double doors and ran smack into a lot of light. They had all their lanterns lit, and sure enough, there were a mess of those show people in there, most of them female. There's some who think females shouldn't be in saloons, but I wasn't one. I sure enjoyed seeing the bunch, seven or eight of the ladies and a few of the traveling gents too, some of them at a table by themselves, but a few bellied up to Mrs. Gladstone's polished bar.

There was a bunch of Doubtful people in there too, most of them taking a gander at the show people. It looked like a convention of whiskey drummers in there, and I swear there were Doubtful businessmen like Hiram Perkins who'd actually washed his face and trimmed his beard and put a little witch hazel behind his ears. The showgirls were bringing every stage-door johnnie in town to the Sampling Room. Well, this was where the entertainment would be this night, so I just smiled, got myself another sarsaparilla, this one from Rudy, the barkeep, and settled back to enjoy the show.

I slipped into a corner and just watched, and pretty quick no one remembered Sheriff Pickens was anywhere around. Them show people were in there hard at work. They was getting to know the locals, getting themselves free red-eye, and getting real close to a lot of Doubtful fellers. Most of those gals were all gussied up, and wearing lip rouge. My ma, she used to tell me never get interested in a gal wearing enamel on her face because she'd be after my money. Well, these gals looked pretty nice if you didn't look too close at the varicose veins. Some had gotten their hair all bleached up, and most were showing plenty of neck and a little chest. But they was just being virgins there at the Sampling Room. Like ma says, I might not be the brightest light in town, but I could see they was working all the locals to come to the show the next night. And there were a couple of the gents there too, but nobody paid them any attention. No one bought the black-haired one a drink, or the redhead juggler a glass of beer.

I got the drift of the action pretty quick. These show people weren't just having a good time after a hard trip; they were aiming for standing room only, and they'd do most anything to separate a feller from his wage. I reckoned I'd do some sheriffing that night.

CHAPTER FIVE

The Sampling Room sure was the place to be in Doubtful that eve. Just sitting there I seen half the town. I saw Reggie Thimble wander in, and Mayor George Waller, and the postmaster Alphonse Smythe. Even Ziggy Camp, who was more or less married. Those fellers hardly ever went to the Sampling Room, but there they were, catching an eyeful of those show people. And then Lawyer Stokes ambled in, and that sure was news. I'd never seen him in a saloon before, and then I spotted my own deputy, Rusty, pokin' his head in just to get an eyeful. And it didn't quit there, either. I actually saw Doc Harrison wander in, eye the crowd, and belly up to the bar. That was like the pope showing up at a Baptist revival. Sure enough, there was Maxwell of the funeral parlor, Turk of the livery barn, and Leonard Silver, who had the emporium.

I just sort of hid out at the rear, watching the

show. Cronk, who ran the poker table, was sitting near me and getting no players at all and shuffling the worn-out deck with one hand, looking sour. So I just sat there looking like a fixture that came with the place, but I wasn't lacking for entertainment with all those show people getting right into it with all the citizens of Doubtful.

And then one of the prettiest of the showgirls, or maybe they were show women, seeing as how some had crepe flesh and varicose veins, came drifting my way, drink in hand. She was all enameled up like the others, but younger and didn't look quite so worn-down as the other ladies. She was tall and curvy and knew it. And it was clear she was heading straight toward me, so I stood, wanting to be civil. My ma always told me to stand when women came around, because it was the thing to do. But my pa never did it, and I was sort of half-hearted about it. Sometimes I couldn't make much sense of being civil.

But there she was, with a glass of amber fluid.

"You the sheriff?" she asked.

"I was last I knew, but maybe not," I said.

She eyed me and my badge like I was loony. "You gonna offer a lady a seat?"

I hastened to pull over the empty chair next to me, and she settled in, eyeing me like I was a five-year-old. My ma had that look.

"I'm Viva Zapata," she said.

"Ain't that some Mexican bandit?"

"I wouldn't know. That's a stage name my agent gave me. Just call me Viva."

"You got a real name?"

"I was born with one and don't ever want to remember it again."

She looked kind of sad.

"Can I buy you a drink?" I asked. "I'm having sarsaparilla."

She eyed my sorry glass and laughed. "Ain't you the prim and proper."

I didn't know what she was laughing about, so I just clinked my glass to hers. I'd never met a show person before, so I didn't know what to expect. But they seemed like other people, only more so.

"Are you Mexican?" I asked.

"No, half Bohunk, half Croatian. That means one half of me fights the other."

"Which half do you like best?"

"The south half, sweetheart. Doesn't everyone?"

That sort of shut me up. I couldn't think of nothing to talk about.

"What are you?" she asked.

"My ma said I was a bad accident."

"That's rich. I could give your ma some advice about that. You want to bring her over?"

"Ah, she might not want any advice."

"You gonna treat us real sweet when we open?"

"What do you mean by that?"

"Some lawmen just itch for reasons to cause trouble."

"I'm not a trouble-causer, Viva," I volunteered. I still didn't know what kind of trouble she was talking about, but I was enjoying the company. She was missing a front tooth, but had an ivory one stuck in there and it looked about right.

"Say, honey, I'll take that drink. Whiskey neat, all right?"

I didn't want to plow into that bar crowd, but there was Cronk a few feet away. "Hey, get the lady a whiskey neat, okay?"

Cronk eyed me, settled the deck on the green baize, flexed his manicured white fingers, arose, and headed for the bar.

"Hey, you got clout in here," she said.

"What's clout?"

"Moxie."

"What's moxie?"

"Aw, you're just being modest, chief. Here." She leaned right over and kissed me on the kisser. I could have fainted. Not only that, but some of that bar crowd saw it, and a few were nudging each other with big elbows.

"Was that Bohunk or Mexican?" I asked.

"Meet me after the show tomorrow and I'll show you," she said. "Say, do you want a couple of front center seats for you and the missus?"

"No missus, but I'm sort of taken."

"Not yet, you aren't. I'll leave some tickets for you at the box office."

She patted my stubble. "You're a sweetheart," she said.

Cronk returned with the drink and handed it to her.

"Here, you drink it, Sheriff," she said. "I got it because no one should be condemned to sarsaparilla for life."

With that, she abandoned me.

"That'll be two bits," said Cronk.

"Viva Zapata," I said. She sure was curvy in all the right places. I finished my sarsaparilla and watched her sashay her way into the crowd. She reminded me of a bucking bronco the way she wiggled her croup. That got me to thinking about Critter.

"You've been had," Cronk said, cutting his deck with one hand.

There wasn't nothing more I could get from the Sampling Room, so I headed out the door. The rain had quit and I saw some stars. I was done for the day, and headed for Belle's boardinghouse where I had a room. Room wasn't the word for it. It was a cot with two feet of space beside it. Home for a lawman who was about to get axed.

I dodged puddles. Step in one and I'd land in China. I walked past the hotel and discovered the lobby had some people in it. There was Ike Berg, with his star still on his lapel even if this wasn't his county, and Madame Gildersleeve, owner of this here troupe, and her male companion, of whatever species I didn't know. They were sitting there enjoying the evening, jabbering away. I peered at them through the window and there they were, polite talk deep into the evening.

For some reason, I decided to check on Critter over at Turk's Livery Barn. Critter and I understood each other, at least some of the time. I liked to talk to Critter about women. He was a gelding so all he could do is nod and whicker, but that was his bad luck, not mine. Turk's was a little out of the way, but I had the yen. There are times when a man needs to talk to his horse, and this was one.

Turk's livery stretched back from the street, with the barn in front and a large paddock and wagon yard behind. I'd kept Critter there ever since they made me sheriff. He sure wasn't the prettiest horse in the world, with his roman nose, wild eyes, ewe neck, and slab-sided croup. But he and I had a working arrangement. He would obey half the time, and I would keep quiet about it the other half.

It sure was quiet. Not a lamp lit in there. Turk was over at the Sampling Room, sampling the showgirls. The barn door was open, so I plunged into the inky dark, knowing that Critter would be three stalls down on the left. So I worked along to his stall and opened the gate and edged in. Behind me the open double doors of the barn let in a little moonlight.

"Where are you?" I asked.

A horse in the next stall shifted its feet, and I could see it peering over the planks.

Critter wasn't there. The stall was empty. Rank, fresh manure squished under my boots.

I must have gotten into the wrong stall, so I backed out and tried the next, and almost got kicked by a big draft horse I thought might be hauling one of those show wagons.

"You sure ain't Critter," I said.

The horse responded by pinning me to the wall until I thought my ribs would crack. But I got out of there, checked the other stalls, and finally realized Turk must have put Critter outside, maybe because of the draft horses that had clopped into Doubtful. So I eased out the back, past all them wagons and buggies and carriages, and into an open pen, where at least some moonlight could steer me to him.

Only thing was, Critter wasn't there.

"Where are you, you rank outlaw," I said.

But those three horses back there weren't Critter.

My horse had vanished. Maybe borrowed. Maybe worse.

I was mad, so I hiked back to the Sampling Room and found Turk, who was fingering his beard and patting the arm of a showgirl and drinking schnapps all at the same time.

"Where's Critter?"

"What are you talking about, Sheriff?"

"Critter's gone. You lend him to someone?"

"Critter's in his stall."

"No, and he's not in any other and he's not out back."

"I guess someone took him, Sheriff."

"You gonna help me find him?"

"Maybe he got out. Try in the morning. He's probably wandering free somewhere. People go in there and let horses loose and I don't know anything about it."

"You let people in there?"

"Cool down, Pickens. He'll show up tomorrow."

"Turk, you leave this here lady and come with me and get my horse."

Turk yawned. "He'll show up. I think I'm going to bed."

"Where are the roustabouts bunking?" I asked.

"What roustabouts?"

"With the show."

"Not in my hayloft," Turk said.

The action at the Sampling Room was winding down, and half the town of Doubtful had gone to bed.

"You're gonna find Critter or buy me a horse, if you're still alive when I'm done with you."

Turk laughed. The showgirl ran a hand along his leg.

I got out of there, and hiked through the moonlight. Back at the livery barn I tried every stall again, checked the pen, wandered the open country back of there, and yelled at Critter to find me. But he was plumb gone, and it wasn't no accident.

Someone took him.

I just plain hated that.

I knew what I'd do in the morning. Find out where those roustabouts were bedding, and rattle their teeth until I found out which one of them stole my horse.

I hiked over to the sheriff office. Burtell was in there, snoozing in the office swivel chair. He's my oldest deputy, with a lot of gray thatch on his face.

"Someone stole Critter," I snapped.

Burtell woke up with a start, eyed me, and slowly got it into his thick head that the sheriff of Puma County was yelling at him.

"Why weren't you out doing rounds?" I asked. "You could have stopped it. We got a town full of strangers and you're parked in that chair."

Burtell yawned, looked annoyed, and then woke up the rest of the way.

"First you get held up, and then your horse gets took," he said. "Ain't any other sheriff in Wyoming gets robbed and rustled in a few days. I guess someone's wanting your job."

"No, it was one of them show people around here."

"Go to bed, Cotton. Critter ain't worth getting into a conniption about. Whoever stole that horse done you a favor, if you ask me."

"He's my horse, and I'm going to find him, and I'm going to hang the horse thief."

"I'll come watch," Burtell said.

"Put it in the log," I said. The office had a log with the complaint and the time of the complaint.

"Ah, just go to bed. I'll find Critter and put him back in his stall." Burtell said.

"You'd better, or you're out the door," I said.

Burtell stood, looking a little ornery. "Cotton, damn it, tomorrow someone's gonna come in here and complain that he's got a horse in his back yard eating all his carrots and radishes. And Rusty or someone will go over there and put a halter on Critter and lead him back to his stall. So go to bed."

"Critter wouldn't do that." But then I had second thoughts. "Maybe he would. Maybe I'll sell him for dogfood."

CHAPTER SIX

By the next dawn I was as ornery as I get. I woke up mad and got madder. I got dressed mad, and ate oatmeal mad, and eyed Doubtful mad, and went to work mad. I snarled at Rusty and De Graff. They had the good sense to duck out and patrol the town and leave me alone with my misery.

My ma, she always said the madder you get, the dumber you get, and if she was right, I was as dumb as I've ever been. Critter was gone; no one found him. He wasn't wandering around loose. He had been hijacked and was probably in a different county by now. I'd be robbed by a hooligan on the street and my horse got stole. Maybe it was just a coincidence, but I thought it was deliberate. Someone either wanted my job or wanted me out of office, and was making me look as bad as possible.

If one of them supervisors walked into my jail,

I was going to yell at him. But no one did. They just let me stew in my office and think about quitting before they fired me. But I knew I wouldn't do that. I'd keep on doing the best I knew how.

I thought a lot about Ike Berg, from over in Medicine Bow County, hanging around here like an executioner. Maybe he arranged these embarrassments so he could take over. I thought about my deputies. Maybe they wanted my job and knew how to kick me in the groin. There was Cyrus Ralston, who wanted me to go easy on his Opera House and the performers. There was the starchy banker, Hubert Sanders, who thought Doubtful had gone to hell when the opera house went up, and wanted me to arrest any performer who walked the streets. Sanders was the one who gave me the willies. Maybe he was behind this crime wave directed entirely at me. It sure wouldn't take much of that to persuade the supervisors I was too small for the job and then Sanders and his rich friends could get me out of office and talk the commissioners into hiring someone else. Like Berg.

Well, there wasn't a thing I could do for it. I'd just live each day of work as best I could. That's how the day played out, me as ornery as a bear with a sore tooth. I spent most of the day hunting for Critter. I checked with the barkeeps about rumors they might have heard. I pushed my way into sheds and stables. I snapped at Turk, who had been enjoying himself at the Sampling Room instead of tending to business at his livery barn.

It all came to nothing. Critter was gone and I'd probably never see him again. I hoped he'd kick the teeth in of whoever stole him. He would enjoy that. If anyone in Doubtful suddenly got stove up, I'd arrest him as a horse thief.

This was opening night over at the opera house and I intended to be there even if I was still as mad as I get. I'd never seen a real live show before. I decided I was going to stand in the rear of that theater and keep an eye on things. If there was trouble in the streets, I could duck out.

"I'm going to be there," I told Rusty. "You're stuck with duty."

"If you've seen one, you've seen 'em all," he said.

"You seen a show?"

"Once in Cheyenne. They're a bore. I left at the intermission. I'd prefer to spend my nickels on a nickelodeon. Give me a good dance hall and some dollies to stomp with, and that's better than being bored in a chair in a show hall."

"Well, the town's yours, then. And watch out for footpads."

"You feeling any better?"

"It's none of your damn business," I said, and stalked out of there, slamming the door hard to make my point. He probably was the one angling for my job.

By seven the new opera house was jammed,

and people were standing along the rear wall. It was too crowded for comfort, so I stood, too. That got me in for four bits. Sit-down tickets cost six bits. I saw half of Doubtful in there, and cowboys off the ranches. I even saw a few women, but they were still scarce in Doubtful, and most of them wouldn't be caught dead in a theater. It got hot in there; I don't think Ralston had given much thought to comfort. But it didn't matter. This crowd was raring to see whatever walked onto that stage behind the velvet curtain.

After a bit, some feller came out and lit the kerosene footlamps along the front of the stage. That brightened up the place. The footlamps had mirrors on the audience side, so they could throw the light back on the performers. But that only made it hotter in there.

I saw the county supervisors sitting in a row, and Mayor Waller and his woman. I saw Boardinghouse Belle, my fat landlady, bulging out of her seat and putting the squeeze on skinny clerks next to her. And sure enough, there was Ike Berg, still wearing his badge, sitting with the woman who ran the show, Mrs. Gildersleeve. She was all gussied up in brown taffeta. Lawyer Stokes was just in front of her, dressed like he was heading for a funeral. I thought I got a whiff or two of whiskey in the air, and I think maybe half of this crowd had fortified itself in the saloons before coming to the opera house.

Then the musicians came out of a side door, and I saw at once that they were also the roustabouts that muscled this show into wagons. There was a skinny accordion player, a fat drummer with a snare drum, a greasy-haired trombonist, and a gray-haired fiddler. That sure was more musicians in one place than Doubtful had ever seen. I pulled out my Waltham pocket watch and noted that it was well past seven and the show hadn't started. That sure was annoying. But at last, the orchestra wheezed to life, and the tooters tooted and the drummer drummed, and everyone got real quiet. Some feller in a tuxedo came out from the curtain. I'd never seen a tuxedo before except in Montgomery Ward catalogs in the outhouse, but there he was, with them flapping black tails.

"Ladies and gentlemen, welcome to the first show ever to appear in Doubtful, Wyoming," he began.

That got me looking around to see who he was talking about, but I didn't spot any ladies and gentlemen in that place, which left me a little wary of this crook up there. He was going to give us a pack of lies.

"And now, we will begin with our National Anthem, sung by the Gildersleeve Variety Singers."

He vamoosed behind the curtain, and moments later it rolled apart, and there were them six gals, all done up as virgin brides in white, but somehow a lot prettier than when I saw them at the Sampling Room the night before. So we all got up, and they ran through it real nice, and the variety show was off and running.

We all settled in for some fun, and we got it. There was stuff I never did see before, like tap dancers, that made the place snap and pop with the cleats on their shiny shoes. And there were singers, and a comic with baggy pants hung from suspenders. He kept pulling stuff out of his pants, like a big string of red sausages, which had all the fellers laughing even if the ladies turned real quiet. And there was some deal called the soft shoe, in which a pair of dancers got up like city slickers, wearing white spats, did a thing with canes and top hats. It sure was grand. I'd never seen the like. I kept wondering what my ma would say if she saw all this stuff.

Then this fellow in the tuxedo, he came out and said there'd be an intermission, and the show would crank up again in twenty minutes. A feller came out and turned down the footlights. So people drifted out and got in line for the two outhouses in the back. And some guy in mutton-chops set up a bar in the lobby and was selling beer and booze, and he had a lot of thirsty customers. I watched Iceberg head into the cool eve and light up a stogie. He saw me watching him.

"I suppose this is your first show, Pickens," he said.

"It sure is wonderful," I said.

"You keeping an eye on the town, are you?"

"I got a deputy on duty."

"But you're not? And the town's half empty and you're not out there?"

"I got a good deputy," I said.

"You got a lot to learn, Pickens," he said.

He turned his back on me, and began a quiet conversation with Madame Gildersleeve, who was half-way pretty, in an antique way, at least in the dark.

Well, pretty soon they got the footlights turned on again, and some feller with a bell rang it and kept saying "Two minutes." And after about five, they got the shebang up and running again, this time with a rousing chorus of them pretty girls, all gussied up in orange dresses with a lot of feathers. Except for one fat one, they were nice-looking, and all the males in Doubtful sat there lusting for them. I suppose they were used to that. They must have a real good life, with thousands of lusting men everywhere in sight.

Then they had a magician in there. I'd never seen one before, and he was real interesting. He wore a black silk stovepipe hat, and kept pulling stuff out of it, including a live rabbit. And then he wadded up a handkerchief in his fist and began pulling it out of his hand, and it got longer and longer until he'd pulled out a few yards of handkerchief and I'd never seen the like of it. And then he sawed a woman in two and I was fixing to arrest him for murder right there on the stage. He put her in a box with her head sticking out of one end and her dainty feet from the other and then he got a big crosscut saw and began sawing that box in half. I was waiting for blood to gush out of there, but it didn't, and pretty quick he'd sawed the box in two, and them feet was still wiggling and the head was still wagging, and I think I got myself tricked. I thought maybe I'd pinch him for defrauding an officer of the law, but ma always said, look before you leap, and I thought maybe I'd better wait until after the show and the magician was burying the corpse somewhere.

I don't think I like magicians. They think we're all dumb and suckers.

After that, the gent in the tuxedo came out. The footlights were sending up smoke, so some feller adjusted the wicks again, and then they announced the next number. It was a cancan direct from Gay Paree—whatever that was. I'd never heard of a cancan. It sounded like a couple of tins of Arbuckles coffee. But the music started up real fast, the accordion wheezing, the fiddler fiddling a lively tune, and the drummer hammering, and next I knew, all the gals in the show, they came prancing out and started a lively jig all over the place. They were dressed in frothy skirts, I can't even find a word for them, but they all wore these skirts that looked like beer foam, and swirled them skirts around like they were weightless. Then the trombonist got real sultry, making long sounds on his horn, and the gals got to swiveling their hips, sort of like they were in their own bedroom, and the next thing, they were kicking high, real high, kicking their legs right up in the air, and everyone in the opera house could see their legs. From there on it got real interesting, with the gals flipping their skirts this way and that, kicking high, the legs up to their heads, and all anyone could see was flashes of white leg as these ladies showed more and more of their undies. I pretty near fainted.

All them good citizens of Doubtful were whistling and cheering, and every time they kicked high, and there was a lot of female leg catching the footlights, why half the audience was clapping and cheering. But there was some sitting there with their hands in their laps, real silent. Like they weren't approving of anything like this. But the cancan dancers just kept on going, just a rainbow of color and flounces and whatever. There wasn't a man in the place but wasn't trying to figure out what sort of undies them gals wore, if any, but the low light didn't allow it.

When that cancan ended, half the audience stood up and cheered and clapped and whistled, while the rest just sat there like stumps. But then the show wound up with the whole company on stage, singing "There'll Be a Hot Time in the Old Town Tonight," and they were taking bows and smiling, and enjoying the clapping, and the velvet curtain came down.

I never saw the like. I thought maybe I'd been transported to some big place, like Denver or

Laramie. People drifted outside into the fresh air, which everyone needed. George Waller came hustling up to me, and straight-off waved a fist in my face.

"Arrest the whole lot. Arrest Ralston. We can't have this. Doubtful's reputation is ruined."

"For what?" I asked.

"For public indecency."

"I don't know any law like that, Mister Mayor."

"Then invent one. I want them out of town by morning."

"Pretty nice show," I said.

"You heard me," Waller said. "This is your last chance, Pickens."

"You mind opening up the city ordinances and showing me chapter and verse?" I said.

"You heard me," he said, and stalked into the soft summer night.

Well there I was, in deeper trouble than before. Seems like that's how my life was going.

I hung around outside as the citizens of Doubtful drifted away, except for a few stage-door johnnies waiting for the girls to show up at the rear door of the opera house. Most of the crowd was heading for the saloons for a nightcap, except for the merchants and their wives, who were escaping the revels and heading straight to bed.

The town was turning quiet, so I decided to head for my room at Belle's, which was half a block off Main Street and real quiet. It was a pretty nice show, actually, and I thought Ralston had done the town a good turn, sinking money into that opera house and opening for business. I thought Mayor Waller would sleep off his anger, and things would be fine tomorrow.

There wasn't nobody awake at Belle's and not a lamp lit either. She'd been the first to vamoose from the show, and was probably tucked between her blankets now. But I found my way up the wooden stairs to my room, first door on the left, and got in there, scratched a lucifer, and lit the oil lamp. That's when I noticed it. My room had been ransacked. There was stuff all over. The bureau drawers had been pulled out and emptied. My spares were all over the floor. I carried the lamp around, looking at everything real close. It was hard to say what was missing, but one thing was gone for sure. My spare holster and revolver, which hung on a peg from the door. The burglar had cleaned that out, and some loose change I had lying on the bedstand.

He'd taken advantage of the show. No one was around the boardinghouse or out on the streets as long as Ralston's place was filled up with folks. I'd started the day mad, and now I was mad all over again. Someone was after my job. And trying to make me look as bad as possible.

If Ike Berg hadn't been sitting right there in front of me the whole show, I'd have gone after him. But in fact, I plain didn't know who, or why.

CHAPTER SEVEN

I did what I had to do. I walked over to the office and put the theft in the logbook. I don't write so good, but I spelled out the letters and got it in. Anyone looking at the sheriff's log would see a mess of trouble for the sheriff himself. He'd gotten himself robbed, had his horse stole, and now he'd lost his service revolver and other stuff in a rooming-house burglary.

I got the letters all spelled out and then sat in that lamplit place alone. Burtell was out, checking up on places. But he'd see the log when I got in and probably have a good laugh on the sheriff.

I sure wanted my gun back. It was an ordinary Peacemaker Colt in an ordinary holster. I'm good with a gun but I don't much care what kind of weapon I've got as long as it's easy to use. This here Colt of mine, it'd been put to use a few times, keeping the peace in Doubtful. It wasn't filed down or slicked up. It didn't have any work done on the trigger or the firing mechanism. That ain't the way I use guns. When I need a gun I don't much care if it's fast or slow. I just want to get it aimed right and make sure it shoots true. All those fellers who work on slick holsters and fast draws are just finding ways to get themselves dead. That's about the whole of it, too. Them that get reputations all end up under six feet of earth in a couple of years. I liked that revolver, with its forty-four caliber barrel and shells, and that's all that needs saying. And now someone had it. Someone determined to push me out of my job, most likely. I'd get this solved one way or another, and then we'd see who might have the job, him or me. A stickup, a horse theft, and a burglary wasn't exactly a recommendation for a sheriff job.

I waited a while for Burtell, but he was off and gone. I was worn out. I'd had a long evening, seen the first show I ever saw, hung around afterward to make sure the town was at peace, and then went to my room only to find myself the victim of a burglary. I thought about going to my room and getting some shut-eye, but the truth of it was that I was not going to sleep that night.

I picked up the sawed-off twelve-gauge from the rack, threw some shells in my pocket, and headed into the night. It was black and cool, with only a sliver of moon to light my way. I needed to walk my town. I needed to walk every street, pass by every house, and check the door of every business. Maybe it was because I was the one who'd been robbed, but the need in me was to be the protector of Doubtful, the guardian of the ones I disliked as well as the ones I liked, the peace officer walking his beat in the depths of the night so that the people behind all those dark windows and closed doors could rest peacefully. I don't know where the need came from; it was just there, guiding me as I walked down Main, checking doors, studying windows. I'd do the south side first, because that was the poorer, the rowdier, the looser side, and then the north side, where the gentry lived in comfortable homes, with picket fences around them, and nice white privies behind big houses.

I was all alone. I wasn't sure what the hour was, but it was well after midnight, and Doubtful had pulled its shades and was slumbering. I carried the shotgun in the crook of my arm, easy-like. I knew how to swing it up and aim it fast, if it came to that, but this wasn't a night for that. I worked my way past Turk's Livery Barn, and saw the darkness within, and a few horses standing in the pens, legs cocked, dozing. I shook the doors of a couple of stores, Alden's Drygoods and Marcella's Millinery. I came to the red brick walls of the bank, and the granite stairs leading to its front doors. It had been built for permanence, unlike the rest of Doubtful. There were places that looked like they'd blow away in the next wind.

The bank stared back at me, dark and cold and mean. This is where calculating men made hard decisions, and stared at columns of figures, and connived to ruin the rest of us. This was Hubert Sanders's place, and from these granite steps he had demanded that I shut down the variety show and drive Ralston out of town, whether or not anyone had transgressed the law. I thought maybe Sanders wanted to live in a joyless world, where happiness was counted in figures and coin and bills. But now the bank was quiet. Its doors were secure. Its windows were black rectangles, vaguely reflecting the sliver of moon.

I was feeling better. This business of walking the streets of Doubtful to keep folks safe was lifting me up some, so I stopped thinking about the missing revolver and my room in a shambles. I'd find out who done it, and I'd keep looking, even if it took weeks or months. I was going to lock up someone and toss the key.

I worked my way east, rattling storefront doors, until I came to the saloon district. There was only one still lit, the Last Chance, where my friend Sammy Upward manned the bar. He was a good man most of the time, and kept an orderly house. If he didn't complain about city taxes so much, we'd get along better. There sure wasn't much light coming out of the single window. But there still were two horses standing at the hitch rail, legs cocked, waiting for the trip out to one ranch or another. I was fixing to go in when I spotted the drunk on the road, between the two horses, sprawled out flat, so the horses had a hard time keeping their hooves off him. Well, drunks was ordinary enough. I'd get him up and haul him to the nearest pool table, or maybe the pokey for the night. It would all depend.

I pushed them skittery horses apart and kneeled down over the man, who was lying on his stomach, his arms pitched outward under the nags.

"Hey, you, get your butt out of here," I said.

But there wasn't no answer from this one. He'd had about six too many. I poked him a time or two, and he didn't budge. He sure was drunk as a sergeant away from the fort.

"Well, all right," I said.

I stepped into the saloon, where Sammy was polishing glasses and waiting for two ancient cowboys, so old they leaned into each other to stay on their stools, to finish up their suds.

"Sammy, I got a drunk out here," I said.

"I plead guilty," Sammy said. "I wouldn't want one to leave here sober."

He wiped his hands on his bartender apron, and followed me out to the street. I got this feller by the shoulders and Sammy got him by the feet. The drunk seemed stiff and cold, and I was having a few doubts about all this, but we lifted him up and toted him in, and laid him across a table, faceup.

He was looking almighty dead. And acting

dead, too, by which I mean he was a cold flop, and there was some blood on his shirt, but in the lamplight it was hard to say for sure. He was dressed in a blue shirt and black broadcloth trousers, and had a trimmed, brown beard shot with gray. His boots looked pretty new. He was about fifty, but I'm not much good at putting the age to a face. His hands were soft and showed little sign of hard use or calluses. He had seen plenty of sun, and his flesh was darkened from outdoor living. He was clean-shaven but for some long sideburns.

"He don't look very lively, Sheriff, Upward said. "In fact he looks more unlively than lively."

"I think you got a point, Sammy."

The barkeep produced a pocket mirror and held it to the drunk's nostrils. It didn't steam up none.

One of the two ancient cowboys at the bar toppled to the floor, and got up cursing. "You're a sonofabitch, Sammy," he said, peering up from the sawdust with rheumy eyes, and fingering his ancient, sweat-stained hat.

"Those your nags out there?" I asked.

"How should I know?" the one on the floor said.

"Don't leave. I'll talk to you later," I said.

"That feller sure took on a load," said the other cowboy.

"Was he in here?"

"Not as I remember," the cowboy said.

"No, this man's never been in here," Sammy

said. "He'd be a one for the Sampling Room, but not likely here. This isn't the sort that comes in here. He's got money, or some comfort anyway."

"I think he's pickled," I said.

"Dead," said Sammy, putting the mirror away. "Should I go for Doc Harrison?"

"Maybe we won't need him," I said, eyeing that nasty bloodstain spreading over the back of the man's shirt. I tried to find a pulse and couldn't. I noted that the man's flesh was plenty cool. I laid my ear on his chest, and heard nothing.

"He's gone, Cotton," Sammy said.

I turned him slowly over to look at that wound in his back. The blood was caked around a wound below the ribs. I pulled the shirt up and exposed the injury, which appeared to be a stab wound.

"Knifed him," Upward said.

I agreed. Someone had killed this party with a large knife, judging from the size of that cut, near here or even out in front of here. He was no one I'd seen in Doubtful before. I wondered whether he was connected to the Gildersleeve Variety Company. So, there was no more peace in Doubtful. I sure hated that. I'd kept the lid on for a long while, and now there was trouble, seemed like everywhere.

I pulled his pockets out, looking for a purse or something that would put a name to him. Except for a couple of two-bit pieces in his trousers, he had nothing in his pockets. No purse or billfold.

Likely his purse got took by whoever stabbed him in the back.

"You think maybe he was with the show?" Sammy asked.

"I'm going to have to ask. That Mrs. Gildersleeve is over to the hotel, and she's the one to tell me. I'm going to wake her up."

"He don't look like one of that traveling company," Upward said. "They're rough. The men got skin like leather, and the women more so. The roustabouts look like they came out of some mean place, like St. Louis or Memphis. All that company got flesh so hard you could turn it into alligator boots."

"Mrs. Gildersleeve was traveling with a gent," I said. "I hardly got a look at him, but this one fits the bill."

I watched that cowboy clamber up on his barstool. The other one stared, his head in his hands, his elbows propping him up.

"You a couple of cowboys?" I asked.

"Cowboys? Cowboys? Scum of the earth, if you ask me," said the wizened older one.

"Cooks, sir. Cooks, and don't you forget it. I cook for the Admiral Ranch, and him, there, cooks for the Baker Ranch. And if you call me a cowboy again, I'll skin you with a paring knife."

"You cook a good meal, do you?"

"Absolutely not, Sheriff. It would offend the universe to treat cowboys to a good feed. The idea, Sheriff, is to produce hog slop for them rannies, and let them suffer."

"Was this here body we took from under your horses there when you got here?"

"I never examine the manure, Sheriff."

"Naw, he got there when we was drinkin' in here," said the other.

"That's right," Sammy said. "I'd have heard about it."

"You know this dead man?"

"I wouldn't want to know him. I refuse to know him. If I knew him I'd have to quit my job and go to Colorado."

"Why's that?"

"Because he's dead drunk."

I wasn't getting anywhere with that pair, and they were too far gone to help. I thought of locking them up and questioning them when they had a morning headache, but thought better of it.

"All right, go on. If I need you I know where to get you," I said.

They didn't move. One was asleep, the other one nearly so.

"I gotta get Maxwell," I said.

Upward shrugged. He woke his two customers and managed to steer them to the billiard table. I ducked out, headed across town, rang Maxwell's gong, and he showed up at the door with a bull's-eye lantern.

"Got an unidentified body at the Last Chance."

Maxwell yawned. "You would, wouldn't you?" he asked.

"I'll be sending people over in the morning to get the story on him."

"Who's going to pay me?"

"You take your chances, Maxwell."

The door slammed in my face. He would arrive with a handcart at the saloon in twenty minutes.

I was tired. I'd been held up, my horse stole, my room burglarized, and now I had a murder, all in two or three days. It was dark and mean as I made my way through the slumbering town to the sheriff's office. Burtell was there, feet up, half asleep. He was startled when I walked in.

"We have a body, no name, no one from here," I said.

"How'd that happen?"

"I found it walking the town. Where were you? Why weren't you out?"

"Outhouse," he said. "When a man has a bad bowel, he sits for hours in the outhouse. I spend half my life in an outhouse."

"I'm going to bed," I said. "You get out there, to Last Chance, and help Maxwell. I'll put what I know into the log."

He nodded, and headed into the deep dark night. I got a pencil ready, and did my best to get them words down, one letter at a time, like I learnt in sixth grade. "Unknown man kilt." That's all it took. I put my shotgun back on the rack and went to my room, hoping for some shut-eye.

CHAPTER EIGHT

I woke up sick as a puking cat. I didn't know what time it was. The sun tossed light into Belle's boardinghouse. My body smelled. My mouth was fuzzy and dry. I was fevered. I don't know how I got so sick, but what did it matter. I'd rubbed shoulders with a lot of people at the opera house, and maybe the sickness rubbed off on me.

I didn't want to get up but there was stuff to do. I had some crimes to solve, including a murder of someone unknown. I started to get up, and fell back. Getting up was a bad idea. I didn't know what to do. I hadn't been drinking and wasn't hung over. I got to testing each part of myself. My head hurt, tongue was fuzzy, neck and shoulders hurt, but lungs pumped away all right. My gut was nauseous, my bowels threatened disaster, and my legs ached.

My most immediate task was to get down the stairs to the outhouse in back. Either that or face disaster. The way I was feeling, it was like climbing the highest peak in Wyoming. I didn't have any choice, so I forced myself up, steadied myself against the dizzies, and managed to pull on some pants one leg at a time. Then I stumbled down the wooden stairs, got to the two-holer, used up half a Monkey Ward catalog cleaning up, and staggered through the yard back to the boardinghouse.

Belle spotted me and blocked my passage.

"You look like a throat-slit hog," she said.

"Feel worse than that," I said.

"You ain't going to the office, are you?"

"I couldn't get past the first block. Belle, I need you to go tell them I'm sick."

"I'll tell them, but first I'm going to get you back in your bunk and get some tea up there."

"My ma used to say tea cures anything. All you got to do is down it. Send me some red-eye."

Instead, she was pushing and shoving me, and with each step I felt a great force hauling me upward. It took some doing, but old Belle finally got me laid out like a slab of meat, and got some tea into me. Don't ever drink tea. It's the awfullest stuff and I think some mad genius invented it to torment the world.

"I'll get Doc Harrison," she said.

"No, don't! I can't afford it. And he'll yank my tonsils out without asking."

"I'll get him anyway. And I'll stop at your office and tell them you're dying and need last rites."

"You're real kind, Belle."

I sank lower into the corn-shuck mattress, which crackled under me. If I had to be sick, I might as well be plenty sick, so I sort of lay there turning lavender, staring at the fly-specked ceiling while snakes burrowed through my gut.

"Tell Rusty and De Graff to find out who the body is. Start with that man rooming with Mrs. Gildersleeve, who owns the show. Or just send one of my men over here, and I'll tell them."

"Whatever," she said. She vanished, and appeared with a white enameled thunder mug.

"You lose anything from any north or south exit in your carcass, you lose it in here. If you lose it on the floor, it'll drip through the planks and wreck my parlor. I'm expecting guests."

"Gotcha, Belle," I said.

I eased back in my bunk. The room was probably going to be my coffin. The ceiling would be the last thing I'd ever see. I might croak in the dark and never see sunlight again. Maybe croaking wouldn't be such a bad idea, the way I felt. The room rotated around and around and then heaved like the deck of a ship in a gale.

I was dangerously near heaving, but it never happened. I'd hold off until Doc Harrison arrived, and then show him a thing or two. If he came. I hoped he wouldn't. He would be full of hearty cheer, and I'd be ready to kill him if he said one more kindly word.

I lay there rumbling away, farting and belching, and then Rusty walked in without even knocking.

They call him Rusty because of his copper hair; I don't know what the rest of his name is; I'd have to look it up in the county ledgers. He's my best deputy, and is real good at terrifying children. He's got a lantern jaw and sings bawdy songs like a sailor on shore leave. He can keep order in Doubtful better than I can. His main fault is that he pinches women's butts.

"How you doing?" he asked.

"I might croak."

"That's fine. The office runs better without you. Don't get well."

"I'll try not to."

"We all went to have a look at that corpse over at Maxwell's. He sure is a stranger."

"Yeah, no one in Upward's joint ever saw him. You get aholt of the vaudeville lady?"

"Yeah, we got her into Maxwell's just as he was bleeding the corpse into a bucket. She said it ain't anyone with the show."

"What about her consort? The one she showed up with?"

"Him? He came with her. That's her fixer. Harry Frost. He does the fixing for the show."

"What the hell is fixing?"

"Every show's got a fixer. He's the one makes things work. If someone quits, he pounds the hell out of the quitter or finds a replacement. If a freight company overcharges, he has it out with the company. If they lose costumes in a rain-storm, he fixes up the show with new ones. If the politicians in the next town want some bucks or free tickets or a concession to sell beer in the lobby, he gives them something. Get it?"

"I wish he'd fix my gut."

"I don't think the deceased had anything to do with the show. He looks like a businessman. Pretty well dressed."

"Rusty, you get Arbenz to take some pictures of him. Prop him up, get the image, and have Arbenz make two prints. We need to get someone to identify him."

"Maxwell wants money."

"My ma always told me never walk into a funeral parlor. Rusty, when I cash in, which should be in ten minutes or so, you put me in a wagon and take me to the supervisors and lay me across their big table in there and tell them to pay."

"They're too cheap, Cotton."

"Ain't that the truth."

"You need a good scrub. Should I get Belle?"

"Stop torturing me, Rusty."

"You should never have took your boots off. How can you stand your own feet?"

"My ma used to say that smelly feet are better than any other smells."

"I'm out of here."

Rusty left, and I settled back to get some rest, but then Doc Harrison busted in unannounced. He was unlikeable on sight, with them little eyeglasses with round lenses and shark teeth wounding his dusty lips.

"Belle sent me," he said.

"There's nothing wrong with me," I said.

He sat on the edge of my bed, poking me with a finger and making me mad.

"And I won't pay you since I didn't ask for you," I said.

He was manipulating my jaw, trying to find swelling in there, and listening to my heart and all that stuff.

Finally he quit mauling me. "You're right. There's nothing wrong with you."

"I told you so."

"It's the vapors."

"What's that?"

"The vapors are the imitation of disease. The county supervisors are firing you, so you get the vapors."

"Tell that to my chamber pot," I said.

"The vapors are induced by stress. They are most common among women but an occasional womanish male gets them."

"I haven't got any vapors."

"That's three dollars. I usually charge two, but you're special."

"Send it to the county supervisors. I didn't ask you to come."

"Belle thought you were goldbricking. She thought you should be out on the street keeping us safe. You discovered a body last night and now you have the vapors."

"Doc, I'm going to sleep," I said, and turned my back on him.

"You should get out of bed and stop cheating the taxpayers," he said.

He stuffed his shiny instruments into his black Gladstone and eased out the door. He was a pretty good doc, except when he wanted to be.

He made me mad. I wondered what the next insult walking through my door would be. I pushed myself out of my deathbed and uncovered the chamber pot, and sat, getting settled just in time. That was just about as satisfying as a chamber pot session can be, and I was congratulating myself when Mrs. Gildersleeve and Harry Frost walked in.

"Take your time, Sheriff," she said, and settled on my bed, waiting for me to finish up.

That's show people for you. They are a breed apart.

This was getting to be a predicament, so I just sat tight and hoped the smell would drive them out. But they just sat there.

"What do you want?" I asked, refusing to budge an inch.

"Death threats," said Frost.

"Not a bad idea," I said.

He dug into his suit coat and pulled out several papers and handed them to me.

I don't read real good, but I got the gist of them. They were saying to get out of town before

sundown or the Gildersleeve Variety Company
would soon be shorthanded.

"What are you going to do about it?" Frost said.

"Where'd these come from?"

"They got pushed under the door of our hotel
room. Ralston found one pushed under the door
of the opera house. And another ended up with
the ladies of our cast."

"Who doesn't want you here?" I asked, still not
budging. The smell was getting real ripe now, so
I figured they'd be escaping in a minute or two.

"Ralston thinks the banker and his friends are
behind it."

"Sanders? That's possible. He wanted me to
arrest your whole show even before it opened."

I looked at the notes. They were printed in block
letters even I could read. Not that script stuff.

"Maybe you should write one of your own and
stick it under the bank door," I said. "You don't
need the law for this."

"Sheriff, these are death threats. 'Get out or
end up shorthanded.'" Frost said.

"This is just some Doubtful prank or other,"
I said.

"You should get off the pot and help us," Mrs.
Gildersleeve said. "Mr. Ralston said you'd help us,
and what have we got? A sheriff stuck on a pot."

I sighed, and reached for the Sears Roebuck
catalog lying there, brought by Belle along with
the chamber pot.

"I'm off the pot," I said. "I'll go talk to Sanders. If he did it I'll deal with him."

I ripped a page of farm implements from the Sears catalog and stood.

"God almighty," Frost said. "You've sprung a leak." He steered Mrs. Gildersleeve through my door and into the hall while I repaired myself. I didn't much feel like getting up and confronting Sanders, but if my vapors allowed it, I'd go over there.

It took a long time to get myself repaired. And I forgot to cover the pot, so the room wasn't improving. But I finally got dressed, and sat down to study them death notices they handed me. They was all hand-printed with a pencil. Someone sure didn't like the variety company.

They all were signed, in small type at the bottom: "Doubtful Mothers for Modesty."

Well, there were two or three of those in town, probably all friends of Mrs. Sanders.

I stood, and got dizzy. If I had the vapors, they sure were plenty powerful vapors. Maybe I'd start with Hubert Sanders himself, since he was the one who wanted me to shut down the show even before it arrived. Or maybe Ralston first. I wanted to get the story. When did these death threats show up? And who did he think was doing it?

I carried the chamber pot down to the parlor where Belle was entertaining the Doubtful Chamber of Commerce, and handed it to her.

"Got it filled right up," I said.

"Oh, crap," she said, and accepted my gift.

I staggered into the daylight, en route to the opera house, hoping I'd survive the vapors. I made a mental note of all the outhouses in town as I headed for the opera house with the death threats in hand.

CHAPTER NINE

Once I got out in the sunlight and the warmth of a summer's day, I felt worse. Them vapors sure had me looser than a calf with scours. I hoped Doc Harrison would catch the vapors himself; serve him right.

I stood in front of Belle's deciding whether I could walk or not. I decided I couldn't but had to, so I began bobbing and weaving my way to the sheriff's office, intending to startle my lazy deputies. Actually it was good to get some sweet air in my lungs. I was feeling pretty fit above the waist, but south of there I was still in trouble. The air in my room was just short of lethal.

I wobbled down Main Street and finally climbed the steps and into the office, where Rusty and Burtell had their feet on the desks while eating marshmallows. They eased their boots off the county furniture as I entered.

"You look like you're seeing a ghost," I said.

"You're supposed to be dead," Rusty said.

"My ma always said a gossip dies a thousand times before his death," I said.

"We haven't got anywhere with the murder," Rusty said. "We were just thinking what to try next."

"What have you done about it?"

"Talked to saloon men."

I pulled the death notices from my pocket and handed them to the deputies. "You fellers got any idea about these? They got put under the doors of the variety company."

Burtell eyed his upside down and handed it to Rusty. "My eyes are no good," he said.

That wasn't exactly right. I could read better than Burtell. He didn't make it past fourth grade.

"It just says for them to git out of town or end up shorthanded," Rusty said.

"That's supposed to be a death threat?" Burtell asked. "Maybe it's a threat to chop off some hands."

Rusty rolled his eyes. I stepped outside into the sunlight for a moment, to pass some more gas. Someone told me that if you touched a match to that gas it'd blow up. I mean to try that some day. When I stepped back in, Rusty eyed me.

"You're pretty pale," he said.

"It's the vapors."

"You better go back to Belle's."

"I've got a murder to solve and death threats, and all you do is sit here eating marshmallows."

"The supervisors were here looking for you. I think they were planning to fire you for being sick."

"Well, if I'm fired I'm still going to solve this murder if I can."

I abandoned them to their marshmallows and wandered toward the opera house. I had one more card to play. I found the door unlocked and Cyrus Ralston in his cubbyhole backstage, waxing his moustache. He had a small revolver on his desk and was ready to grab it when I wobbled in.

"Oh, it's you, Sheriff. Doc Harrison says you have the vapors."

"I'm fit as a fiddle," I said.

He was amused.

"Ralston, we got an unidentified male over at Maxwell's Funeral Home. He's not local. He's too well-dressed. No one in Doubtful dresses like that. None of the barkeeps had ever seen him. Maybe he's with a show. I'm wondering if you'd mind having a look."

"I enjoy bodies," he said. He tucked the revolver into the breast pocket of his black worsted suit, and we headed out the door for Maxwell's a block away.

"Your show doing well?" I asked, mostly to keep him from getting ahead of me.

"Sold out every night, Sheriff."

"That cancan does it," I said.

"That's what's causing the death threats."

"How long will they be here?"

"Tomorrow night's the last show. Then they're off to Casper. I tell them there's nothing good in Casper, and they'll have to play in a root cellar or a church basement, but they'll give it a try."

We steered into Maxwell's parlor. It was just a tiny place, on the theory that no one in Doubtful had any friends or family or money, but it was the only burial palace in town. It started as a log store with a false front, but now looked like a cottage, with green shutters on fake windows and white-wash covering all the bad carpentry.

Horatio Maxwell answered the door chime, and yawned. "Up half the night squeezing blood from that turnip," he said.

Without my asking or nothing, he led us through a couple of parlors to a dark room in back, where the unknown lay on a zinc tabletop.

"Nothing in his pockets," Maxwell said.

"That you'd admit to," I added.

"No gold teeth," he said.

"Except what's in your pocket," I said.

Meanwhile, Ralston studied the ghostly white body, which wore underdrawers and no more.

"Pinky Pearl," he said. "Oh, no."

"You know him?"

"Advance man for the next show. I spent yesterday afternoon with Pinky. Oh no, this is terrible."

Now we were getting somewhere. "Who *is* this fella?"

"He's with the next show, the Grand Luxemburg Follies, doing advance."

"What's that?"

"He works ahead, making sure the show has what it needs when it gets here. If a magician needs a live chicken to pull out of the hat, the advance man gets the chicken."

"Now there's some job for you," Maxwell said.

"Advance men book rooms, book meals, book transportation, make deals with theater owners like me, fill special needs," Ralston said.

"What did he want yesterday?"

"Actually, he wanted to know whether his company would be safe."

"Safe?"

"The Follies are a little daring."

"Well, the less safe the better," Maxwell said, and I worked that comment around in my noggin a little and decided Maxwell was drumming up trade.

"We've got to notify next of kin."

"The show will know," Ralston said. "It's leaving Cheyenne in the morning. Be here the following eve."

"We've got a killer around here," I said. "You got any clues, Ralston?"

"The deceased is a show man. So am I. That means I'm staying armed."

"Who runs the Grand Luxemburg Follies?"

"The Camel Brothers Circuit."

"What's that?"

"There's organizing outfits, some in New York, some in Chicago, that create circuits and put shows on them and hire or own shows themselves. My theater's a Camel Brothers house."

"Roll him over, Horatio."

The undertaker flipped the carcass with a practiced hand.

The stab wound was low, below the rib cage.

"First stabbing I've dealt with," I said. "Cowboys, teamsters, and vagrant males all use six-guns."

"I've seen a few," Maxwell said. "This killer knew enough to thrust upward from a low point."

"A professional, then?"

Maxwell nodded. "We've an experienced killer loose in Doubtful. Who'll he strike next?" He cleared his throat. "Now, Sheriff, about the fee— my little recompense?"

"Wait for the Grand Luxemburg Follies. They'll take care of him, all right?"

"But it would be helpful if the county paid from its Poor Fund. You never know about show people, beg your pardon Mr. Ralston."

"Bury Pinky Pearl and send me the bill. And give him a good send-off," Ralston said. "I'll tell his company when they roll in. Oh, and Maxwell—get a man of the cloth too, and some flowers if there are any, and something better than a pine box. And a marker on that grave."

Horatio Maxwell scribbled away. "Ah, yes, a

marker. We have a thousand-dollar granite obelisk, plus shipping from Vermont. Shall I sign you up? The incised legend would be extra, of course. We'd have to bring in an artisan from Denver. So far, you're at two thousand seven hundred forty-nine dollars."

The theater owner sighed. "Pour a rectangle of cement, and put his name in it, and I'll pay twenty dollars."

"That's seventy-nine for the concrete, and forty for the name in it, Mr. Ralston."

Ralston inflated like a bladder. "Cancel that. Some of us will pick up the body in an hour."

"And do what?" Maxwell asked.

"Bury Pinky Pearl," Ralston said.

"I'll get the deputies to pitch in. We've got a couple of spades," I said.

"But you can't! It's not legal."

"Ralston and I'll pick up Pearl in one hour. Have him ready."

"I won't let him go until I'm reimbursed."

"That killer stabbed the wrong man," I said.

Ralston moved briskly. "I'll go rent a dray, Sheriff, while you get the deputies."

I didn't expect to do much shoveling, not the way I felt, but I'd fetch two deputies with strong backs. Only trouble was, they weren't in there. They'd been out to lunch for three or four hours. I did collect the spades, and by the time I got back to Maxwell's, Ralston had one of Turk's drays ready, and he also had four of the roustabouts bunking in Turk's hayloft. We marched into Maxwell's and found him back there with Pearl, who was wrapped in a winding sheet.

"Where's a coffin?" Ralston said.

"I can't release the deceased or supply goods or services without reimbursement."

"Well, bill the county," I said, easing past the dapper little mortician.

We eased Pearl into a box from a stack of boxes, and then carried him out to the dray, while Maxwell caterwauled behind us.

"I'm going to talk to the county supervisors about you," he said.

"That's fine. The line's only a block long now," I said.

The roustabouts laid Pearl's box on the dray, and led the horse toward the Doubtful cemetery, which was just west of town. We were a sorry bunch, in sorry clothes except for Ralston, who always wore something that suited his station in life.

We pulled in there, just the six of us and that pine box, and we picked a good spot, next to Mrs. Stokes, the lawyer's luckless lady. The roustabouts took over, carving the rectangle in the earth, prying loose a few rocks, and finally climbing out.

With a nod from Ralston, they eased Pinky Pearl into the hard soil of Doubtful, and then shoveled that tan clay back into the hole, until there was only a mound.

"I'll say some words," Ralston said.

We stood there in the summer afternoon.

"Some people don't much care for show people. But Pinky Pearl was as fine a man as I've ever met. His handshake was his bond. Like all of us in the business. We try to brighten people's lives, bring them the things that they never would see in their own worlds. We bring dreams to people. We bring them smiles and tears and beauty. We remind them that life is something to enjoy, no matter how hard it may be. Pinky Pearl was one of us. May he rest in peace. May God welcome him as one who spread happiness across the land, and brought beauty to those who had never known beauty."

Ralston looked like he was going to say more, but then subsided, and stood with head bowed, perhaps offering his own silent prayer.

One of those roustabouts had found a wild aster, and now he placed it gently in the yellow clay, where it would serve as an honor and a blessing and a remembrance.

We took the horse and dray back to Turk's, and I checked in at the sheriff office, and found no one around, and my deputies out to lunch until supper. I was pretty worn out, and far from well, so I settled in the swivel chair and dozed. There needed to be someone watching over Doubtful.

CHAPTER TEN

By the next morning my south half was healing up but my north half was worse. I had a mean cough and some sniffles. Given a choice, I thought that north-half disease was better than south-half. My ma, she always told me to dose myself with cod liver oil, but I'm against livers in general, especially fish livers, so I dodged her advice. But I'm real good at blowing out snot.

I got myself outfitted in britches, boots, and a shirt, and wobbled down the stairway. Belle eyed me suspiciously, worrying that her boarding-house would be quarantined and she would lose rent money, so she let me pass without the usual howdy-do. I made my way down Main to the sheriff's palace, wondering how many crimes had been committed in the night and how many would be blamed on my negligence.

When I got in there, Rusty looked at me and

nodded toward the jail. Sure enough, a local drunk named Arty was snoozing on a bunk in a cell.

"Drunk and disorderly?" I asked.

"No, Ike Berg dragged him in late last night and we booked him for burglary."

"Ike Berg? He's got no legal right. This ain't his county."

"Well, he did it. He booked Arty."

I was feeling a little put out. "He's playing lawman around here?"

"He wants your job, and he's getting in thick with the supervisors, so he decided to show off a little."

"Read me Ike's log," I said. I could never get much out of that curvy handwriting with all them letters tied together like they were bent out of shape, so I'd just let Rusty figure it out.

"Suspect was found rifling a cashbox in Rosie's House of Heaven at about midnight, June 11, and had put seventy-one purloined dollars in his pants pockets while Rosie was entertaining a customer in another room. Rosie reported she had been robbed of her life savings and retirement funds while entertaining a client, and identified Arty as the thief. Suspect said he had gotten the money from swamping saloons and picking up change dropped in the sawdust. But most of the greenbacks were two-dollar and one-dollar greenbacks, along with a twenty. Suspect arrested and booked. Ike Berg, Sheriff."

"Ike should have got a deputy," I said.

Rusty was grinning. "De Graff was Rosie's customer just then, so he was busy."

Well, that was a turn. I'd always wondered how Deputy De Graff screwed around all night, and now I knew. Wasn't a bad way to spend some duty time, I thought. But he was spending faster than he was earning, if I knew Rosie.

"Guess I better find Iceberg," I said.

"Oh, Cotton, the supervisors are looking for you."

"Tell 'em I'm here."

"I think they're worried about this crime wave."

"I think they want to fire me," I said.

"Well, I didn't want to say it," Rusty said.

I clamped my ancient Stetson on my unruly locks, picked up the county's sawed-off scattergun, and headed into the June sunlight. It was the wrong time of year to have a mean cough. I could see that Doubtful was having a peaceable morning. Ralston had changed his marquee to read FINAL NIGHT THE GILDERSLEEVE COMPANY.

I headed for the Beanery, which is where I likely would find Sheriff Berg. I meant to have a word or two with him, and maybe discuss a few rules in my county. Sure enough, the skinny man in black occupied a corner seat and was nursing a java.

"You owe me lunch, Pickens," he said.

He had a wry grin pasted on his skinny lips. I could paste one on mine, too, so I nodded and sat down uninvited.

"Somebody had to stop the crime wave around here, as long as the local peace officers couldn't manage it, so I was elected," Iceberg said. "I'll have steak and beans."

"I see you nabbed our local saloon swamper Arty," I said.

"Sure did, with a pile of stolen greenbacks in his britches."

"I hear you hauled him off and put him in my jail and booked him."

"I did. Your deputy De Graff was nowhere in sight. In fact he wasn't even dressed for business."

"I hear that Arty thought you were a lawman," I said.

"It sort of surprised him, Pickens. He was used to getting away with murder."

"And your star persuaded him? Even if it came from the wrong county?"

"A peace officer's a peace officer, Pickens. I'll nip anyone, anytime, especially when the locals don't manage it."

"You after my job, are you, Iceberg?"

"I already have it. They just haven't told you yet. They want this crime wave stopped, and you're not doing it."

"What are they going to pay you?"

"Seventy-five. I came down a little when they threw in a few perks."

"And what are you earning now?"

"Fifty."

"And why aren't you in your own county?"

"Pickens, you just don't get it. I've got no crime in my county. I stamped it out. And I've got two deputies watching the store while I'm here. No one's even seen a burglary since I took over down there. Medicine Bow County's the cleanest place in the country. I've got the best enforcement in Wyoming. The last arrest was six months ago, when I caught a little girl playing hopscotch in the middle of the street. She spent three days behind bars before I cut her loose. So, naturally, your supervisors are eager to have me, and send you packing."

"Well, my ma always used to say, when someone's busting the law, arrest him. So put your paws up, Iceberg." I moved the barrel of my scatter-gun straight into his midsection.

He looked plumb flummoxed.

"You heard me." I waggled the scatter-gun.

"For what?"

"Impersonating a peace officer. You ain't sworn in this county, and you're pretending you are. Now git up slow and easy, and we're going to walk real careful toward the jail."

He smiled. "Forget it, Pickens. This is a joke."

"You see these twelve-gauge barrels aiming at your ribs? Back in there are two loads of double-ought buckshot, and if I pull these here triggers I'll separate the Ike from the Berg real permanent."

It dawned on him that I meant it. He was staring real hard at my trigger finger, so I wiggled it a few times for show.

There sure was a bunch of Doubtful folks watching this in the Beanery, and enjoying every minute. Two men with stars, and one holding a scatter-gun on the other. The customers would be gossiping about this one for weeks.

Iceberg got real smirky. "My fifteen minutes in the sun," he said.

But he got up slow and easy, and kept his hand away from that piece he had strapped to his hip because he knew I'd do what I said. We eased out the door, and he was too smart to try any tricks, so I let him walk ahead of me toward my office, while more of Doubtful's finest citizens watched.

Iceberg started to enjoy himself. He waved at the gawkers, and nodded and bowed and saluted. I didn't care what he did, long as his hands didn't get anywhere near that Peacemaker he was carrying. He knew he'd be a big red blood spot after about thirty lead balls tore him into dog food. I was sort of enjoying it myself, and waved a time or two at the spectators. My ma always said when they shout for an encore, go ahead and give them one.

But finally we climbed them steps and stepped in, and I was ready for some trick. Rusty got to one side real quick, and eased around and opened the jail door, and then a cell door, and then stood real wide, at the ready.

"All right, Berg, real slow, unbuckle that gun belt and let it down real slow, and remember I don't even have to aim to turn you into fish food."

He obeyed, still real smirky, and even stepped away from the weapon on the floor, and into his cell, which Rusty clanged shut.

I headed for the log and wrote the information, getting it down in nice clean block letters: ARRESTED SHERIFF IKE BERG FOR IMPERSONATING A PEACE OFFICER AND USING ARMED FORCE TO ARREST A CITIZEN OF PUMA COUNTY.

"Can you spell my name, Pickens?" Berg asked.

"Good enough. The judge and the county attorney can read it."

"When do I post bail?"

"Oh, in a few weeks," I said. "I tell you what. You can leave here anytime you want—so long as you get your kit at the hotel and get out of my county just as fast as you can manage it. You'll get out and stay out. You ain't coming back. You ain't gonna work here, even if I get fired. If the supervisors want you, you'll say no. You think about that."

Berg stood at the door, his hands clamped around the iron bars. He was so skinny he looked like he could almost squeeze through the six-inch gaps between the bars.

"Nothing to think about," he said. "I'm your guest—for a little bit. After that, maybe you'll be my guest here. I expect a supervisor will swear me in anytime now."

He prowled in there, plain unhappy. He was still wearing his star, which was fine with me; a little more evidence for District Judge Alvin Rampart. Berg finally settled down on the metal bench and stared at Rusty and me.

"I never forget anything," he said. "I will not forget that I came here to help you, that I put a dent in your crime wave, and that you treat me as if I'm the criminal instead of that reprobate there."

Over in the next cell, Arty stared at all of us. "He's not a copper?" Arty asked.

"Not here," I said. "He's the sheriff over in Medicine Bow."

"I shoulda shot him," Arty said. "It would have only been a misdemeanor."

"You would have done Puma County a favor," Rusty said.

"If I wasn't nabbed by a legal peace officer, then you got to let me go," Arty said.

It wasn't a bad argument. "When you see the judge, tell him," I said. "Maybe you're right. The judge listens to jailhouse lawyers."

I headed back to the office and found Rusty with his feet up, reading a Captain Billy Whiz-bang comic.

"I'm going out. You tell De Graff when he comes in, on county time his pants stay on. Dinner hour he can wear nothing at all, that's fine with me. But I expect him to be on the job instead of on Rosie during work time."

"I'll tell him," Rusty said.

"Tell him we've got a crime wave."

Rusty yawned.

I stepped into the afternoon and headed across the village square to the Puma County courthouse. I coughed my way in, and started hunting supervisors, and finally found Reggie Thimble in the county assessor's office jacking up the taxes.

"Ah, are you feeling better?" Thimble asked.

"South half is," I said. "My ma used to say that's the important half. North of the waist I've got leprosy, a cough, pneumonia, catarrh, and yellow spit. In other words, nothing."

Thimble cringed. "We've been looking for you, Pickens."

"I don't fire easily," I said. "And I just tossed Ike Berg in my jail."

"Berg? Jail?"

"He's not a peace officer here. He ain't sworn here. His office runs to the boundary of Medicine Bow County. But he's wearing a star and arresting people, and so I'm charging him."

"But we're going to swear him in as soon as we get rid of you. In fact, we've unanimously voted to hire another sheriff. We've a crime wave in Doubtful and so far you haven't even slowed it down. Sorry, Pickens. You can take that star off your chest right now, and that will end it."

"My ma always said, never argue with a man with a gun," I said, waving my scatter-gun a little. "You're going to give me thirty days' notice. If I don't bust this here crime wave one month from now, I'll hand you this star."

"But we've fired you."

"Thirty days' notice, Thimble. And Iceberg is going to enjoy my hospitality the whole time. If I don't restore public safety by then, I'll cut him loose and you can pin this here star on him and ship his star back to his county. And if you mess with me before the thirty days are up, I'll toss you and Ziggy Camp and George Waller in there, too, and you can play poker with jailhouse cards all day, every day, with Iceberg, and he'll clean you out of everything you own."

"Pickens, you imbecile," Thimble yelled, but I didn't hear any more because I was out of there.

CHAPTER ELEVEN

Soon as I got my weary carcass back to my office, I discovered Delphinium Sanders intimidating Rusty. She was the banker's wife, and she could cow anyone or anything. She was built along the lines of a perfect cylinder, and if there was anything female in there, she took pains to hide it. Her brown skirts touched the ground, and the rest of her from neck to wrists was swathed in brown also. She had a brown parasol, folded up now, she used to jab at anything that slowed her progress through towns. She'd been known to wound dogs with it, and kill cats.

Rusty sat sort of low in the swivel chair, and seemed to get lower and lower as she berated him. But when I walked in there she turned on me.

"You've been fired. What are you doing here?" she asked.

"I've given myself a thirty-day notice," I said.

"How can you do that? We told the supervisors to fire you."

"Well, I did it," I said.

"Where's Sheriff Berg?"

"He's my guest back there," I said, pointing toward the lockup.

"How dare you put him in there? He's the new sheriff!"

"Well, he's there."

"Let him out immediately."

"He can leave any time he wants, ma'am."

That puzzled her, but only for a moment. "Give me the keys."

"My ma used to say, never lock a woman out," I said.

"Why are you keeping him back there?"

"For impersonating a peace officer. He got busy arresting a feller and flashing his badge, even though he ain't sworn here."

"What difference does that make?"

"Well, ma'am, if you was to start arresting people, they might object."

"Well, I just might. It's come to that. There's no enforcement of the law and the constitution in Puma County, and I intend to take matters into my own hands."

"Then I'll toss you in there, too, ma'am."

"If he can leave when he wants, why is he there?"

"The deal is, if I let him out, he goes back to

Medicine Bow County and gets his skinny butt out of here."

"You're talking to a lady, young man."

"Who would have thought it?" I said.

If a glacier had eyes, she'd be a glacier. "Why haven't you shut down that immoral opera house?"

"You want to show me a law says I should?"

"There's a higher law, Pickens, that tells us all how to behave, and that is why theaters and playing cards and whiskey and dancing are illegal in the larger scheme of things. That is why I've organized the Doubtful Watch and Ward society, and why we'll be picketing the opera house tonight. To drive this shameful public display of licentiousness out of the city."

"License what? I don't cotton to them fat words, ma'am, but I'll license whatever needs licensing."

"Oh, forget it. I'll get the supervisors over here and my husband and we'll have this distasteful business done with in five minutes. We're going to clean up this town for good. It's going to be so clean that it squeaks. We're going to shut down every saloon and every disorderly house and every theater. We're going to drive out aliens and noncitizens. And you're at the top of our list, Cotton Pickens."

"I wish I never had that name hung on me by my ma and pa, ma'am. It sure is embarrassing. I'm inclined toward Thaddeus myself. Do you figure that'd be a better handle than what I got stuck with?"

"You're an imbecile," she said, and huffed out the door.

Rusty sure was grinning like hell, but I didn't get mad at him. "Go lime the privy," I said. "And while you're at it, empty Ike Berg's pisspot. And after that, lime the courthouse privy."

Rusty, he sure was smirky, and I thought maybe I'd fire him if he didn't shape up.

I still didn't feel well. Doubtful was on the warpath, and my nose was running snot, and I had a crime wave. I missed Critter. When a man can't stand humans, he can always go talk to his horse, and Critter had heard an earful from me over the years. Critter always listened, and if he thought I was feeding him a line of baloney, he just sunk his big horse teeth into me to remind me to talk true to him. I'd trade in all my deputies as a down payment on Critter. If I ever found out who stole Critter, there's likely to be a necktie party right on the spot, with me operating the necktie.

That woman was on the warpath; or maybe her banker husband talked her into it. I sort of wondered what it would be like to be married to that battle-axe. Old Hubert, no wonder he was so cranky. They seemed to have the whole town in their pocket. Didn't she say something about telling the supervisors what to do?

I pinched a nostril and blew some snot out the

other, picked up a billy club, and headed for the opera house. The marquee said this was the "final night" for the Gildersleeve Company. "Next: The Grand Luxemburg Follies," with a cast of "twenty beauties." I sure was ready for some beauties, and planned to watch every show.

I liked carrying the billy club. I had quit wearing my six-gun long ago, because it wasn't needed, and was heavy. Anyone who thinks it's fun to haul around all that weight is nuts. I found the opera house door was open, so I went in there looking for Ralston. It sure was dark in that cavern without them footlights lit, but there was some light coming from that cubbyhole of an office, and I found him in there.

"Last night, eh?"

"For the Gildersleeve Company. They'll wagon over to the rails tonight after the show."

"You're going to have some company, tonight."

Ralston settled back and waited for the bad news.

"Banker's wife, Delphinium, she's got some ladies together in a Watch and Ward society, and they're going to make a fuss at your doors."

"Good," said Ralston, "get the word out."

"Good?"

"You bet. That should fill the house. I was thinking the gate was all played out for this show, and we'd be lucky to have a few dozen. But this'll crank it up."

"But they're a mean bunch, Ralston. I sure

wouldn't want Delphinium Sanders for my ma. My ma always said, choose your ma carefully."

Ralston cocked an eyebrow. "The longer I know you, the more I like your ma."

"There'll be a few ornery ma's out there tonight," I said.

"I hope they beat up a customer or two. That'd be even better," Ralston said. "Put the opera house on the map."

"You sure you don't mind?" I asked. "I'd pinch all them ladies if they start disturbing the peace."

"You don't understand show business, Sheriff."

"I don't understand sheriffing either."

"Do me a favor and tell all the barkeeps that these ladies will picket tonight."

"Hey, Ralston, I'm a peace officer, not a war officer."

"That's my boy," Ralston said.

Well, sure enough, at about six-thirty them Watch and Ward people showed up with signs they'd painted on pasteboard. There was a bunch, all right. Delphinium Sanders was the top dog, organizing them people in a sort of line around the box office and the front doors of the opera house, so it'd be real uncomfortable to slide between them and into the theater.

There was the wives of some of the businessmen in town. Like Mrs. Sawbridge, whose husband ran a dry goods store, and Mrs. Vermont, whose husband sold men's clothing, like longjohns and flannel shirts. And there was Mrs. Bullock, whose man was a cobbler and sold boots and shoes and fixed old ones. And there was that old Mrs. Perkins, whose husband ran the feed store and sold horse tack. And there were a few men, too. The blacksmith, Mickey Mann, was right in there with a sign he was waving. And the feller who ran the hardware and sold lime for privies and garden fertilizer.

I watched them collect there, and studied on their signs some, but it wasn't easy for me to read all them words. One said THE WAGES OF SIN IS DEATH, or something like that. And another said DRIVE SIN FROM DOUBTFUL, and another said, SWEEP EVIL FROM PUMA COUNTY, and another said WALK IN AND ENTER HADES. Mickey Mann's seventeen-year-old daughter Melodia had her own sign: PURE MAIDEN DEMANDS A PURE TOWN. Someone had painted up them signs pretty fine, big black letters so everyone could read 'em easy, and none of that script where all the letters bleed into the others and no one can make sense of it all.

I got to thinking that nearly everyone there was connected one way or other to a local business, and all them people wanted the cowboys coming in to see the show to buy union suits and boots and haircuts and not spend their money in Ralston's place. And it made all them people feel real bad to think that the Gildersleeve show would soon leave town with a mess of money gotten in Doubtful in its cashbox. That sure was interesting. Maybe all these folks were less interested in morality than in keeping their cash in town and keeping shows from latching on to the ranch and mine payrolls.

And that was plenty interesting, too. So I stood there, with my billy club, keeping the peace. Those sign carriers could stand there, but if they tried to block people from going in or coming out, I'd step in. I figured Ralston's patrons would have a bad enough time just sliding through them merchants and their wives, and I'd not let it go further than that. The Gildersleeve show people wandered by, real pretty gals, and gawked at the crowd, but then they went down the alley and entered the stage door. No one molested them, so I just kept an eye on things. The comic and the magician showed up, eyed the crowd, whistled at Melodia and tipped their top hats to the picketers, and meandered down the alley. This here was real entertaining.

"Arrest them for lewd behavior," Mrs. Sanders said.

"Arrest who?"

"Those men who whistled."

"They were just appreciating a local girl, ma'am."

"Appreciating! That's a sinister insinuation, Sheriff. They were virtually disrobing the girl with their gaze. Demeaning her. Reducing her to their own animal lust."

"Well, that's kind of nice, ma'am."

Man, the look she gave me had a hangman's noose in it. I thought maybe she'd whack me and I'd have a good reason to haul her off to my friendly jail. She whirled away, leaving me staring at her rigid back. I saw Hubert Sanders standing back away, watching all this. He looked like he was the field marshal for this whole Watch and Ward business.

Pretty quick, customers began arriving, and mostly just grinned, bought their tickets from Ralston himself in the box office, and entered the theater. They didn't have any trouble slipping between all them sign-wavers. They were mostly cowboys off the neighboring ranches, and had probably seen the show two, three times. Cowboys don't see women very much, and here were a mess of pretty ones, with a little leg showing, too.

They drifted in, and the women waggled their signs, and the customers just ignored them, and headed for their seats. The only real interesting thing was Lawyer and the second Mrs. Stokes, who studied the picketers, decided to go in, bought tickets, and entered, even as Delphinium began a chant: "Shame, Shame, Shame," she said and the chorus started up.

Then came Lemuel Clegg, a logger out of

town. He studied them signs, and approached Delphinium Sanders. "How come you ain't picketing the cathouses?" is all he said.

She whacked him, and I stepped in between them and pushed her back with my billy club.

"Arrest him!" she cried.

"You're the one hit him," I said. "He didn't hit you."

"He insulted me!"

"How'd he do that, ma'am?"

"You wouldn't understand," she said.

"Guess not, ma'am. You hit anyone again, and I'll lock you up for the night."

Clegg bought himself a cheap balcony seat and winked at me.

"He winked at you!" Delphinium cried.

"Pretty awful, ain't it?"

"You're in league with the devil."

Then she whacked me with her sign.

I sighed, and took her by her arm. "Guess we'll walk over to the sheriff office and I'll book you," I said.

But Hubert Sanders swooped in. "You touch my wife and you're dead," he said.

I decided not to argue against the snub-nose revolver in his hand, pointing in the general direction of my heart.

"I'm temporarily outgunned," I said, and let her go.

"We're going to close this show. Right now. And you won't interfere."

They was plumb serious about it, and that revolver never wavered.

I done what I've tried a few times, and brought my billy club up from below before he could think about things, and whacked his arm to one side as he pulled the trigger. The shot went up in the air. Then I whacked his hand, and he dropped the gun and howled. A couple more whacks put him in a real howling mood.

My ma, she always said be kind to dogs, so I quit. I picked up the piece, and motioned to them both. "You go ahead of me," I said. "You'll have Ike Berg for your cellmate."

CHAPTER TWELVE

That banker and his old lady, they weren't just mad. Mad is shouting and carrying on, but this pair, they just turned silent, and it was so cold they frosted over half of Wyoming. But they walked right along ahead of me and into my sheriff digs.

Rusty, he'd gone home, and De Graff was around somewhere, maybe with his pants on. I thought of booking the two, and I didn't have any trouble thinking up a few laws that got trampled on, but then I decided I'd just let them cool off for a couple of hours and let them go. They were mostly just trying to be good people and had gotten a little violent about it. They were the most powerful couple in town. Bankers are like that, I guess.

So I just ushered them into the jail, eased them into my last empty cell, next to Arty, who was next to Iceberg, and slammed the door behind them.

It clanged shut real hard. They didn't say one word. I guess they thought I was beneath talking to. But Arty was staring, and Iceberg, he had himself a leer on his skinny puss, like this was the best entertainment he'd seen.

The Sanderses, they stared at me like I was already in my grave, and I stared back. They didn't even ask what I'd charge them with, or when they could get out, or get bail, or whatever they wanted to know. They just glared. Then Delphinium stared at the slop bucket, and at the males in the other cells, and closed her eyes real tight. I sort of enjoyed that. I hoped she'd keep them eyes tight shut for a while, and think about what she done.

They sort of wanted me dead. My ma used to tell me I wasn't the sweetest voice in the church choir, but I never paid much mind to it. Tossing the powerful banker in there—and his rain-barrel wife—now that would set some sort of record for folly in Doubtful. So I just smiled.

"That there pail's for your needs," I said.

Hubert Sanders, he was clamping his hands around the bars so tight his knuckles were white. That was fine with me.

I headed out, after locking the jail door tight, and went back to the opera house. Sure enough, all them Watch and Ward people had fled after I nabbed the ringleaders. And the last of the theater-goers were slipping in. I followed. Ralston nodded, an eyebrow arched, but I didn't tell him nothing. The house lamps were dim, but I could see the place was only half filled. They didn't get the last-night crowd they hoped for. About the time them fellows lit the footlamps, I decided to vamoose. What I wanted was to keep an eye on Doubtful when so many were in the opera house watching the show. So I headed out.

"You send Sanders home?" Ralston asked.

"No, they'll cool their heels awhile. I'll let 'em out when I'm good and ready."

"I hope you have nine lives," he said.

I smiled.

It sure was a nice summer's eve in Doubtful. The June light lingered, and the town seemed at peace. I decided just to patrol, and steer clear of the saloons. So I headed over to the north side of town, where all the swells lived and ordinary people like me weren't ever invited, and walked through those three blocks of comfortable homes on Wyoming Street. Most of them picketers lived around there, and now they were back inside of the white frame houses, many of them with shiplap siding. I could look through all them big glass windows, framed by curtains, and see nice rooms lit by kerosene lamps, all pleasant and secure.

Most of the trouble in Doubtful was south of Main Street, so I didn't get over to this area much. The town sort of faded into grassy fields with long gulches full of cottonwood trees, and after that, the foothills. All those people in their comfortable houses treated the country behind them as a sort of village green, where they would go picnicking and walking. There was sort of an unwritten rule: that was for the business people in Doubtful, and ordinary folks weren't welcome there. I don't think I'd ever been back in there.

What caught my eye was a mess of ravens and crows and magpies loading up some cottonwoods back in one gulch. I didn't like the looks of that. When all them black birds collected, it was for a funeral. Every once in a while something would stir them up, and they would rise in a cloud of wings and settle again. I eyed the crowd, and figured someone's dead dog had been tossed back there, or something like that. I was fixing to return to Main Street, and maybe join the intermission crowd at the opera house, but my feet kept hauling me past them nice homes and out on the meadow and finally into the gulch, where I sure stirred up not just a bunch of birds, but a lot of little animals that kept busting loose when they saw me working my way up the gulch.

I finally got to the heart of it, and discovered a horse lying there, or what was left of it. It was mostly picked down to the bone, and there wasn't much left to feed a crowd of scavengers like that. I thought maybe I knew that horse, because I knew the color of the hide, and when I got in a little bit, I found myself staring at Critter. His throat had been slashed and he'd been left to bleed to death. It was him, all right. His empty eye sockets were full of blackness. None of all his kicks, all his life, kicked me as hard as I got kicked right then, right in my gut. I got kicked so hard I could hardly think.

Critter was gone.

I thought of all the places we'd gone together, over mountaintops and across meadows and through canyons. And how he'd stood over me when I climbed into my bedroll. And how he had notions and I had notions and sometimes he won. And the time he stopped dead and refused to move and I was spurring him and trying to make him move, but all he did was crow-hop. And then I saw the big prairie rattler on a high rock, ready to sink his fangs into me or into Critter.

I stared at the mess of hide and bone and gristle. It was getting dark.

I backed out of there, knowing Critter hadn't been stolen from Turk's Livery Barn by some ranny who wanted a horse; Critter was stolen to hurt me as bad as a man can be hurt. It wasn't a very good feeling. Someone killing an innocent horse to get at me. Some holdup man sticking me up on Main Street. Some burglar getting into my room at Belle's, and taking my good revolver and belt and holster. It had come together as a pattern. These here weren't random acts; they were all intended to get at me one way or another. And that meant someone sure didn't want me around Doubtful anymore, or maybe someone just wanted to make me as miserable as a man can get.

Which I was. Losing Critter was like losing a friend. Maybe like losing one's own pa. Critter was like a pa sometimes, teaching me stuff I was too thickheaded to teach myself.

That discovery up there in that lonely gulch, in June twilight, maybe half a mile above Main Street, sort of changed my life. It didn't matter whether I wore a star or not; whoever was doing this stuff to me would be brought to justice, whether I was sheriff or Iceberg had the job.

I headed back into town. I'd missed the intermission at the opera house, when half them cowboys were outside puffing away on their cheroots. So the final act of the final night for the Gildersleeve Company was playing in there. I walked past Turk's and found some of the roustabouts from the show harnessing them wagons. That show would be off and gone within minutes of the final curtain.

I found the sheriff office real quiet; De Graff was gone somewhere, as usual, and nothing but a smoky lamp burned, its bad wick needing a trim. I unlocked the jail door and headed through the dim light back to the cell where them Sanderses were enjoying a little visit. Iceberg stared. Arty stared. The Sanderses sat side by side on the single iron bunk, staring.

I unlocked that cell.

"Go home. Don't ever pull a gun on a peace officer again," I said.

They stared at me, not quite believing they were free to go. Finally Delphinium rose, dusted off her clothing as if it was full of lice, and pulled Hubert up, and they walked out, ahead of me.

"Where's my revolver?" Hubert said.

"I'm going to keep that for a day or two, until you quiet down," I said.

"It's not your property."

"It's my peace. I'm a peace officer. You'll get it back when it seems fitting."

At least Sanders was speaking. All the way from the opera house to the jail cell he had not said a word, but those burning eyes spoke a lot better than his tongue and lips ever could. I could see Iceberg smirking in there.

"Kill a horse, did you?" I asked, not knowing why I said it. I just felt like saying it. Iceberg stopped smirking.

I locked up the jail and escorted the banker and his wife to the door.

They neither thanked me for cutting them loose nor cursed me nor said one word. Instead, they showed me their backs, and walked stiffly into the twilight. I watched them turn north. They had the biggest house on Wyoming Street, which is the way bankers live. Maybe they'd watched that convention of black birds up the gulch a way behind their place. Maybe they'd enjoyed the sight.

The show must have ended. I saw some fellers wander out of the opera house and head for the saloons. Hardly anyone in Doubtful went straight home after one of them shows. They went to the Sampling Room, hoping to mix with the girls. But even as people poured out of the theater and vanished into the summer darkness, the roustabouts and teamsters were driving those wagons and coaches straight up to Ralston's place, and began piling in all the theater stuff, the settings and lamps and all that. One freight wagon already had the trunks of the cast in it; they must have packed up before the show. The gals hardly got their greasepaint off before they were crawling into the coaches, while Madame Gildersleeve and her fixer, Harry Frost, were huddled with Ralston. I watched that a little, knowing that they were summing up the take and who got what. But eventually Ralston handed over some packets of cash and coin, and Frost pushed it into his black portmanteau, and headed for the mud wagon that would carry the madame and some of the top people in the show.

That looked like a heap of money to me, but Ralston had told me it didn't amount to a whole lot. What the businessmen in town saw was a lot of cash leaving Doubtful for good, cash that could have kept circulating right there, making all the local folks real happy. That mud wagon apparently had a lockbox in there somewhere, because I could make out Frost pushing his hand down in and clamping a padlock on it. That wouldn't stop a holdup gang for long.

My ma, she always said to see guests to the door, so I wandered over there and had my say to the madame.

"Awful nice of you folks to come by, and you come again now," I said.

"Next time, we'll want some rooms and some box office," she said, sort of tart.

"I thought you filled it up pretty good," I said.

"Good? First night, maybe. Let me tell you a thing or two, Sheriff. This was the make or break night. We'd win or lose in Doubtful depending on a full house. We lost. If you'd chased those crazy women off, maybe we'd have sold out. But you didn't."

"They had a right to wave their signs, long as it was peaceful, ma'am."

"Sheriff, if you want Doubtful on the show circuit, you'd better welcome us real nice."

"It sure was a good show," I said.

"Legs," she said. "They wanted bare legs and undies so we gave them legs and undies."

"Those are pretty gals you got, ma'am."

"The prettier they are, the more impossible they are, Sheriff. There's some need a harness and a whip. If I could put a show on the road without a single broad in it, I'd do it in a trice."

"It's a hard world," I said. "All them male singers and comics and magicians and the cowboys of Wyoming don't cross your palm with silver."

She eyed me like I was a snake. "You're a card, Pickens."

"My ma always said I was the two of clubs," I replied.

She smiled, and climbed into that mud wagon, and Frost climbed in beside her. I watched them getting settled down in there, while the driver climbed up on the box and got aholt of all them reins.

In an amazingly short time, that show was loaded up, and the girls settled into a wagon, and the roustabouts and teamsters were lining out the drays and teams, and next I knew, just as a big moon tipped the horizon, that Gildersleeve Variety Company was rattling out of Doubtful and into the bright June afterglow.

It somehow seemed kind of lonesome.

Chapter Thirteen

Ralston joined me.

"They'll reach the railroad tomorrow," he said.

"They're carrying some cash."

"Not as much as you suppose. It cost them plenty to board the company. More to take them to the next stop."

"The merchants are all whining."

Ralston laughed. "After gouging the company for meals, rooms, supplies, booze, animal feed, and all the rest. Whine away, I say."

"They think the company's simply walking off with cash that should be theirs."

"And right now Harry Frost is blistering Madame Gildersleeve's ear about how Doubtful euchred them out of a profit."

"How do *you* see it?" I asked.

"Doubtful profited. It added to the town's business. It brought cowboys off the ranches in droves."

"I think so too, but you'll have trouble persuading Hubert Sanders of it."

"He'll change his tune. Just wait until the Grand Luxemburg Follies open up."

"What'll happen?"

"It'll draw every last male off every last ranch in Puma County, and half the males in the next counties over. And they'll spend."

"Guess that should please our barkeeps," I said.

"It'll please the barkeeps, the madams, the merchants, and the banker—if he's got eyes to see. Doubtful's going to do a land-office trade."

"If the show opens up," I said. "If I can keep Ike Berg locked down, maybe it'll be like you say. But they're all ganging up on me."

Ralston eyed me quietly. "I'm depending on you," he said.

"Right now I'm worried that the Gildersleeve outfit'll be jumped."

"There's hooligans in every town on the circuit who think they'll clean out the company when it leaves. If they try to set up an ambush around here, they'll be in for a surprise. Those traveling companies expect it, and know how to deal with it."

"I thought it might be something like that."

"They'll keep Doc Harrison busy, and it won't be patching up the Gildersleeve company, either."

I was real tired, and it had been a bad day. My old horse was dead, murdered in a gulch. I had a cough. My night deputy couldn't keep his pants on. And I was trying to hang on to my job, which someone wanted me out of real bad.

"Guess I'll fold," I said.

"Guess I'll lock up," he replied.

I made my way to Belle's, ready for a week of sleep.

It finally got good and dark. Sometimes I thought June days never quit.

I got as far as Colorado Street when a stickup man hit me.

"Hands up, Sheriff, and don't swing the billy club. I'm too far behind you."

That sounded authoritative so I slowly raised my arms.

"Higher!"

"You got everything last time and the county hasn't paid me."

"Higher!"

"Ah, hell, if you're going to shoot, then shoot."

"Pull your pockets out."

"I got my hands up."

"Lower them and pull your pockets. I want your jail key."

"Don't have it on me." I pulled my pockets and dropped a couple of dimes. He ignored them.

"Head for the jail," he said.

It sure was turning into a long night, but I done as he said, and he followed behind, and we hiked back to Main and up the stairs and in. De Graff was still off somewhere.

"No tricks, Pickens. Get the jail keys and drop

them on the floor. If you pick up anything else, you're Maxwell's meat."

"I forget where they are," I said, trying to turn my head around to get a glimpse of the holdup man. It was dark in there, with one lamp lit and its chimney smoked up. There were a couple of shotguns and a couple of rifles in the rack on the wall, none loaded. The jail keys were kept out of sight. Mine were in my desk drawer. I wondered if I could reach the sawed-off scatter-gun I'd been using, which was on my desk.

"Don't," he said.

"I plumb forgot where them keys are," I said.

The shot lifted my hat plumb off my noggin. It sure made a lot of noise.

"I just remembered," I said.

I pulled the bottom drawer and pitched the keys in his direction. He scooped them up, and now I got a glimpse. He had a kerchief over his face, and was wide and short, and dark-haired. He could have been any of a dozen people I'd seen around town.

"Pull your star off," he said. "You got fired and now you'll stay fired."

I got an idea where this was heading. I unpinned my badge and laid it real gentle on my desk.

"Leave that billy club on your desk."

I done that, too.

"Now, head out the door," he said.

I walked out, and the door slammed behind

me and I heard him bolt the lock. It sure was quiet and dark in Doubtful.

I slid off into the shadows and waited. It didn't take long. The door opened up, spilling lamplight, and the holdup man and Ike Berg emerged. Ike was wearing a star, and I thought it was probably mine. My sheriff job had come to a screeching halt.

At least that's what they thought. Me, I'd keep right on with it, whether they liked that or not. From my shadowed view, under a store gallery, I eyed the pair. I thought the stickup man was the same as robbed me earlier, and when I thunk about it, maybe he was a horse thief, a horse killer, and worse, all rolled into one.

I sure was tired. I kept on watching and saw them head for the hotel and go in. It was so dark I couldn't be sure. I edged over to the hotel, trying to see into the lobby, but there wasn't anyone in there, and not one lamp was lit. I waited awhile, thinking the stickup man might come out, but he didn't.

I got to coughing, and knew I'd better get to bed or get worse again. But first I hiked over to Rusty, and knocked on his door. He had a little shack behind the cathouses. He opened up real fast, his six-gun in his fist.

He looked me over and invited me in with a nod. Then he lit a lamp.

"What?" he asked.

I told him. And then I told him about Critter, too.

"I'm Berg's deputy now?" he asked.

"Looks that way."

"The hell I am. I'll quit."

"I'd like you to stay on, Rusty. That stickup man's gonna wander in and you'll figure a few things out, like who he is. They haven't run me out of town yet, but that's next. They might fire you, too, might fire all my deputies and put in their own. If they do, will you join me? We've got us a crime wave, and now it's in my office."

He eyed me awhile, and simply grinned. That's what I like about Rusty.

"I've got an old iron to lend you," he said. He headed into the rear room and came out with a battered gun belt with a Smith and Wesson parked in it, and handed it to me. I strapped it on, and it felt real good.

"It doesn't fire true," he said, "but it makes lots of noise."

"They even took my billy club," I said. "And I was partial to that sawed-off scatter-gun, but that's the county's."

"Look, Cotton, they won't want us around. They know we'll stick together. I'm expecting I'll get my marching orders when I walk in. The rest, too. I don't know what your plans are, but I want to tell you something. Whatever they are, deal me in. I think the others will agree."

"The thing is, I don't know what's behind it," I said. "I've been a good peace officer, kept the lid on, and now this."

"Yeah, it's a mystery. The supervisors, they're itching to get rid of you. Something's pushing and shoving them," Rusty said.

"Care to guess who?"

"Somebody with a lot of push and shove," he said, yawning.

I got out of there. I hiked across the south side, past the saloons and cathouses and all that stuff, which were still lit up. It felt strange, not having that badge on my chest. I was just another citizen now, without the power to do much. I got to my room, glad to throw myself into my bunk, barely taking time to unbuckle Rusty's hardware. I had intended to lie there and speculate a little, try to figure out what tomorrow would bring. But all I managed to do was drop into a deep sleep, and I didn't break out of that until the next dawn, when sunlight tickled me awake.

It occurred to me I had to make a living. On Monday, I'd owe Belle for another week. And somehow I would need to pump some chow into me. I didn't even have a horse to take me out to the ranches, where I might hire on to do a little cowboying. The thought of Critter, his throat slit, lying in that gulch, sure didn't make getting up and facing the day any better.

I rifled the stocking where I kept a few singles, stuffed them into my pocket, and headed out the door. Belle waylaid me before I could escape.

"It's all over town," she said. "You're out, Skinny's in."

"It's a mystery," I said.

"No, it ain't. The banker's wife, she's been pushing to shut down all the saloons and the, ah, pleasure places, and clean up Doubtful, and you're the obstacle. She wants Doubtful to turn Baptist, or whatever she is, and get dipped in the river."

"You think so? How do you know that?"

Belle glared at me. "Sometimes, Cotton Pickens, you don't know where your feet are."

"That's what my ma always said."

"Maybe I should go get myself baptised before they shut me down," she said. "Once you've been pushed under water, wearing all white, they leave you alone."

I got out of there. The Beanery was a likely place for some cheap chow, so I barged in—and discovered my whole crew there.

"We knew you'd show up," Burtell said.

I stared at them. No badges.

They waved me to their table. "We're out. They collected our badges. We don't know who Iceberg's naming as his deputies, but it ain't us," said De Graff.

"Where were you last night?" I asked.

"Patrolling the tenderloin."

"Yeah, every room," Rusty said.

De Graff smiled cheerily. "I keep 'em all from overcharging customers," he said. "Personal inspection."

Billy Bono, the proprietor, set a bowl of oatmeal before me, which was fine. I could breakfast for one thin dime.

"How come they fired you?" he asked.

"Because of the crime wave," I said.

Bono laughed. "Word sure got around."

Rusty waited for Bono to vamoose. "What's gonna happen next?" he asked.

"Me, I'm going to find out who killed Critter, who robbed me, who stole my gun belt. And why. What are you fellers going to do?"

"Help you," Rusty said. "Until we run out of money, which won't be long. But we'll help out. We've been making a few plans of our own. Something's gone real wrong in Doubtful, and there ain't nobody but ourselves to put it straight."

"That would be mighty fine, mighty fine," I said. "We've got a friend, Cyrus Ralston. It's also a place for us to meet on the quiet. Cy's plenty worried that this is all directed at him, that the goal of half the merchants in town is to shut down his opera house and keep those variety companies from playing here. And we're the only help he's got, especially now with the county supervisors, the sheriff, the banker, and all the town's merchants lined up against him. There's something we can do, starting today when the next company rolls in. We can protect it, and keep Ralston's doors open."

"What for?" De Graff asked.

"It's a girlie show," I said.

CHAPTER FOURTEEN

The Grand Luxemburg Follies rolled into Doubtful in style. This was obviously a high-class outfit. Outside of town, they'd taken time to polish up. The lacquered coaches had been wiped down. Them actresses, all dressed in gauzy white and wearing big straw hats, were all bunched on a big wagon covered with red bunting. Man, were they a sight. I never saw such a bunch of pretty girls.

Even the harness on the draft horses was loaded with nickel-plate, so everything shone bright and fancy. Four wine-red coaches and six wagons came in that June afternoon, with the company musicians tooting away on one wagon, them trumpets and trombones all brassy in the sunlight. And then came the one with the ladies. They was so pretty it was all anyone could do not to rush up there and do some kissing. I'd trade my sheriff job for two or three of those ladies any day. My ma always said, it ain't what's under a dress but under a skull bone that counts, but I wasn't of a mind to pay her any attention. It didn't matter what they had in their heads. They were plumb delightful, tossing kisses at the gathering crowds, smiling, standing in that wagon in them gauzy dresses that looked like the wind could blow them away. I knew half the cowboys around Doubtful were going to spend their last dime seeing that show every night it played.

Ralston had got his promotion men busy pasting up red and black and yellow broadsheets on every fence and barn in the area, so the show was getting the attention it wanted. Those sheets were everywhere. Most of them said

GIRLS, GIRLS, GIRLS
THE GRAND LUXEMBURG
❧ FOLLIES ☙

Thirty-Six Beautiful Ladies.

Ballet Straight from Paris, France.

The Royal Flemish Opera *singing*
Arias from Milan.

Tableaux Vivants from the Louvre Museum, the
Galleries of Florence, the Prado of Spain.

☙

And the UNFORGETTABLE *"Beaux-Arts Ball."*

Well, if that didn't start an itch in every male in Puma County, nothing would.

So there was the outfit, rolling down Main Street, and people rushing to see what was what. There sure weren't thirty-six ladies on that wagon, but ten or fifteen would do just fine. And none of them had varicose veins neither, like the ones in that Gildersleeve outfit. Maybe these were all painted up, but they looked younger than the ones that rolled out of town.

"Hey, Rusty, do you feel like you died and gone to heaven?" I asked.

"Nah. If you've seen one, you've seen 'em all," Rusty said.

I don't know why I ever deputized him if he thought like that.

Speaking of that, along came Iceberg, wearing the Puma County star on his black frock coat, a skinny lawman that looked like he'd just escaped from the bottom of hell. And he had him a new deputy with him, short and wide and built like a butcher's block, with the muscles of a blacksmith pushing through his shirt. That sure interested me. I'd never seen that one before, and marked him as trouble. It was pure instinct. He was strong. He could stab with a finger, slap with the back of his hand, and send me sprawling. I decided just to call him the Butcher, since I had no name. Them two just plain ticked me off.

But for now the pair was just gawking. At least the Butcher was. I think Iceberg must have been immune to women, because he just studied on everything and said nothing and let people see who was in charge. One glance landed on me, but then he was looking off in other directions, like he was casing his new town. He seemed like a pool of darkness there on that sunny day when everyone in Doubtful was having a fine old time.

But he left me alone—for the moment. I kept expecting he'd find some excuse to make me his guest in his iron-barred parlor.

The new company rolled right past the opera house, where Ralston stood watching, and headed for the far side of town. Then it rolled back and pulled up in front of the theater. I crowded in. The girls stepped down from their wagon, and waved at all them merchants and cowboys gawking, and at a few frowning ladies who didn't like all the competition getting off the wagon. Sure enough, there was Delphinium Sanders, a cylinder of lavender velvet, scowling at the actresses like they'd done something wrong just by being in Doubtful. I had a hunch she and her bunch would be out picketing tonight, and they'd have Iceberg on hand to block theater patrons from going in. Maybe things would get real rough.

One gal, cutest thing I'd ever seen, with a mess of curly red hair and ruby lips, gave me a big smile and I big-smiled back at her, and thought about proposing matrimony, but decided I'd wait a little bit. I wanted to see her perform. Pretty soon the opera house swallowed the new company, and its roustabouts were unloading sets and gear and hauling it in there. They didn't have much time if they were going to run the first show this very night.

"Guess I'll buy a ticket," Rusty said.

"We don't get in free anymore," I said.

"I'd like to marry about six of them, all at once," he said.

"I couldn't handle more than one," I said.

Rusty shook his head at me. "Poor devil," he said.

The last person out of the coaches was a little feller with a potbelly, almost a dwarf, skinny except for the bowling-ball belly. He wore a black silk stovepipe hat that added a couple of feet to his person, and the rest of him was all encased in a black broadcloth suit, along with them shiny patent leather shoes that never saw a scuff.

He stared around, eyeing Iceberg and his new deputy, and the crowd, and the dour-looking women in it, and the views up and down Main Street. He smiled, lighting up one side of his misshapen, off-center face. His black-eyed gaze finally settled on the lavender and formidable Madame Sanders, so he approached, removed his big old silk hat, and bowed clear from the waist, with an elaborate sweep of his hand.

"Ah, madame, it is a pleasure to be in Doubtful at last. We've heard good things about this place, and appreciate your warm welcome."

Delphinium glared back icily.

"I am Alphonse de Jardine, the author and

proprietor of the Follies, late of Paris, Monte Carlo, Madrid, and Barcelona."

"You purvey wickedness," she replied. "You bring shame to Doubtful."

"Culture, madame! You will see samples of the great arts of Europe. Opera! Ballet! Comedy! Symphonic music! I invite you. I will give you and your beloved a pair of free tickets, so that you may enjoy my little extravaganza. It will delight the eye, balm the spirit, lift the heart, bedazzle the mind." He reached into his black suit coat and pulled out two purple tickets. "Here! Free passes to the greatest show on earth!"

Poor old Delphinium. The lure was too much for her. Instead of declining, she snatched the pasteboards from his tiny hand, even while her trout-lips were pursed in disdain. The little feller was delighted, and soon had handed out another ten or twelve purple ducats to assorted gawkers. That seemed to me a pretty good way to make a few friends. Two of them tickets went to Iceberg and his new deputy, who could've walked in free anyway. But there was the sheriff, eyeing them purple tickets like he never seen the like.

After that, the impresario vanished inside the opera house, and there wasn't much to see. The town's women kept their eyes on the door, half expecting someone naked to rush out of it, but all they saw was the stagehands and teamsters hauling stuff inside. Fancy sets full of glitter, and big trunks, stuff like that. And some of the other roustabouts had a wagon over at the hotel, and were hauling trunks in there. Looked like the actresses would all be squeezed in there, and would find their travel trunks in their rooms after the show.

This here was a real show, all right. There ain't many kids in Doubtful, but now a gang of little rascals was collected around those big drays, most of them dappled gray Percherons, which were about as big as horses get. The squirts had never seen horses like that, or a nickel-dressed harness before. While everyone else was gazing at the beautiful showgirls, them kids were studying the horses. In a few years that would all change.

"I guess we buy our own tickets," Rusty said, sounding a little blue. Neither him nor me could afford a seat in there, and there were no free passes to ex-sheriffs or fired deputies.

The crowd was thinning now, the excitement over. And pretty soon the streets of Doubtful were half empty again, except for all them fancy carriages and wagons.

"I want to find out who that new deputy is," I said.

Rusty and me, we hiked over to the Last Chance Saloon and found Sammy Upward in his usual white apron, polishing his shiny bar. Sammy plucked two tumblers up and started to load them up, but I slowed him some.

"Sammy, we don't have badges anymore."

"I know that," he said, and poured our favorite hooch in there, bourbon for me and red-eye rotgut for Rusty. I never could figure out why Rusty liked to scorch his tongue out of his skull.

"Okay, what happened?" Sammy asked.

"Supervisors didn't like how I was keeping the peace and got rid of me, and the new man fired my deputies."

"Iceberg," Sammy said. "We've been hearing stuff. Is it true that Iceberg's going to shut down the saloons and close the cathouses and boot the tinhorns out? That's what I'm hearing. Also, no one does business on Sundays. Is that true?"

"If it is, some of our best citizens will lynch him," Rusty said. "I may join the crowd."

"I don't know. I have no idea what's happening. It all seemed to crank up when Ralston built his opera house. Now there's a regular army of mean old ladies out picketing, and I get robbed, my horse is stolen and killed, and my room rifled and my stuff stolen—and the politicians call it a crime wave and blame me. And then fire me. And put into office a feller who's not resigned down in Medicine Bow County, far as I know."

"Someone wants you out," Sammy said.

"Maybe it's not me. Maybe it's a way to shut down the opera house."

Sammy polished a glass and smiled. "I don't get it."

"I don't get it either. But I will."

"That man that was killed outside of here. Who was he?"

"Pinky Pearl, Ralston told us. He was an advance man for this show."

"Like making arrangements?"

"We buried him, and Ralston said a few words."

"That was aimed at this show," Sammy said.

"Or at Ralston and his opera house."

"These shows siphon a lot of cash out of town?"

"Ralston says no; they actually bring cash in. Cowboys come in and spend."

"Yeah, they spent in here and Rosie's place," Sammy said. "I did a good trade."

"And over at the mercantile, they didn't sell one union suit or one bandana."

Upward smiled. "Now you're getting somewhere. I got one question. What's Medicine Bow County like, with Iceberg law?"

"They voted themselves dry," Rusty said. "So Iceberg shut down the saloons. And threw out the madams. And shut down all businesses on Sundays. It sure is silent there. I visited there a couple of years ago, and it was like staying in the back room of a funeral parlor. The ranch people, they headed for Laramie if they wanted a good time. No one ever heard of prohibition in Laramie, and what's her name, Carrie Nation, she never showed up in Laramie, busting bottles with her axe. You know what it is? That there Temperance Union. It's all women. Next thing you know, they'll be wanting to vote. Makes me pine for the old days, five years ago, when a man was a man and a woman knew how to be a woman."

"There's our future," Upward said. He looked

pretty bleak. "And that's what the Puma county supervisors are heading toward. Next thing you know, we'll have women in office here. And maybe that's why you were axed."

"My ma, she always said that women already are the supervisors," I said. "She says women tell men how to vote and they do it if they want peace in their house or a little kiss at bedtime."

Rusty shuddered.

It sure was pretty grim to think about. Doubtful would have to change its name to Desolate. And call itself the county coffin instead of the county seat. The sporting people were all waiting for the axe to fall. I sort of wondered where Reggie Thimble and Ziggy Camp and George Waller came up with a mess of bad ideas like that. Or maybe they didn't. Maybe they was being pushed. Maybe some of them merchants were putting the squeeze on the supervisors. It sure wasn't anything I could figure out. And there wasn't much I could do about it, star or no star.

Rusty and me, we finished our drinks and got out of there. The world was coming to an end. The good times, anyway. That was the trouble with civilization. When things are still wild, it's every man for himself, but once the women and children start rolling in, things change, and no one can have fun anymore. I wondered how long it would take for all them bluenoses to shut down the Grand Luxemburg Follies. About two minutes, is what I decided. I'd see soon enough.

CHAPTER FIFTEEN

Rusty and me, we found ourselves in that little cubbyhole of an office Ralston had. Across from us was the show's boss, Alphonse de Jardine, still wearing his stovepipe hat over his straight black hair.

"So we buried your man," I said. "We don't know who done it. I've got the saloon men listening. They hear things."

"Doubtful seems a little inhospitable," Jardine said. He had some funny accent and I had to listen hard. "Pinky Pearl was a gem. By the time we would roll into a town, he'd have the theater ready, the broadsides pasted on every barn and fence, the tickets printed, the rooms ready. He was the best in the business. I can't replace him."

"I feel real bad, sir," I said. "We got some trouble here. There's some folks, they don't want a show in Doubtful. They got rid of me, and my deputy Rusty here, and they put in a man who don't have no vices at all. He don't even drink coffee. He's got his county so locked down it's like Sunday mornings all the time."

"He's the sheriff here now?"

"He's wearing the star. And them supervisors, they told me I was done for."

"What'll happen tonight?"

"They'll look for some reason to shut you down."

"I offer many reasons, and take great pride in it. We're avant garde."

"Avant what?"

"Progressive."

"That ain't how that's spelled, but I'll take your word for it."

"Will they wait for the show to end?"

"Beats me, Jardine."

"It's monsieur. Call me monsieur."

"Well, you're a friend no matter what you get called," I said.

"We offer splendid *tableaux vivants.*"

"What are them? Draft horses?"

"No, *mon ami*, they are living art. We create in living flesh and blood the art of the Louvre, the Prado, and all the great art museums of Europe. You will see Rubens, Rembrandt, Goya, and a host of other splendid paintings brought to life with live models."

"I reckon I don't get the half of it, but my ma always used to say, wait and see."

"You think these live paintings will get you into trouble?" Rusty asked.

Jardine smiled crookedly, revealing two silver teeth and one gold. "Monsieur, a man who will not sip wine, who will not puff a pipe, a man who makes the whole world a sepulcher, ah, my friend, the Follies puts a halt to all funerals, and this angel of death will not favor it."

"You don't say!"

"You will be my guests, and I have a small request. Keep order. Protect my company."

"I don't wear the badge any more, man-sewer."

"Pretend that you do," he said.

"I sure want to see one of them tables," I said. "Even if my ma wouldn't like them."

Ralston ushered us out. The place was a dim madhouse, with sets being assembled, and costumes getting unpacked, and the footlights getting charged with fresh kerosene. I saw that redhead and smiled, and she smiled back.

"You in one of them tables?" I asked.

"Tables? Oh, *tableaux*. Why, yes. I play Lady Godiva in one. And I'm in three others."

"I'll be looking," I said.

"Anytime, anyplace," she said.

That was real friendly of her. In all my life, no woman ever said "anytime, anyplace" to me, and the more I chewed that around, the more I thought I might be falling in love. How many men ever met some gal who said that? I thought maybe I should pack up and move to wherever she was from, and try to find more of those. I sort of wonder if I was destined all my life to get hitched to a redhead.

Well, the biddies showed up with their signs when the box office opened and a lot of Doubtful people came flooding in. There was Delphinium, still in purple, or lavender, or whatever, waving a black and white poster that said KEEP DOUBTFUL PURE. And the rest of them ladies with posters talking about sin and death and evil and stuff like that. The crowd, they mostly just grinned and enjoyed the ladies and ignored them as they lined up to shell out their seventy-five cents for a good seat or fifty cents for one of the rear ones, or two-bits for standing room. They were off the ranches, most of them, and some had even scrubbed up a little and wiped the manure off their boots and put on a fresh shirt if they had one. They were wearing their usual slouch hats and that was going to cause a mess of trouble if they blocked views in there, especially of all them real pretty girls. And there sure were some, which I got a good look at with my own eyes. That Frenchie, he must have had a good hiring man to hire gals like that. These girls were young, too, not ones with leathery skin and varicose veins.

I watched Iceberg and his new deputy wander close, and eye all them lusty cowboys buying seats. He stood there, sort of starchy and skinny, looking like he didn't approve of nothing. The other one, the deputy, he was a block of beef on legs, and looked like he wanted to punch anyone that got an inch too close to him. They both were armed. But it was Ike who interested me most. He'd been in town many days and I'd never seen him spend much time at a bar. He was running on dry, is how I figured it. If all the merchants and their ladies here wanted Doubtful to become another Medicine Bow, they'd hired the right man. The pair of them wandered inside, not bothering with tickets, and I waited to see if they'd come out. But they didn't. There wouldn't be any law looking out for Doubtful during the show. But maybe that wasn't so bad. About half the nights I had De Graff on the night duty, he'd be gone somewhere, pants up or down.

I sort of thought they were in there for some purpose. Maybe they was looking for some excuse to shut down the show. I followed them in, and watched them sit in a couple of seats down front, but on the side aisle, and just stretch themselves waiting for the action. The place was filling, and those show people were lighting the footlights, which meant it would get hot in there pretty fast on a soft June night.

There wasn't a whole lot of light in that dark opera house.

The orchestra came in, five fellers with some brass and fiddles and a gal with a harp, of all things. Then, about five after seven according to my timepiece, that music outfit lit up a tune, and the audience quieted. The Follies would crank up now.

That dwarf with the silk topper, he came out waving a black walking stick, and addressed the crowd. All them cowboys and locals were sitting real still.

"Ah, my friends, we are pleased to be in Doubtful, Wyoming. It is the most beautiful city we have ever been in. It is filled with good people. It is surrounded by a natural world unsurpassed. It moves our hearts to be here, and to present our little entertainment to you," he said. "And now, our national anthem."

"What's that?" I asked Rusty.

"The country's song."

"How come no one ever played it before?"

The orchestra sawed away, and them cowboys stood up.

"How come they're all standing up?" I asked Rusty.

"It's what everyone does."

That sure was an awful song, squeaking and sawing away, and hardly a cowboy sang. But then about halfway through, there was a regular parade up there, all them young pretties in gauzy white dresses, marching in a row, carrying little flags, smiling with painted lips, and then they all lined up either side of Jardine, and sang away. They sure were pretty. I spotted the redhead down at one end, and she had ruby lips and orange hair, and she choked me up, and I wished the anthem would never end so I could just watch her sing away.

But finally it ended, and the ringleader, or whatever you call him, peered out from beyond the lights, and said that now we'd see the Ballet de Monte Carlo, direct from the Riviera, wherever that was. And next I knew, just as all the cowboys and shopkeepers were getting seated again, the harpist starts in on that thing, fingering them strings like she wanted to kill them, and the fiddlers and one feller on a clarinet, and they play a lot of goopy loopy stuff, and pretty soon a bunch of actors came leaping and stomping out on stage. I'd never seen the like. There were a couple of men dressed in white underwear and they must have stuffed rags in their crotch; either that or they were very peculiarly made. And then the ladies came out and they were showing a lot of leg beneath itty-bitty pink skirts that looked like frosted doughnuts, and the rest of the pink outfits sort of fit real tight from waist to neck. And then they were leaping and whirling, and them two males in the underwear were tossing the gals around, while the harp and clarinet sawed away.

The fellers would lift the gals and toss them, and the gals would leap at the fellers and get caught, and it sure looked pretty familiar to me. I wondered if those ladies and gents were as familiar offstage as they were right in front of everyone. I wasn't against familiarity, but maybe they should have done this out in their summer kitchen or some place, and not in an opera house in front of half of Doubtful.

Then the ladies did a twirl on one toe. I don't know how they done that. They had little slippers and they'd get up on their toes and stay that way a while and then run like deer. They sure had nice legs. I hadn't seen so much leg before and it made me glow. Them fellers in the long underwear didn't seem to notice, and I wondered what was wrong with them, not admiring all that leg. I looked around for the redhead, but she wasn't in this number, so it wasn't as interesting to me. But pretty soon all the leaping and twirling stopped, and them people were out of breath but pretending not to be, and they all stood in a line and bowed, even though no one was clapping. The cowboys, they didn't know what to make of it either. With all those half-naked people up there, you'd think they would put a bed in the middle of the stage. Then them people run off into the wings, and the music flared up again, and the little gent with the black silk hat paraded out again.

"*Magnifique!*" the little guy says, and claps his hands, and all them people in their underwear came out again and bowed and scraped and blew kisses to the cowboys, who whistled.

"And now, friends, the finest tenor in the Republic, direct from Brooklyn, New York, Sanfred Stolp."

Some guy in a tuxedo came out, flapping his

tails around, and nodded at the cowboys a few times, and then began singing "Little Miss Sunshine." Then he sang "My Beloved Mother's Passing Away." Then he started in on "Roaming in the Gloaming." I'd heard that one once. The crime is usually laid on the Scots.

"What's a gloaming?" I asked Rusty.

"Beats me," he said.

That lasted too long and we were all mighty glad to get him off the stage so we could see the ladies again. But he stayed on, and the music struck up again and this time he sang while all the gals in the company, each with a big fan made of ostrich feathers, came swooping out. You couldn't hardly see the gals for the feathers. Them fans were so big all you saw was a face or a hand or a few dancing feet. But it sure was pretty, all them fans swaying and whirling around together, while that feller sang away up there like someone was paying attention to him.

About the second chorus, it got more interesting up there, as the gals sort of brushed the fans a little farther down so we could see their tops some. They were all in powder-blue outfits, but there was a little shoulder and arm and neck showing, and I liked that and wished I could grab those damned fans and toss them out of there. I didn't want to see the fans; I wanted to see the girls. If I wanted to see ostrich feathers, I'd buy an ostrich. But at least them fans kept whirling and dipping, and by the third chorus, they were

sliding past a little womanly hip. I finally found
my redhead gal, and she was edging her fan past
her legs real slow, and I almost ran up there so I
could catch that fan and toss it away. And all the
rest of the fans, too.

They was wearing real short skirts that almost
came up to their knees, and the fans were showing lots of ankle and leg, and it was a real pretty
sight. I'd never fallen for ankles before but now I
was crazy for ankles. I think I'll hate ostriches the
rest of my life for blocking the view.

Then when that feller was on the final chorus,
the gals, they pretty much were pushing the fans
over their heads, and wiggling them up there,
and it sure was nice to see the gals at last, but it
took them about ten minutes to get there. I sure
liked this show, and all them gals in their little
blue dresses. The Grand Luxemburg Follies were
the best thing that ever came to Doubtful.

The little guy in the big black top hat came out
and said there'd be an intermission, so all them
cowboys and people could go smoke. They piled
out of there into the June twilight, and lit up,
and the older ones headed for the two outhouses
back behind the opera house, but the young
ones just slid over to the alley and cut loose.

Pretty soon some lady with a cowbell came
around ringing, and that was how they corralled
all the citizens of Doubtful for the second act.

CHAPTER SIXTEEN

Before we headed back in there, I scouted around a little to see where Iceberg was, and I found him fast enough standing in deep shadow, along with that blocky deputy, in a rear corner trying to look invisible. That was a bad sign.

When we all got lassoed down, the orchestra whipped up a tune or two, and they started in on a chorus that had them gals dressed in pants. All the pretty gals in the show was wearing boiled white shirts and black tuxedos and top hats. I didn't like that one bit. A woman is a woman and a man is a man, and they were pretty fast ruining my evening. I thought maybe I'd talk to Jardine about that one, saying it don't go over very well with a mess of cowboys and other good folks.

Then that singer who nearly drove us out the door came back on stage, and began talking at us. He said that long ago in England there was an evil nobleman whose taxes were so heavy they were ruining his town, a place called Coventry, and driving the citizens into despair. The man's wife, named Lady Godiva, took pity on the suffering people whose rents were much too high, and begged her husband to lower the rents. But he refused time after time. Finally, weary of her constant begging, he told her he would lower the rents if she would ride through Coventry wearing nothing at all.

Well, that story was getting real interesting, and all them cowboys in the audience was all perked up. This singer continued. Lady Godiva, he said, agreed to do it. And so the town of Coventry prepared for the ride, shutting all windows and doors, and hanging curtains. But there was one feller, a tailor named Tom, who drilled a little peephole in his door and watched as the beautiful woman rode by on her beautiful horse. But because God is good, the tailor was struck blind right then and there.

"And now, ladies and gentlemen, Lady Godiva's ride!" he said.

I could hear a horse stomping around back there, and sure enough a feller dressed like a knight was leading a nag onstage, and there she was, my redheaded friend, buck naked, her lithe body glowing in the footlights. I swear, it was real quiet in there. She was plumb pretty, sitting bare on a bare horse, walking slowly across the stage. There was a mess of heavy breathing in the audience. I'd never seen the like, and I was sort of hoping she'd take the reins and steer that horse into the aisle and out the front door so I could have a closer look. But all they did was stop in the middle of the stage, and she looked around some, and we could see more of her when she did that. Then a little door in the back of the stage creaked open, and some runt of a man peered out, and stared at her, and then someone in the orchestra hit a drum and there was a flash of light and the little peeper, he clasped his arm to his eyes and staggered back and then the red-head, she and her horse slowly walked across the stage and vanished.

It was real quiet in there, but then the clapping started, and we all wanted her to come out for an encore, but she didn't. Instead, that little feller playing the peeper, he staggered around clutching his eyes, and then vanished.

That sure was the best scene I ever did see. I didn't know what my ma would think of that one, but I sure liked it. And I'd pay to see it the next night, too.

It got real noisy in there for a while, and a few fellers whistled and plotted to get her and that horse and bring 'em out again, but in the end they didn't.

Next they gave us the Royal Opera of Madrid, and some people came out and screeched a while until I wanted to vamoose, but I kept my seat, and Rusty stared at the floor, and pretty soon the screeching was over. It had to do with some old gal suffering consumption, and as she lay in bed screeching, everyone around her was sobbing away until she sort of gave up the ghost and the orchestra whined a little and the curtain came down.

The little feller with the big hat came scrambling out, and kept lifting that hat and lowering it, and pretty soon all them bored cowboys quieted down some.

"Now, esteemed ladies and gentlemen," he began, "we will celebrate the virtue and goodness of this new nation, this republic built on freedom. We will honor Lady Liberty, the Goddess of Freedom, the divine spark that has turned this republic into the bountiful and golden land of dreams. Now, my dear friends, let us applaud the Goddess of Liberty!"

Them curtains rolled back and there she was, up on a big box, standing there with a golden crown on her head, a scepter in her hand— I think that's what them things are called, and not much else. There was some sort of gauzy, filmy stuff draped over her, but not much more, and she sure was pretty and there wasn't no part of her we couldn't see through that gauze. There she was, every inch of her celebrating Liberty and Freedom and all that stuff, and the cowboys sure cheered. There wasn't nothing hid; from her bright red hair down to her pink toes, she was Freedom itself. That sure was a dandy moment, and we never loved our republic so much as we did then. She stood real still, like in a painting, and hardly moved an arm or turned her face, and we sure had a fine old time studying on Liberty. I was all for liberty and freedom, and now I could think of nothing else.

Well, all good things shut down, and pretty soon the curtain shut her off from us, and we soon were getting more choruses and that ballet outfit came back, and another round of the ostrich feather fans, and all that. It was a nice show, but that Goddess of Liberty was the standout.

I glanced around, and there was Iceberg staring at the stage, like he was ready to cause trouble, but he just stood there in the shadows. I knew something was up, but I didn't really know what.

They had a tap dancer going next, some feller with shiny shoes that had metal on the soles and he thought it was pretty fine to make a racket, while the fiddles fiddled and the drums drummed. He sure rattled around too long, and I was ready to give him to the woodpeckers so they could all tap on tree bark, but finally he got off of there, and the next act was a chorus of pretty girls singing Stephen Foster. I'd never heard of that feller, but the little dude in the big hat told us he was America's favorite songwriter.

Anyway, the gals singing those songs were all dolled up real nice. Those were lively airs, and I got to tapping my feet. They sang "Jeannie With the Light Brown Hair," and sure enough, a real pretty gal with light brown hair came drifting through. She was dressed proper and we couldn't see anything except a real pretty gal with a real pretty face.

They switched over to "Oh! Susanna," and that was one I'd heard a couple of times, and it went just fine. And then came "Camptown Races" and how some fools bet on the wrong nags, so I didn't like that one. And next was "My Old Kentucky Home," and I feared this Foster feller might be a Southerner. I don't like Southerners, and wish they'd all move to Argentina. But the song was pretty nice. And finally these gals sang "Old Folks at Home," and that was real sweet, but it sounded pretty southern to me. I'm not sure where that Swanee River is, but it ain't around Wyoming and I wouldn't want to drink the water.

Them gals hustled off, and the little feller announced the Grand Finale.

The orchestra thundered up, and the gents were in tuxedos and the gals in long gowns, and they were doing a waltz. But up on that box behind them was three women, bare-ass naked, the Goddesses of Abundance, Joy, and Beauty, according to them signs. They just stood there wearing haloes on their heads and not a stitch, and I was all for Abundance, Joy, and Beauty for the rest of my life, Especially Joy, because she was the redhead that caught my eye. You can't quarrel with Joy.

"I like Abundance," Rusty said.

"Then don't work as a peace officer," I said.

He gave me an elbow.

But all too soon the curtain cut off the view, and the show was over. We sort of waited around for an encore, but that was it. And all the cowboys and such drifted out. The few women in the audience sort of stared straight ahead, not looking at any of the men around them, and pretended that hadn't seen nothing unusual. I was so taken by the whole show, and Joy in particular, that I wasn't paying much attention until Rusty elbowed me again.

Then I saw Iceberg and his beefy deputy make their way forward, as if to talk to the management, and I got up fast and followed. The little feller, Jardine, and Ralston wanted me on hand to slow down trouble if I could; that's how we got in for free. So me and Rusty pushed forward, and followed Iceberg into the backstage area, just in time to see Iceberg throw manacles onto Jardine while the deputy cuffed Ralston.

"You're under arrest," Iceberg said to them.

"For what?" Ralston asked.

"Violating public decency."

"What statute is that?" Ralston asked. "I don't know of any. Show it to me."

For an answer, Iceberg cuffed the manager, who tumbled to the ground. Some of those gals were watching, and they screamed. There sure was some commotion back there as people scattered.

Them fellows who were dousing the footlights quit and got away.

Ralston was slow to get to his feet but the beefy deputy yanked him up. There was blood on Ralston's lip.

"Guess that'll teach you not to resist arrest," Iceberg said.

That sure was unfriendly.

Iceberg spotted Rusty and me. "What are you doing here? Get out."

"Guests of management," I said.

"Out," Iceberg said.

"I'm a guest here," I said. "Think I'll stay."

I was half expecting Iceberg to draw his cannon and aim it, but maybe he didn't like the odds, and instead ignored me and Rusty.

"Come along," he said to his prisoners.

I think that little feller Jardine could have slid his hand out of the manacle easily enough, but he left his wrist in there and nodded at me. I guess I was doing the right thing, not making too big a fuss.

All them show people gathered now to watch as Iceberg hauled Ralston and Jardine out the door and toward the sheriff office and jail. At least that's where I thought they were headed. I followed along, and watched Sheriff Iceberg haul them into the county courthouse rather than the jail, and straight into the courtroom, which was all lit and ready. And there was Judge Rampart, waiting behind the bench, and there was Lawyer Stokes.

And there was the banker, Hubert Sanders. So this here little party had been planned in advance.

They hauled Ralston and Jardine straight before the judge.

"The charge is public indecency. Guilty or not?" Rampart asked, leaning forward and licking his lips.

"This sure is a fancy welcoming party, your holiness," said Jardine.

"Contempt of court. Ten dollars," said Rampart.

"Your majesties, I scarcely know what to plead because no such law exists," said Ralston.

"Contempt of court, ten dollars for you, too."

"Yes, indeed," said Jardine, "if we plead guilty to a law that does not exist, what does it gain us?"

"Five hundred dollars or six months, your choice," said Rampart.

"But if we plead not guilty to a law that does not exist, what does that gain us?"

"The exact same. Except that Lawyer Stokes and Sheriff Ike Berg will spend thirty seconds testifying that there was nudity on that stage."

"Well then, we won't plead guilty, and we won't plead not guilty," Jardine said.

"That's nolo contendere. The fine is your box office receipts," Rampart said.

"Right here," the beefy deputy said. In his hand was Ralston's black metal cashbox.

"Ah, capital," said Rampart.

The deputy dumped the loot onto Rampart's

bench, and the judge and Hubert Sanders swiftly counted up the evening's take by the light of three kerosene lamps brought to the bench.

"That's it?" said Rampart, sliding the last two-bit piece into a pile.

"That's it," said Sanders.

"Your fine for public indecency is five hundred seventeen dollars and fifty cents. Sheriff, unloose those cuffs and let these gents go. Hubert, you take this fine over to your bank and lock it up tight, and don't let any vermin get at it. The wages of sin belong to Puma County."

That was mighty fast justice.

Rampart turned to me. "You. Why are you here?"

"My ma always told me not to stick around where I'm not invited," I said.

Rampart rolled his eyes. "How long, oh Lord, must the good citizens of Doubtful suffer the presence of this buffoon?"

"What's a buffoon, your grace? I never did hear that before."

"Out!" Rampart was waving his finger at me and Rusty, and Ike Berg was making mean gestures, so we headed into the warm night and waited. Sure enough, a moment later Jardine and Ralston came ripping out the door, fined and freed.

For two gents who had just taken an awful whipping, they didn't seem too upset.

"Nice of them to store the box office for us," Jardine said.

"We'll try it again," Ralston said.

"That's plumb crazy!" I said. "You'll go broke!"

"No, it'll keep Ike Berg from stealing the boodle," Ralston said.

CHAPTER SEVENTEEN

Alphonse de Jardine steered us all into the opera house and Ralston scratched a lucifer and lit the lamp in his cramped office backstage.

"We'll do a little planning," Jardine said, eyeing Rusty and me. "That is, if you wish to join us. If not, we'll bid you a pleasant evening."

I peered at Rusty. The flame in that lamp was tossing so little light around that I could hardly make him out. "I'm in," Rusty said.

"Likewise," I said. "But we ain't got much to offer. No badges, no weapons inside city limits."

"You'll do," Jardine said.

I was sort of offended. I'd do? Maybe there were others who'd do better. But Jardine had an odd little smirk in his odd little face, and I quieted down.

"These contretemps happen," he said.

"Contra what?"

"Difficulties," Jardine said.

"Are you fellers gonna pack up and get out of here in the morning?" I asked.

"No, the show'll go on. And we're adding matinees Wednesday and Saturday."

"And you'll get your box office took away each time?"

"We'll see," Jardine said.

"My ma, she always said I'm slow, but now I'm feeling slower."

"Your mother, my dear Pickens, was a genius."

"Quit pickin' on her!"

Jardine didn't reply, Instead, he sprang up to Ralston's desk and sat on it, which gave him a little height and he didn't need to stare uphill at me.

"Is there trouble in this world?" he asked.

"I imagine."

"Ah! You have arrived at wisdom."

I was starting to get annoyed at this feller and just wanted to get to my room at Belle's and think about that naked redhead in his show. Maybe I could steal her.

"There is always trouble," the man said. He had not removed his silk stovepipe hat, and that made him seem like he was two feet taller than me. "The Grand Luxemburg Follies were born to trouble. We have played in countless towns, and never been without trouble. There is no place in this republic that has allowed the Follies to play, keep its earnings, and depart in peace. We are the most sinned-against road show in North

America. The ways that the towns on the circuit show their displeasure are endless, devious, cruel, harsh, and cunning. How do you think a show like this survives, Pickens? We survive and prosper. How can that be? Every town has its Watch and Ward Society. Every town has its politicians on the take. But here we are. Have you given it any thought? This miracle of survival, eh?"

"How'm I supposed to think surrounded by naked women?" I asked. "You put me in an opera house with naked women and I cease to think. I don't have even a pipsqueak of a thought between my ears."

Jardine, he was smiling at me like I just rung a bell.

"Ah, that is how we all are in the presence of the divine. You have eyes for Ambrosia, and that fries your brain."

"Who's Ambrosia?"

"She of the auburn hair."

"My brain got fried before she showed up, Jardine."

He smiled benevolently. "The ways of the local enforcers are endless," he said. "That black box containing the evening's cash is a magnet to politicians and peace officers. It is so simple, really. They want a percent. Usually fifty. Give them half of each night's collections, and they won't harass us. Or, sometimes, they'll only make a show of harassing us, for public consumption.

Hand out the greenbacks and we can stage our shows. Quite ordinary, my friend."

"But they took your whole wad," I said.

"But they didn't close us down."

"I guess I ain't following this," I said.

"Ah, my friends, let us reconstruct how it is here. On the one hand, you have the moralists, the Watch and Ward people, led by the banker and his wife, Hubert and Delphinium Sanders. They really are a small minority in a frontier town like Doubtful, and powerless. Indeed, there's not even a city ordinance governing anything that happens in this opera house."

"No law that I ever did read," I said, "but I guess Lawyer Stokes could invent one or find one under a rock somewhere."

"Ah, yes," said Jardine. "Now then, you have other factions in Doubtful. The politicians, the county supervisors. The mayor. Judge Rampart. Now for them, the Grand Luxemburg Follies is a fine chance to fill county coffers, as well as to line their own pockets, wouldn't you say so?"

"Oh, they're not all that bad, I'd say. They only do that when they know they won't get caught. I guess that puts them above most politicians."

"There, Pickens, your mother's son absorbed some of her wisdom after all."

"You insulting her again, are you?"

"No, I'm insulting you, not madame. You need a daily dose of insult. Now then, my friend. Another faction is the merchants who see the opera house as rivals. For them, any money a touring company earns is that much money taken out of their pockets. It doesn't work that way, but they think it does. If the cowboys aren't buying tickets to shows at the opera house, then they could buy longjohns and boots from the merchants."

"Makes sense to me," I said.

"I wouldn't suppose otherwise," Jardine said. "Now then, there's another faction in town that profits with every show: the bartenders, the madams, the gamblers, Turk's Livery Barn, the sporting crowd. They support the opera house. They supported you as sheriff because you kept the lid on the sporting district, but didn't shut it down. Doubtful was safe, and they made money, eh?"

"You got her figured out," said Rusty. "You must be talkin' to Ralston there."

"Even long before the show arrived. I was talking to their advance man, Pinky Pearl."

The thought of the murdered man quieted everyone for a moment.

"Then we've got Ike Berg showing up, sheriff down in Medicine Bow, and we've got the supervisors deciding to get rid of you and your deputies, like Rusty here," Ralston said. "And they succeeded. The one thing we know about Berg is that he's a Puritan."

"Ah, Ralston, you insult the Puritans!" Jardine said. "Puritans aren't against sin, they're against not profiting from it. The New Englanders made fortunes in the rum trade, and the slavery trade, too. No, Iceberg isn't a Puritan, he's worse. He's a Messenger of Death. He's murdered Medicine City, and now he's out to murder Doubtful. And after he's murdered Doubtful, he'll get bored and find some other town to gut. When Doubtful's so quiet that a dog crossing Main Street is the only life in sight, then Berg'll arrest the dog, execute it for trespass, and move on."

I guess I never did think of Iceberg as a feller like that. It gave me the chills.

"He doesn't want money," Ralston said. "He doesn't want fame. He doesn't want women. He doesn't want wine and song and cigars. He doesn't want anything but to murder the town where he's the law, and then find himself another. He's arrested boys for playing marbles. He's arrested old ladies who light up a pipe—and there are a few. He's arrested women for hanging their undies on a clothesline. He's arrested county clerks. He's arrested justices of the peace. After he's strangled a town to death he gets bored and finds another town."

"Holy cats," I said. "You fellers sure got notions about Ike Berg."

"It's there, it's in the record. Before Medicine City, Berg was sheriff at Red Rock, and he murdered that town too. And before that he murdered Rock Springs. And before that he strangled Dogwood. That's all he wants. That's all he'll do when he gets to the next town."

"Who's that deputy of his?" Rusty asked.

"He's known as the Butcher. He usually shows up a few days after Iceberg, and gets hired on," Jardine said.

"How come you know so much?" I asked.

"He is a person of interest. He was sheriff in three towns we've played in."

"You know the feller?"

"We're well acquainted, let me say."

That sure was a lot of stuff no one ever told me about Iceberg. I just thought he was the usual sort of lawman. He should change his name to Grim Reaper. I'd never heard of a lawman who was sort of a one-man town-killer.

"Well, that's all news, but now tell me how you fellers are going to make money when they just take away every cent and stuff it in the bank."

Ralston and Jardine glanced at each other, and eventually Ralston spoke.

"The first show, we find out what the city wants. If it wants to shut down the show, it does so. There's not much we can do. The show pulls out and everyone loses. But that didn't happen here. They went for the money. And hope to make more money if we open again. That's important to us."

"Beats me how to get around it," I said.

"Oh, there are ways, Pickens. One is to pay our people as fast as the cash comes in; as fast as the box office takes in cash, it's going out to our cast and crew and suppliers. By the time the show's over and we're being booked, there's not a dime in the cashbox. But that has drawbacks. If we're fined, we're still liable, and the local pirates attach our wagons and goods," Jardine said.

"So, what then?"

"We cover up. The next show will be, shall we say, fully gowned. If we're still hauled in, we'll be forced to take measures. And that's as much as I can reveal to you."

"Why have you got Rusty and me hanging around? What have we got to offer you?"

"Your presence is very valuable to us," Ralston said. "You were, and maybe still are, the sheriff and deputy."

"I don't know what's boiling in your noggins, but there's nothing an ex-sheriff can do for you," I said. "I can't even carry a sidearm in Doubtful. If you're arrested I can't unarrest you. If you go before Judge Rampart, I can't change what he does. I'm not on the county payroll, so get that straight."

"Just be present and stay close. Tonight there'll be two front-center seats for you two," Jardine said.

This sure was beyond my fathoming, but if I got a chance to see that redhead, Ambrosia, dressed or not, I'd go for it. "Count us in," I said, and Rusty agreed.

"Do I get to meet Ambrosia?" I asked.

"Keep your pants on," Jardine said.

"Not if we can help it," Rusty said.

It ended like that. Ralston turned down the wick, and we worked our way into the starlit June night. I knew what I'd be doing the next day. I'd get back on the trail of whoever stole my horse and killed him; whoever rifled my room at Belle's; whoever held me up; whoever killed that advance man, Pinky Pearl, in front of the Last Chance Saloon. I might not be in office, but I had some sheriff work to finish up, and that's what I'd do.

I stopped in there and found Sammy winding up the night, rinsing out some tumblers. All but one lamp had been turned down, and the saloon seemed full of gloom.

"We're closed," he said, his back to me.

"Yeah, so we can talk. You know anything about this new deputy of Iceberg's?"

"I don't even know his name."

"He looks like the holdup man that caught me a few weeks ago."

"You saw him well enough?"

"No, but wide and short and built like a box."

Sammy just shook his head. "You think Iceberg's playing two sides of the law?"

"Someone had to start up a crime wave to push me out the door."

"I'll ask a few questions, and get a name."

"I think he's called the Butcher."

"He looks like one."

"Critter, he died from a cut throat, a single clean cut from one side to the other. One swipe of a sharp knife. Isn't that how butchers slaughter beeve?"

"It is."

"If I find out he done it, I'll cut his throat from ear to ear."

Sammy stopped arranging his glassware. "You're not the law anymore, Cotton."

"That's right, and it gives a man a little more freedom."

Sammy smiled. "I'll ask a few questions and let you know."

I left there and walked to Belle's half hoping I'd get stuck up again so I could pound the hell out of someone.

CHAPTER EIGHTEEN

I decided to have some java at the Beanery and spend a nickel from my dwindling pile of coins. I woke up blue; life sure wasn't getting any better. I was missing Critter like a lusty widower misses all six of his wives. I hadn't a job and no prospects. I was mad and mystified by all the stuff going on in Doubtful.

I thought maybe I should ask Ambrosia to marry me, but she didn't know my name yet, and I was not about to tell her because I never did like Cotton, the one my folks hung on me. Cotton Pickens was their idea of a good joke, but it didn't seem like a joke to me. So unless I got up more courage than I could muster, I wasn't going to turn Ambrosia into Mrs. Pickens. But I sure liked what I saw of her, and I saw a lot. Without even a sheriff salary, my chances of lassoing her weren't very good.

So it was time for a cup of coffee. I indulge once

in a while. Coffee gets my blood running and clears the cobwebs out of my mind. There's some that say I don't have a mind for there to be cobwebs inside of, but I pay them no never mind. I got dressed, remembering to match up the socks, like Belle always wanted me to do, so I wouldn't have blue on one foot and white on the other. Once I tried to boil up my old white longjohns I'd worn a month with a new red shirt, and the result was pink longjohns, so I went out and burned them before I got into serious trouble around Doubtful. I don't seem to learn fast. I got into my boots, which were down at the heels, and finally meandered into a fine June morning and made it to the Beanery, the foremost eatery in Doubtful, Wyoming. I sat down at the counter, staying two seats away from that supervisor Ziggy Camp, who I didn't want to talk to.

I laid a nickel on the counter and Pedro Perkins filled a mug and clapped it down hard, slopping some over the counter. I never tip, and he remembers it and tries to spill a little coffee and burn me in the crotch, but I ignore it.

Camp eyed me dourly and decided to talk anyway, even though I halfway turned a shoulder against him.

"Town ain't the same since you quit, Pickens."

That's what he said, and it made me mad. "I didn't quit. You kicked my ass out of office."

"You quit," he said. "It's in the minutes."

"I didn't quit, and stop trying to cover your

behind," I snarled. The coffee hadn't started to improve my attitude any, but it would in a while. "If you don't like Doubtful now, you got what you deserve."

I sipped, burned my tongue and had to wait a while, which annoyed me as much as Camp did.

Ziggy Camp wouldn't quit. "Ike Berg told us you quit and handed the badge to him," he said. "We didn't axe you. We were looking at it, with all the crime around here all of a sudden, but we were waiting to see what happened."

I started to feel even worse. "Iceberg, he told me to fork over my badge because I was no longer sheriff of Puma County and the supervisors said for him to take over. So I done what I was ordered to do by you politicians."

Ziggy set down his fork and stared at me. "Is that how it happened? You're saying you didn't resign?"

"Why would I quit? I like being sheriff here and I was doing a dandy job, too."

"Well, that's debatable, Pickens. The town was becoming unsafe."

I wasn't going to debate that fool. The only unsafe person in town was me, because someone was robbing me and killing off my family, namely Critter. So I turned my back on the idiot and nothing was said for a bit, which was just as well because other of the regulars in there, the fellers that spent half the morning nursing one five-cent cup of java, were listening.

Camp finished up his three scrambled eggs, his strips of side pork, his bowl of grits, his glass of prune juice, and his four slices of toast, and the last of his coffee. Them supervisors could afford anything and their big bellies proved it.

"Come with me," he said.

I drank up and followed, and he took me over to the Puma courthouse and into the county clerk's office, and dug into the supervisor's minutes. Then he pointed, but I couldn't read that script, where all them letters bleed into the next, and he took pity on me.

"It says here that Berg, of Medicine Bow County, said you quit and handed him your badge, and the supervisors accepted your resignation and appointed Berg to you office and agreed on a wage of seventy-five a month."

"I got forty!"

"We had no sheriff except Berg, so we went along with him."

"Well, ain't that a piece of cake."

"Yes it is, and it looks like Berg was not being square with us."

"That's no help to me."

"I'll talk to the others. I've been hearing a few things about Iceberg, how he slowly strangles a town to death. And how bad things happen in his towns."

"That don't help me any."

"The county's making money with Berg," Camp said. "So it's going to be hard to change things.

But even so, things ain't right. I'll get back to you, Pickens."

"I'll starve before then."

"Give me one day."

"I'll starve by this noon."

"Then starve." The supervisor gestured me out, so I quit the place.

It sure was a fine morning, bright and sunny, in a town where a feller snookered me out of office. I sure felt dumb. I wondered what them supervisors would do. Put me back in, when they were fixing to get rid of me anyway? Maybe they'd get rid of Iceberg, like they should if he tricked them, but hire someone else since they weren't too happy with me.

The other possibility was that Ike Berg would scare them into keeping quiet. He was a rattler, all right. He never had a feeling, as far as I could tell. His inside was all dry and parched and dust, with no life going on in there. If that was true about his strangling every town he worked in, then his only pleasure was to bring a town down to dust and watch the stores fold and the people leave and the whole place die up because he was the man with the guns.

I sure didn't know what would happen. I glanced over there at the sheriff's office, on the square, and it looked real quiet. I sure wanted my job back. I guess I'd have to wait a day and find out if them three supervisors had the same idea.

It was like a good shot of coffee working through my blood, just thinking about that.

I headed over to Turk's Livery Barn to talk to Turk, who knew a lot more than he let on. People are always talking in front of hostlers like they don't exist, and Turk always passed along things that might help me keep the peace when I wore the badge. I found him cleaning out a stall, his scoop shovel full of fresh horse apples, browning on the outside and green straight through.

"You got a minute?" I asked.

"Grab a shovel," he said.

That's how he was. If I was going to waste his time asking questions, then I could shovel right alongside of him. So I found an old scoop shovel and got into the stall where there were piles of apples. He had a wheelbarrow in there. So I scooped up a shovelful and another, and pretty soon we got that barrow loaded up.

"Draft horse in here," I said.

"The show," he said.

There was one of them big Belgians in the next stall, where Critter had lived. I hardly wanted to look there, knowing how bad I felt about Critter.

"This new deputy, the blocky one. He been around?"

Turk lifted a heavy load and dropped it into the barrow, and we began cleaning around the edges of the stall, where there was a lot of wet, stinking straw.

"He came awhile before Iceberg, and hung

around here all the time, like he was memorizing who owned what."

"He ask questions of you?"

"Hardly said a word. Kept to himself. But he'd sit on that bench out front with a stick and a knife and whittle sticks. I knew he was looking hard, but I didn't know the what of it."

"He interested in Critter?"

"Not as far as I could see. He was just another loafer."

"He ask for a job?"

"Nah. He had some cash. He'd quit whittling and go over to the Beanery and eat when he felt like it."

"Where'd he stay?"

"He'd give me two bits and sleep in the hayloft."

"He ever say what he did?"

"Butcher. He said he was thinking of starting a butcher shop in Doubtful. I told him we could use one. I never thought he'd end up Berg's deputy."

"He ever start some new routine?"

"Yeah, when Berg showed up from Medicine Bow, the two sometimes ate at the Beanery. They knew each other."

The stall was cleaned out, so I lifted the wheelbarrow and took it out to the manure pile at the back of the livery. It was getting to be a mountain back there. Turk tried to sell it for gardens, but mostly people just helped themselves, and Turk didn't mind. He had more manure than he knew what to do with.

When I got back, Turk had moved the Belgian to the cleaned stall and we started in on Critter's stall. I didn't like that much. Critter sometimes chewed wood, and I could see where he'd mauled a post or two, gnawing at it. That made me feel bad.

We started loading the wheelbarrow again.

"He ever say where he was from?"

"Medicine City. He never said it to me but when Berg showed up they talked about Medicine City."

"He ever ask questions about people here?"

"You. He wanted to know about the sheriff."

"Like what?"

"Were you a good man? He said maybe he'd apply for work."

That big draft horse had left mountains in there. He made Critter look like an amateur when it came to dropping apples. So we scooped up a lot of apples and straw. I always liked the smell. Horse apples and horse piss were real pleasant to be around, but city folks wouldn't know that. When I was a boy and my ma and pa couldn't afford to keep me in shoes, I'd walk around barefoot, and there never was anything nicer than stepping into a hot steaming pile of horse apples to warm my frozen feet.

"That time I got held up. Was he around then?"

Turk hesitated. "Cotton, I can't squarely say for

sure. I don't want to nail that down when I'm not sure. But I think so."

"Did anyone call him a name?"

"Luke. Berg called him Luke once, when Luke was whittling sticks, and I was harnessing up a trotter right there."

"A butcher named Luke from Medicine City."

"You could get his name off the county payroll," Turk said.

"Anything else you remember about him?"

"Yeah, there was one thing that made me pretty near spit. That was when Mrs. Sanders showed up and asked him to help her."

"With what?"

"I don't know. Just help her."

"What did she say?"

"She said 'You man there. Will you help me, my good man? There's a bit in it for you if you are the one I've heard about.' Then the woman, Delphinium, dressed in purple as she often does, and the whittler on my bench, they wandered off by themselves."

"That don't make no sense," I said.

"I never saw them together after that. Just that one time. They didn't go toward the bank. They went down that alley."

"One last one. Was this Luke the Butcher around when that stranger got stabbed in front of the Last Chance Saloon?"

"I can't say for sure. He'd come and go," Turk said. "Some days I wouldn't see him at all."

I sure couldn't make anything of it, but maybe if I worked at it some, I'd come up with an idea. I set the shovel aside and thanked Turk, and headed for my boardinghouse. I'd have to scrape myself clean if I was going to watch Ambrosia on that stage again.

CHAPTER NINETEEN

Rusty and me, we got front-center seats again, thanks to management. I sure didn't mind because I'd get to watch Ambrosia real close. I was thinking about waiting at the stage door and asking her to marry me. I thought maybe to take her out to a cabin I know about and show her a thing or two. That's all I thought about. I wasn't going to let Ambrosia go. I hadn't really met her yet, but that didn't make no difference. Anyone who'd say "anytime, anyplace" to me I'd keep in Doubtful if I could.

That next show was even more packed than the opening one. They sold every seat and there must have been fifty people lining the walls, ready to whistle at the girls. It was pretty much the same show, except the girls were covered more. Ambrosia wore a white gown when she played Lady Godiva, which wrecked the scene as far as I could tell, but maybe if I was going to marry her, it'd be best not to have all them people gawking at her like that.

Later in the show, when they did all them imitations of art with the bare girls, they got 'em all covered up. And Ambrosia wore a light blue gown when she played the Goddess of Liberty, which saddened me. I'd been looking forward to the Goddess of Liberty scene all evening and was feeling a little cheated by all that drapery she was wearing. It annoyed me that Ralston and Jardine had caved in so easily to the county, but they had. I guess they needed to make some money and not have it fined away like last time. It was a dandy show, with ballet, choruses, dancers, and all that stuff, and I couldn't see how anyone would get upset by it.

But I was wrong. No sooner was it over than Ike Berg and his deputy Luke pounced, grabbing the cashbox and hauling Jardine and Ralston over to the courtroom where Judge Rampart and Lawyer Stokes and a few other people were burning lamp oil waiting. Ralston motioned for Rusty and me to come along. I guess the owner of the opera house wanted some witnesses.

But it went just like before. The warrant was for violating public decency, and the fine was the contents of the box office cashbox for that evening. Ralston and Jardine had to defend themselves since the only lawyer in Doubtful was also the county attorney. So Ralston asked to see the written law, and was denied. Rampart said the law

was the public sensibility. Jardine asked what in
the show violated public decency, and Lawyer
Stokes said the show itself did, through and
through, and even the music was a crime against
decency. He was sort of smiling. Jardine asked the
court to find them innocent, since there was no
law and no evidence of violating the nonexistent
law, but Judge Rampart threatened to fine him
ten dollars for contempt, and then found the
two guilty.

That sure was fast. I'd heard of deals like that
but I never saw it before. Justice was a sort of
greased tube, in one end and out the other in
two minutes.

The bailiff, he counted the loot in the cashbox,
and pronounced it to be six hundred and twelve
dollars and change, and the banker Hubert
Sanders, he toted the boodle off to his bank to
lock up real good in his black-enameled safe, and
the bailiff blew out the lamps, and pretty soon
everyone was out of there. So far, the Grand Luxemburg Follies hadn't been allowed to keep one
dime, and a lot of town merchants and the hotel
and restaurants hadn't been paid by the show. It
sure seemed like a mess.

Meanwhile, Puma County was over eleven hundred dollars richer, and at that rate it wouldn't
need to charge taxes the way it had to pay for all
them useless people in the courthouse.

Me and Rusty, we went with Jardine and Ralston back to the opera house, which was dark

now, with all them actresses gone for the night. I was hoping Ambrosia was around so I could ask her to marry me, but no luck.

Once we got back to Ralston's little office and got a lamp lit, I plumb asked Jardine.

"I'm fixing to marry Ambrosia, and don't know what to ask her," I said.

"She won't do it for less than a million dollars," Jardine said. "But you can ask her any way you want."

"All right, I'll ask her for a million," I said.

Ralston had other things on his mind. "You going to open tomorrow?" he asked Jardine.

"We can't run a show on wooden nickels," Jardine said.

"It doesn't matter how you drape the show," Ralston said.

"No, it doesn't. They'll find a way to take the box office for every show."

"You could pull out in the morning."

"I've got a cast to pay; a pile of bills to pay. We can't even get our animals out of the livery barn without paying."

"You've dealt with this in other towns."

"In other towns there were actual laws on the books, and the fines were twenty-five or thirty dollars for each infraction. Here they're inventing laws, the only lawyer in town is acting as county attorney, and the sky's the limit on the fines."

"Can we appeal?"

Jardine laughed. "To whom? We're a road

show. We'll be in the next town in a few days, and then the town after that. It's all here and now. There's no tomorrow in my racket."

"How come you don't get mad?" I asked.

"Anger's a wasted emotion. If I showed any anger in that kangaroo court, I'd only end up behind bars and fined all the more. And the anger would keep me from calculating the troubles. This is a difficult town. There's a lot here I don't grasp."

"Mr. Jardine, you know there's different folks with different notions here," I said. "There's some like the banker's wife and those women who think having a theater in Doubtful's real bad. There's others, like most of the storekeepers who think the show's taking cash out of their pockets. But they're also seeing a lot of trade since the shows started coming in. Like the saloon men. The whole thing's a mix. Then there's the politicians. They're stuck with Ike Berg. And it's Ike Berg who's running this here town now. He's the one making the arrests, collecting the box office, hauling you fellers off to court, telling the judge how much is in the box each night."

Jardine sighed. "What are we supposed to do about that?"

"Leave it to Rusty and me, and maybe my old deputies. Maybe we can fix it."

"How?"

"I don't think Ike Berg's in there legal," I said. "I think he took over, and scared the supervisors into going along with him. I think maybe you'd get to keep your take each night if Berg and that Luke the Butcher didn't jump your ticket window before people hardly get settled for the show."

Them fellers were staring at me, and so was Rusty.

"You keep the show going, no matter what," I said. "Me and Rusty, we've got some work to do."

"What sort of work?"

"I'm going to take my badge back."

"You think you can? And that they supervisors would go along? Weren't they getting rid of you?"

"I've been doing a little poking around," I said. "That crime wave that got me in trouble, I know where it came from. I haven't got real hard evidence yet, but I know. I know who held me up that night, who got into my room and stole my gun, who killed your advance man, and who stole Critter and killed the best friend I ever did have."

"Who?"

"I ain't saying yet. You keep your show going. Me and Rusty, we have a job to do, and maybe in a few days we'll get your money back to you. Maybe not. Ike Berg, they call him Iceberg for good reason. And Luke the Butcher, the one who's deputy now, he's even more dangerous than Berg."

"I'm not quite following you, Pickens," Jardine said.

"I ain't quite following myself," I said. "I'm out in front of my thoughts. My ma always warned me about getting in front of my head."

Rusty rolled his eyes. Rusty never was very patient with me.

"How would Doubtful look to you if there was another sheriff around here?" I asked. "A real sheriff, who reads the law and doesn't invent it. A real sheriff who doesn't scare the judge half witless. A real sheriff who tells Lawyer Stokes to back off?"

"Who'd that be?" Ralston asked.

"That badge belongs right here," I said, tapping my chest.

"But you were fired."

"It ain't so. My badge got took from me by Iceberg. He told the supervisors I'd quit but I hadn't. Then he scared them into accepting him as sheriff, and he's been keeping 'em scared ever since. When he wants something, they jump. But I'm still sheriff, far as I can figure, and I aim to get my badge back real quick now, and if I do, you'll get your money back."

"That would be an improvement on robbing the bank," Jardine said.

"That sure is an interesting notion," I said.

"How do you propose to return our box office to us? It's the county's."

"I'm not real sure yet," I said. "But I will, soon as I get Iceberg and Luke the Butcher out of here."

They was staring at me like I was nuts. Maybe I was. But when I get stubborn, somebody bends and it won't be me. "You run your show tomorrow as you see fit," I said.

"Two shows. Matinee tomorrow," Ralston said.

"Two shows then. You run both, even if they make off with your box office take again."

"Are you trying to help us or enrich your county?" Jardine asked.

"Do what you want," I said, feeling testy. "Hit the road if that's what you want. Let that Watch and Ward bunch shut down your theater, and drive you out."

Ralston smiled suddenly. "I'm going to invite Delphinium Sanders to the matinee. He turned to Jardine. "For the sake of art."

I didn't think we solved anything back there, but Ralston turned down the wick, and we slipped into the night. Rusty headed to his shack, but I was restless and headed for the Last Chance, intending to buy a five-cent mug of beer from Sammy Upward.

It was a real nice idea, because there were them showgirls in there, with a lot of fellers crowded around, and everyone having a real cozy time. I got my beer from Sammy and headed over there, because Ambrosia was sitting there, her coppery hair drawing me like a magnet.

"Hey, it's the stage-door johnnie," she said.

"That's me, I said. "I was asking your boss if I could marry you, and he said you'd do it for a million dollars."

"Make it two," she said.

"That's real nice," I said. "You can bring it with

you and we'll get started as fast as I can line up a preacher."

"Anytime, anyplace," she said.

Now there was that invitation again. I swear, I'd never heard a woman issue a greeting like that. "How about now?" I asked.

"Are you sure you want a preacher?" she asked. "I don't like preachers."

"Well, there ain't but one in Doubtful, and he'd be asleep by now," I said, "but we can start this honeymoon in advance, and fix everything regular in the morning."

She laughed, and I sat there remembering what she looked like as Lady Godiva, but that was nothing compared to how she looked as the Goddess of Liberty. I'd never thought of Liberty as being red-haired before.

Iceberg and Luke the Butcher wandered in just then, and it got real quiet real fast in the Last Chance Saloon. No wonder Berg was called Iceberg. It was a cold wind blowing through the place, cold and mean and bleak.

Berg, he spoke real soft. "This is a disorderly house," he said. "I'm shutting it down. And for good. This place is closed. And all of you, I'm taking you in. You're all inmates of a disorderly house, and you'll face justice in the morning. Come along now. And you, Upward, bring your till with you. You're going to be paying a lot of fines."

"What the hell are you talking about?" Sammy snapped.

Luke the Butcher slammed a billy club into Sammy, who yelled and dropped behind the bar.

"Get up," the deputy said.

Sammy did, real slow, rubbing his head where the club had conked his skull.

I couldn't remember what the fine was for all that, but I didn't have it, and I knew I'd be spending the night in the Puma County jail, along with these people, and maybe ten days more if I couldn't come up with the price of my freedom. But I wasn't the only one who was real unhappy just then. The only happy ones were Iceberg, who had a glint in his dead eye, and Luke the Butcher, who was looking us over like we were slabs of meat.

CHAPTER TWENTY

Iceberg and Luke the Butcher herded us all into a single cell. It was going to be a lot tighter in there than anyone cared for. And with nothing but a single slop pail for us all, men and women.

"I'd like some water please," one of the showgirls said.

"Morning," Iceberg replied and locked the door with a clang. It was dark; a single lamp burned in the distant jail office.

"What's the fine?" someone asked the man with the badge.

"Two dollars for being an inmate; ten for running a disorderly house."

"What if we don't have it?"

"Tough luck," the lawman said.

"When do we go to court?"

"When I feel like taking you."

"Where can we get bail?"

"I'm fresh out," Iceberg said.

"Hey, sheriff," Sammy Upward said. "I'll bail everyone out from my till."

Iceberg smiled. "You donated everything in it to the Puma County Retirement Fund."

"Then you won't ever see any of it," Upward said.

"Will we get out in time for the matinee?" someone asked.

"I hope not," Iceberg said.

"It's cold; can we have blankets?"

"You sure didn't catch cold up on that stage with nothing on."

I thought that was kind of clever of Iceberg, but I wasn't going to laugh any.

He slammed the jailhouse door and disappeared. And we started to get ourselves comfortable. It didn't look like there would be enough space for us to get settled on the bare concrete, but we worked it out, sitting down real tight. I sort of wondered how long that would last. Pretty quick, someone would need to take a leak.

I caught a glint of red hair, and worked my way down to sit beside Ambrosia, who was looking pretty grumpy.

"Would you marry me?" I asked.

"You from Doubtful?"

"Sort of."

"You bust me out of here in the next ten minutes and get me a thousand miles from Doubtful and I'll marry you if you're nice."

She accepted! I was a happy man, and began dreaming about our honeymoon.

"I'd sure like a lot of babies," I said.

"I've been in enough jails," she replied.

The odor of all them unwashed men sure took over, and it got pretty rank in there. Pretty soon one of the fellers who'd been sitting at the bar began groping around for the bucket, and cut loose. It didn't bother no one. The showgirls, they didn't care. But it bothered me. Iceberg, he should have put the women in one cell and the men in the other. But I'm just a fool when it comes to things like that. It helps to think that others have a little dignity.

Keeping a disorderly house, or being an inmate in a disorderly house, were common infractions in western towns. They were sort of a catch-all that could be applied to anyone or anything. Most often, when the city was broke, it rounded up madams and their girls and fined them using that sort of law. I used it a couple of times on a barkeep in the Sampling Room who allowed his customers to brawl with broken beer bottles. He finally got the message that a mess of ten-dollar fines was sending to him, and kept better order and there was less blood in the sawdust over there.

"Something's crawling on my leg," a girl hissed.

"I hope it's just a cootie, but it could be a sewer slug," I said.

She bolted to her feet, and announced she would stand the rest of the night.

It sure was a long night. I tried to woo Ambrosia and tell her I like gals who have red hair all over, but she just snarled at me, so I told her I'd wait until we got bailed out.

She jabbed me with a hatpin or something to shut me up, so I just patted her hand and told her I'd take her to Argentina tomorrow.

Dawn finally filtered through the little window high up, and I thought maybe something would happen, but nothing did. I was sure getting thirsty. People could see each other now, and I never saw such a miserable lot. The girls were not very pretty that morning, and looked pretty broke down, like old nags.

Nothing happened. The sun rose, and the place warmed a little, and the smell got worse because so many people had to use the bucket, but still no one showed up. I was wondering how long this would last until we all got real sick, jammed in like that. That slop bucket was running over now, and it was sure tiresome, that stink that we couldn't get away from. The stuff was puddling on the floor, getting into our boots and shoes, and it was getting about as bad as a jail cell can get. The women, they weren't sitting anymore, and none of us could sit on that floor now, and I wondered how long it'd be before one keeled over.

A commotion out in the sheriff's office caught our attention, and I heard Ralston and Jardine in there, and hoped they would bail us out. I caught enough of the talk to know they were trying to free us, but finally it quieted out there, and we were still rotting behind bars, so thick in there we were like a pile of dead rats.

Finally, in the middle of the day, Iceberg opened up the jail door and came back to the cell and looked us over.

"I'll be taking you to county court now," he said. "So clean up. Judge Rampart will convene court at two, and you will be fined then."

"Two? We'll miss the matinee," Ambrosia said.

Iceberg smiled slightly.

It seemed like another half hour slipped by and then Iceberg and Luke the Butcher showed up.

"You didn't clean up," Iceberg said. "Judge Rampart won't like that."

We'd all gotten smart enough to keep our traps shut.

But Luke the Butcher unlocked our cell door and motioned for us to follow him, while Iceberg stood at the cell door, watching us crowd out and into fresher air. I just wanted air, clean air, sweet air, and soon I'd have it.

I was going to be the last out, and was standing behind the others as they crowded past Iceberg, so I plucked up that overflowing slop bucket, and when Iceberg saw it, it was too late. I splashed the whole thing right in his face. It splattered him, blinded him, and oozed down his white shirt and black suit coat, and while he was trying to wipe that crap out of his eyes and nose and mouth I got a hand on his sidearm and yanked it and clobbered him on the skull, and he sank senseless to the ground. I shoved ahead and clobbered Luke the Butcher. He didn't go down, being built like a bull, but he was dazed long enough for me to shove him back toward that stinking cell, and I pushed him in, and I dragged Iceberg in, and got their keys away from them, and locked them the hell in there.

The stink was so bad I didn't hang around, but got out of the jail and locked the jailhouse door. But the stink followed me into the sheriff's office, and I wondered where I could go to wash it off of me, and doubted that I could.

Outside, I saw the people who'd been in there with me vanish this way and that. We were out, but the trouble was only beginning. I returned to the sheriff office and found my own gunbelt, the one that got stole from me at Belle's, hanging there, so I took it back. There was one more thing I wanted, and that was my badge, so I went back to the jail cell, where Iceberg was sitting, trying to wipe the crap away.

"Toss me the badge," I said.

He froze.

"Toss it to me or I'll kill you."

He studied me a while, and then he unpinned it and pitched it through the bars. He had sense enough not to say anything, because if he'd said anything I'd probably have killed him for saying it. He stared at me with those dead eyes, eyes without life back behind them, and I knew it wasn't over. The Butcher was just sitting there holding his head.

I had the badge. After a bath and a change of clothing I might put it on.

Me, I wanted to clean up. I hiked through the middle of the day, got to Belle's, scrubbed my flesh raw, and got into some fresh clothing, leaving the rest to stink until I could get to it. Then I headed for the county courthouse and hunted down a supervisor, finding Reggie Thimble in there soaking his tonsils from a flask.

"What are you doing here?" he asked, from hooded eyes.

"Here is what I'm doing," I said. I pulled my sheriff star from my pocket and pinned it on, and he stared at it, and me.

"I never quit. Iceberg told you I did, but that was a lie. You may have been fixing to fire me, with some help from Berg, and I told you I wanted thirty days. And until that time's used up, I'm still sheriff. And if you want to know where Berg is, you'll find him stinking up a jail cell with his favorite hooligan, Luke the Butcher. If you want me out, you can call a regular meeting of supervisors and do it and tell me proper, in person, and give me notice in writing. Until then, I'll enforce any law on the books, and protect anyone from being harassed by made-up laws. You give me a law to enforce, and I'll do it. And that's what separates me from Berg."

"That's quaint," said Thimble. "Imagine that."

I had a feeling he was smirking behind his moustache.

"And what are Berg and the Butcher in for?"

"See this gun belt? It's mine. It's what went missing in the crime wave that got your knickers in a twist. It was hanging right there, property of Berg and the Butcher. So maybe I'll just go back there and make some charges."

"That would be entertaining," Thimble said. "Never a dull moment around here."

He was drunk, so I let him stew in his juices. He'd heard from me. I'd told him what needed saying.

I debated what to do with Berg and the Butcher, and decided to deal proper with them, so I went back there, found them stinking and glaring, cleaned the pisspot and handed it to them, and brought them clean drinking water, and dug around for clean stuff for them to wear, all the while saying nothing. I also got them some soap and a bucket of scrub water, and slid it into that stinking cell. It wouldn't do any good. Some people, they just stink from inside, and even after they're cleaned up outside, they still stink.

Berg, he just eyed me with those dead eyes.

"When you get cleaned up, I'll decide what to do with you," I said.

Berg actually smiled.

I headed out of there, and entered some items in my arrest log, which hadn't been tended during Berg's brief stay in my office. I charged them with the theft of my gunbelt, stolen property found in their possession. Maybe I'd come up with a few more items real quick. I thought that impersonating a peace officer was a crime, but I'd have to get Rusty to look it up. My ma, she always said crooked men walked crooked ways, and Iceberg couldn't walk a straight line if he tried.

I headed back there, let the Butcher out first, frisked and cuffed him, and then did the same for Berg, and walked them across the square to the courthouse. Judge Rampart was in there, and sure looked like he'd seen the Second Coming of Beelzebub when I herded my prisoners in.

"What's this?" he asked.

"I'm booking them for theft, your eminence."

"You're not the sheriff."

"I'm the sheriff."

"Would you mind explaining?" Scowl lines corrugated his brow.

I told him real plain, and I couldn't tell whether he favored liars pretending to be lawmen or a real lawman trying to send liars up the river. Alvin Rampart was part of the bunch who wanted Iceberg around, and me out, but now I was wearing the star, and I had the sidearm, and I had two prisoners.

He sat there awhile, chewing on his Bull Durham–stained lip, his sandy muttonchops wiggling around his hairy ears. I got the impression he itched to have a little conference with the county supervisors and half the businessmen in Doubtful before he proceeded.

Iceberg, he just stood there with his dead eyes, while Luke the Butcher sort of sneered at us all.

But sorting it out would take time, and just now Judge Rampart had two men before him who'd never been sworn as Puma County lawmen, and who'd gotten my badge by fraud. And he liked them two frauds more than he cared about me or the law.

"I will need to consult with the county attorney and supervisors," he said. "I'm releasing you two on your own recognizance. Don't leave Puma County. Report to me daily." He turned to me. "Release these gents."

"They ain't gents," I said, but I pulled off the cuffs.

CHAPTER TWENTY-ONE

Two fellers who were nothing but trouble were loose, and there wasn't anything I could do about that. I had other stuff to take care of, and lining up my deputies was top of the list. I needed some backup, and right away.

I simply locked up the sheriff's office to keep Iceberg and the Butcher out, and went hunting for my old deputies, Burtell and De Graff. I wasn't at all sure I wanted them or they wanted to work with me. My instinct was that they would blow with the wind. If they thought Berg would be sheriff, they'd try to hire on; if they thought I might be, they'd look for a badge from me. They wasn't what I'd call loyal. I wanted men who'd walk with me, just as I'd walk with them, through any kind of trouble. I needed to know.

I thought I might find them in the Sampling Room, and sure enough they were in there sucking beer and playing darts. They looked pretty rough, like they hadn't scraped off their face-hair or wiped their butts for a few days. Burtell's red darts were closer to center than De Graff's blue ones.

They quit tossing darts, eyed me, studied my badge, and nodded uneasily.

"I've kicked Berg out. You want to come in?"

"Where's Berg?"

"Him and Luke the Butcher are roaming free because Rampart cut them loose from some charges."

"Rusty in?"

"He will be."

"The supervisors, they took you back?"

"They never got rid of me but they was working at it."

"How's that?" Burtell asked.

I told them the whole thing.

The two eyed each other, and I could pretty well see all them cogs spinning in their heads.

"We'll think about it," De Graff said, looking like he wanted to get back to tossing darts at a cork target.

They looked real nervous, like they was hiding something.

"Do that," I said.

I made up my mind I didn't want them. Rusty and me, we'd hold the fort until I could lasso some good men. I headed for Rusty's log cabin and found him sewing up a torn shirt. It didn't take long for me to tell him how things stood.

"I'll come in shortly," he said. "Glad to have a job."

"Maybe you don't," I warned, and he laughed.

Rusty was as loyal as anyone ever could be. I was glad. Now I had someone to man that office or help me. Rusty was as good a peace officer as anyone, and had a real skill at buffaloing dangerous men almost before they knew what bounced off their skulls.

I still was outmanned, and Doubtful didn't have much law, but it was a start.

I stopped at the opera house on my way back just to thank Ralston for trying to bail me out. Much to my surprise, the matinee was starting up. I could hear that orchestra crank out a tune. Ralston himself was in the box office.

"How come? I thought you'd cancel," I said.

Ralston laughed. "The show goes on, even with half the cast. We've got a full house again."

"All them gals, they're in the show?"

"They're troupers, Pickens. They're washed up and getting dressed."

"But they was half sick and awake all night and scared, so how can they do a show?"

"Troupers, every one. And thanks for springing them. I heard the whole story. A slop pail tossed into Iceberg."

"You get to keep your box office take, Ralston, but I'd sure hide it."

He turned solemn. "It's a good thing, and don't think we're unaware of how it happened.

You've got friends here. The girls, for instance. They sure love you."

"Yeah, I'd like to marry that Ambrosia, but she isn't interested."

"You could pop in and see her. We're going undraped for the matinee."

"Ouch! Now you've got me, Ralston. I'd give a week's salary to go in there and watch her do the Goddess of Liberty. But I've got a thousand troubles to deal with, and fast. The judge cut Iceberg and the Butcher loose."

"I'll send her your fond best wishes." He sure was looking amused, but I didn't care.

"Your show's safe as long as I'm sheriff, which may be not long if the county supervisors yank my badge."

"Matinee and another tonight. That's twelve hundred clear if we pack the house," Ralston said.

I guess that's how theater people thought.

"The girls in this show, they got a hard life," I said. "They're never far from trouble and hardly get a good night in a clean bed for weeks on end. I don't know why they do it."

Ralson stared. "Most of them come from a life that was worse. Being on the road, with all its trouble, is paradise for some compared to the places they escaped from, the mean fathers, the cruel brothers, the men who treat them like dirt. They're tough, and they're loyal, and de Jardine treats them well, actually. He's turned the girls into a big business."

"Them women are runaways?"

"Some, and from worse trouble and pain than you or I can imagine."

"Well, I'd like to run away with Ambrosia," I said. "But I'd want her to quit taking her undies off in front of people."

I wanted to watch Ambrosia real bad, and the rest of those leggy girls, but wearing a star changed everything again, so I headed back to the sheriff's office. Rusty was there, working a mop on all that slop on the jail floor, the windows wide open. Not that fresh air helped any. That whole place stank, and I couldn't tell what was smelling the worst, that slop pail of crap, or the air Iceberg and the Butcher stunk up in my office.

I was half expecting Ziggy Camp or some other supervisor to come in clutching a letter firing me, but no one showed up—yet. So I was still the law in Puma County. I wondered how long that would last.

"I'm going to find out where them two are hiding," I said. "I want to see what else Luke the Butcher might have of mine."

"You think he was the crime wave?"

"I think he was it. And if I can get into his cubbyhole, I'll probably find a thing or two."

Dusty quit mopping up that awful slop. "Listen,

Cotton, that one's not just dangerous and powerful, he's tricky too. He's a knife man."

"If he killed Critter, he won't be any of those things for long."

I headed for Turk's, thinking Luke the Butcher was in there, but Turk said the man had got his bedroll out of the hayloft and gone away. After that I tried the Wyoming Hotel, and two flophouses back behind the saloons, and checked three cathouses for good measure. I found the county supervisor, Reggie Thimble, in Aunt Alice's Parlor House, and Al Smythe, the postmaster, in Sing Long Sally's House of Joy smoking a hookah, but I didn't see Iceberg and his pal puffing dope or getting cozy with tarts. But I didn't expect to. Iceberg was no more interested in women than in mynah birds. And the Butcher, all he wanted was to ruin anything alive. Wherever Iceberg and the Butcher were, it wasn't anywhere in Doubtful where you paid for a room. I wondered if maybe the two had just quit town since they was out of a job. I decided to wait and see. My ma always said, quit poking if you don't know where the skunk's hiding, so I decided just to keep my eyes open. If them two were hiding around town, I'd know it soon enough.

The matinee got out and all them rannies off the ranches were pouring into the saloons for some liquid refreshment. I'd be parched, too, from panting my way through that Grand Luxemburg Follies. I thought it'd be a quiet evening in the saloons. Them cowboys were too busy thinking about women to get into a fight. They'd get drunk and ride out, wondering why the hell they were cowboys on ranches where there wasn't a female in sight.

I had to knock to get Rusty to let me in, and even then he had his six-gun drawn. He locked the door behind me. I saw in a glance he'd got the office polished up, and the jail, too, and had opened the windows to let the stink outside.

"No sign of Iceberg and the Butcher," I said. "But they're around."

"You line up any help?"

"Just you, Rusty."

"You know something? I knew it'd work out like that." He was giving me that red-haired cock-eyed grin again.

"I haven't got a night shift, but we got no one locked up. After the town quiets down, you go on home. We'll have to work days and evenings for now."

"Hell, I'd sleep in a cell and make myself comfortable."

"Your smeller's weaker than mine.

"I'm going to prowl tonight. I want to find out where the Butcher's bunking. If I can find anything he lifted from my room at Belle's, I've got him."

"Iceberg's the one to worry about," Rusty said. "He doesn't steal anything."

I headed out into a June eve just in time to discover a ruckus at the Ralston Opera House. Them women from the Watch and Ward Society were at it again, and Delphinium Sanders was leading the charge. They'd been real quiet for a couple of nights, when Iceberg was wearing the star, but now they were waving posters and signs and marching like angry hornets. Some cowboys were coming up to the box office to buy some tickets, and the women started shouting.

"Shame on you. What would your mother think?" yelled Mrs. Stanford.

"I think my ma'd say enjoy the sights," the ranny said.

"Don't you dare walk into that theater and defile womanhood," said another old gal.

"Hey, I've got the nicest little heifers on the ranch, just like these gals."

"Got some prime bulls, too," said another ranny.

It was getting toward curtain time, and bunches of cowboys showed up suddenly, and they were pretty well liquored up. In fact they was likely the same fellers that saw the matinee, and they'd come back for second servings. That's what pretty girls do for fellers. They'd headed for the nearest bars, soaked up some red-eye, and here they were, real smiley.

They lined up to buy tickets, eyeing the ladies

with their posters, and looking pretty cheerful. But them women were yelling now, and waving posters at the ticket-buyers. And then Delphinium cried to her squad of old babes, and they set down their signs and formed a line across the doors, and held hands real tight and wouldn't let no one walk into the theater.

"Ladies, you can't do that. You've got to let them in," I said.

"The wages of sin," one hollered.

"Never, never, never," yelled another.

Delphinium, she addressed me. "Our hands are locked together in purity. We will let no one enter here. Do violence to us if you must, but we'll hold on as long as we can, until brute force carries us away."

The women cheered. All them boozy cowboys, they sort of stared awkwardly.

"You mind if I get around here?" one asked Delphinium.

"Over our dead bodies," she cried.

This here was getting serious. A big bunch of cowboys was waiting to get inside, and these Watch and Ward women were blocking the path. I didn't like it.

"Ladies, you're trespassing, disturbing the peace. I'd hate to have to take you in," I said.

"Just try it," Delphinium said. "You brute."

Ralston waved me over to his box office.

"You'll get rid of 'em?"

"Well, it's like this. Them ladies, they're the banker's wife, the wives of the merchants, the wives of the trade people, the ones who run this here county. I could haul 'em in and book 'em and lock 'em up. By tomorrow morning, Iceberg would be sheriff. And you could kiss your opera house good-bye. I'll nab 'em if you want. They're trespassing. Up to you."

Ralston sighed. "Take the customers around to the stage door on the alley, but a few at a time so these ladies don't get their knickers in a twist."

"Count on me. I'll get all them rannies seated fast."

I went to some of those cowboys. "Head for the stage door in small bunches, and don't be obvious. Pass the word."

"You the sheriff or something? Why not just nab these dames?"

"Believe me, that's not a bad idea," I said. "But you just slide around there in the dark, and they'll take your tickets back there."

The cowboy, he just shook his head like I was some sort of lamebrained idiot, and maybe I was. But there was a mess of stuff at stake here. If I arrested those old gals, pretty quick the opera house would shut down, and then Doubtful would shut down, and I'd sure be looking for work.

I drifted back to the stage door on the alley, arriving ahead of the rannies. It sure was quiet.

I felt steel jammed into my gut.

"They're not going in," Iceberg said. "And those debased women aren't coming out."

I have learned not to argue with a revolver muzzle pressed into my belly.

"You're a bad joke," Iceberg said. "Tell the cowboys to go home; no show tonight. Tell them loud and clear, or you'll be a dead joke as well as a bad joke."

So I did.

CHAPTER TWENTY-TWO

All them cowboys were lining up at the box office to get their money back, and them old biddies was still barring the front doors, arm in arm, looking pretty smug. Inside, the orchestra was cranking up even if there was hardly anyone in there to watch the Grand Luxemburg Follies.

Ralston, he was sure unhappy in his box office as he began to dole out all them coins and greenbacks. But then he yelled at me to come over there.

"I've changed my mind. I'm making a complaint. They're on my property. I asked them to leave. They refuse."

"You want me to clear 'em out?"

"I have nothing to lose," he said.

He turned to the cowboys at the head of the line. "You'll be going in as fast as the sheriff clears the way."

The orchestra was playing "My Old Kentucky

Home" in there, and all them customers were sure itchy to get in.

I went straight to Delphinium Sanders, who stared down her nose at me like I was a caterpillar.

"Sorry ma'am, I'm taking you in. Mr. Ralston, he's filed a complaint with me. You're trespassing."

"Do you know who I am?"

"I know who all of you are."

"We won't budge. We're here to stay."

"If you don't come peaceable, ma'am, I'll add some charges of my own. Disturbing the peace. Resisting arrest. The trespassing, that's a civil offense. You want to make it criminal?"

"Over my dead body."

"We won't budge," said one of them ladies.

"You come peaceable, or face what I'll have to do."

"You wouldn't dare."

"I'll have Turk send a wagon and you'll get yourselves hauled."

This sure was entertaining that crowd of cowboys, who thought it was better than the show starting up in there.

"We'll help load 'em up," said one cowboy.

Delphinium glared at him with a look intended to wilt spinach, but he just smiled back and looked real eager.

She turned to me. "You'll pay. You'll pay the rest of your life. Very well, we will go. Take us to our fate. We will go with dignity, and as martyrs to our cause, the cause of purity and womanhood."

But she quit blocking the doors, and all them biddies, in their long skirts and bound up hair, and puffed sleeves, they huffed along toward my office. Behind me I saw that mob of theater patrons pouring into the opera house at last. It sure was strange, me herding them old gals along like they was a bunch of milch cows. All I needed was a good herding dog, like an Australian ridgeback. They kept turning to wither me with their glares, but I didn't wither up, and just kept prodding them to the sheriff office and the jail. The old bats, they was a mean bunch, but I was meaner. I wouldn't trade any of them for my ma.

"You realize, young man, that your hours as sheriff are numbered," Delphinium said. "I will see to it."

"I do what I have to do, ma'am. I received a complaint; I acted on it. It don't matter to me who's what. The law covers everyone, and that includes you same as some vagrant wandering through here."

"That's why Mr. Berg will replace you," she said.

"You just head up them steps and into there, and me and Rusty will book you."

"Our husbands will have words with you," one gal said.

"Oh, I'm sure they will," I said.

But the ladies swept into the office like they owned it. I guess they thought they did own it.

Rusty, he was so rattled by all this femaleness coming into his male precinct that he just gaped.

"Take their names and then take them back to the jail," I said.

"The jail! The jail?" Delphinium Sanders was ready to explode.

"That's what we do, ma'am. We put people in jail."

It sure was entertaining, watching them turn pale. One looked ready to swoon.

"You can sit there on that bench, ma'am."

"I demand to see Judge Rampart at once," Delphinium said.

"He'll set bail in the morning," I said, enjoying myself even if I thought I was committing myself to hell.

"I refuse to spend a night in that loathsome place."

"You had your chance not to, ma'am. I told you to disperse and you didn't. I told you to let people through, but you didn't."

"I will be a martyr for a noble cause," she said.

I got their names in the logbook, along with the charges, one by one, except for one woman who wouldn't say who she was. But I knew anyway. She was Mrs. Ruble, wife of the bank teller Gannymede Ruble, so I just put that down, while Rusty, rolling his eyes and whistling, and making odd noises, escorted them biddies back to the cells. I have to give them credit, though. They held their chins high, and none of them got the vapors or busted into tears or any of that stuff. They were tough, and I sort of admired that. I like tough babes.

I put them into both cells so the gals would be able to sit on the bunks rather than the cement floor, and I could see them staring at them two pails that Rusty had cleaned out, and a couple of them just closed their eyes real tight, not wanting to see what comforts the Puma County lockup provided for its special guests.

I left a lamp lit and waited. It wouldn't be long before there'd be hammering on the office door, and a mess of the town's foremost and outstanding citizens would swarm in, probably armed with buggy whips and artillery.

Sure enough, it took about half an hour before the gents arrived, wild-eyed and ornery from what I could see out the window.

Hubert Sanders was leading the assault.

"Open up immediately," he bawled.

"You got business here?"

"I've come to fetch my wife."

"She's in for the night, trespassing. Lucky for her I quit right there because I could have added a few more."

"She's going to leave there right now or your head will roll."

"It rolls already. My ma says I need a stiffer neck."

I heard them slamming themselves against the

door, a human battering ram. From inside the jail I heard tweets and twitters.

"Save us," one gal moaned.

"You out there. You force the door to the sheriff office and you'll walk into buckshot."

That didn't slow them down none, and I was starting to get itchy. They were hammering and thumping on that door, and the old door rattled on its hinges and threatened to cave in.

This sure was getting entertaining.

Rusty, he was looking a little pale at the gills, but you could never wipe a smile off Rusty's mug. He wasn't born red-haired for nothing.

The thumping on the office door kept on for a bit, and then things quieted down out there and I wondered what was what. It didn't take long for me to find out.

"Pickens, this is Judge Rampart. Open this door."

"Not if there's going to be a stampede."

"I said open it."

I got to thinking about it a little. "You can come in if you come alone and the rest of them rioters clear out."

"I said open up."

"You move them rioters back, and I'll open up. You're the only one coming in. Agreed?"

"I don't agree to anything. Release those women. That's a court order."

"You come on in alone, and we'll see about it."

There was a lot of muttering out there, and some snarls and some shouts, but then Rampart addressed me. "I'll come in alone. The rest are off the steps and under orders not to rush."

I nodded to Rusty, who could just see some of the mob from the barred window.

"They've backed up some."

"All right, Judge, you'll be walking into the bore of a scatter-gun, and if there's a rush on this door, you'll get hurt."

"Are you threatening me?"

"I'm keeping order and keeping the law."

There was a long pause, and then he agreed. "You have my word. I'm ready."

I unbarred the door, my scatter-gun ready, and let the man in. He was sure steaming. I closed and barred the door behind him.

The ladies, they all cheered and twittered back there.

Rampart glared, took stock, and faced me square. "I am directing you to release them."

"Soon as they've posted bail," I said. "They've been charged proper, according to the law, and they can post bail and I'll unlock."

"Now," he snarled.

"If it wasn't your friends, would you be yelling at me? You got a law for your friends and their ladies, and another law for the rest of the world?"

"Now," he snapped.

"Tell you what," I said. "I swore to uphold the law without favor. I'm doing it. You set bail for these persons, and I'll collect it or your clerk can, and then I'll let them loose."

"Stop pointing that shotgun at me."

"You stop threatening to break the law, and I will."

He looked like he was about to get seized up inside, so I lowered the bore a little. That seemed to do it all right.

"I am declaring court in session. I am setting bail at five dollars," he said.

"You tell that to them outside, and collect it. I'll give it to your clerk in the morning. Here's the log."

He studied the arrest log. "You certainly know how to get your tail in a crack, don't you, Pickens?"

"I'll put it in a worse crack if I charge them with disturbing the peace, but I will straight off if this ain't done proper."

Rampart fixed me in his cold eyes and didn't blink. Me, I blink any old time.

He walked to the door and waited for me to unbar it, and stepped out. I closed it and heard some angry talk out there, like that mob wanted to string me up from the nearest eave. But for the moment it was peaceful. Not even the biddies was making any noise. Rusty, he just stood there with a cockeyed grin pasted on his face.

"What are you smiling at?" I asked.

"Thinking about where you'll be tomorrow," he said.

A knock on the door. "It's Rampart," a voice said.

"You got them people backed off and not coming in?"

"I do."

I let him in, while Rusty covered that door with the scatter-gun, and I locked it behind the judge. There were some greenbacks in his hand.

"Bail," he said. "Thirty-five."

"I'll give you a receipt," I said. I wrote numbers real good, and gave him his receipt.

"Release them," he said.

"You tell them when they're going to appear in court," I said.

He looked ready to uncork again, but he nodded.

I went and unlocked the cells. Them seven gals didn't put on airs this time. They didn't even stare me down. They just flooded out fast as they could and into my office.

"Oh, thank you, Judge," Delphinium said. "You're a saint."

"I'll expect all of you in court at nine tomorrow. You are charged with trespassing."

A fleeting rage floated across her face, but she swallowed it.

She approached me and spat. I sure wasn't expecting it. That gob, it landed on my star and oozed down and dripped to the floor. Then she stalked away.

"I'm glad you don't chew, ma'am," I said. "Never liked brown spit."

I let them ladies out the door and into the night. Their men were out there, bellowing like bulls.

The judge lingered so I closed the door again.

"I thought Ike Berg was the new sheriff," he said.

"He fooled me out of my badge, so I took it back."

"You mind explaining?"

I didn't mind one bit. "The supervisors was thinking of firing me, saying there was a crime wave around here. Berg showed up and was angling for the job. One day he told me the supervisors had made him sheriff and I should turn over the badge. So I did. Then he went and told them supervisors I'd resigned, and he'd take over. So he fooled them and fooled me. Meanwhile, I found out who was bedeviling me, robbing my room, killing my horse, sticking me up. It was Berg's new deputy, Luke the Butcher. He killed my horse but I'm having a bad time proving it. I had a chance to toss Berg out and I done it, and took back my badge. And I'm keeping it until I get a written thirty-day notice. And I'm pressing charges against both, as you know."

The judge just stood there in the lamplight, absorbing all that.

"I'm not going to support you," he said. "We need a new sheriff and you're not it. This town's a cesspool. But I'll see what I can do to keep Berg out of this office. I've got some difficulties ahead of me on that score. Like Delphinium Sanders, a mad moose if ever there was one. I don't know what'll happen to the republic if women get the suffrage."

"My ma would make a good sheriff," I said. "She'd arrest me if I busted the law."

Rampart stared and stared, and smiled.

CHAPTER TWENTY-THREE

I was in Rampart's courtroom at nine, and so were Ralston and Jardine, all ready to testify. But them old gals never showed their faces, and Rampart, he finally fined them the amount of the bail, and that was that. I thought he was glad that the biddies didn't try some weepy theater in his courtroom.

Outside, I asked those fellers how the show went.

"There were some empty seats," Ralston said. "All that trouble scared people off."

"I'll try to keep the peace tonight, but no telling what the dingbats will do," I said.

"The show went well enough, all things considered," Ralston said. "You have to give those showgirls credit. They'd been jailed all night, and barely made it to the matinee, and then did an evening show, too."

"You tell Ambrosia I'm ready anytime she is. I'll get Rampart to tie the knot."

"Pickens, I don't think she's very fond of Doubtful," Jardine said. "But good luck stealing my star from me."

"Doubtful's a real nice town," I said. "She'd be real happy here. I can put up a cabin near the creek."

"Doubtful's the second-worst town we've ever played," Jardine said. "Sorry to disparage your grand metropolis, but it's been a hard haul here."

"What's the worst town, Alphonse?" Ralston asked.

"Unquestionably, Livingston, Montana. There's a town to peel the hide off a bull."

"What's the trouble with it?"

"It's a railroad town, and that should tell you what you need to know. If you think cowboys are wild, just try some drunken track-layers. Cowboys are sissies compared to that bunch."

"I guess I'm sort of dumb, so tell me," I said.

"They shut me down every night, stole the box office, tore the theater apart, stole all my girls and impregnated every one, so I had to sell the girls to them and get a new cast back in New York."

"That's not so bad," I said. "Doubtful's worse than that."

"All the founding mothers of Livingston are showgirls," Jardine said.

"I wish I was lawing up there," I said. "I could have made off with Ambrosia."

"Not if you want to keep your gray guts inside your tender pink belly," Jardine said, "and your privates attached to the rest of you."

"Maybe Ambrosia has talents I never thought about," I said. "But I'd still marry her."

Them fellers went back into their theater, and I went back to sheriffing. Now that the town was sort of cooled down a little, maybe I could work on that murder, the knifing of Pinky Pearl a few days earlier. The man lay buried in Doubtful's little plot for the dead, but I'd not caught the killer. I pretty well knew who I was looking for, but that kind of knowing, and proving it, were different deals.

If Iceberg and Luke the Butcher weren't hanging around where there were rooms to let, then someone was putting them up, and I knew where to start now. I had unpinned my Puma County badge and washed it real good and put it back on. The last time I'd got spit at, it was a mad raccoon under a porch, but that fracas was settled with a piece of canvas. This time I got spat at by Doubtful's nobility, and it had me thinking that the Sanderses had them a carriage house behind their big house, with carriage and stalls below, and a hayloft above, just right for summertime visitors. I was pretty sure that was where them two were hanging.

The Doubtful Bank was the fanciest building in town. It started as a frame structure but then it got gussied up with yellow sandstone, with white enamel doors and windows. In a town that was still half frontier, it looked like it was permanent. It proclaimed that Doubtful, Wyoming, was here to stay. It cast a reassuring and benign glow upon the town. Some had argued that it shouldn't be called a "Doubtful" bank, but others said that the name was just right. There it was, a sandstone monument to Doubtful, radiating good will, providing financial services to the businesses, cashing checks, doling out cash for the tills of stores and saloons, and reminding everyone on Main Street that Doubtful was civilized.

I hardly went into the place. A forty-a-month sheriff hardly needed a bank. I got paid in greenbacks in a manila envelope by the county clerk. I paid Belle her rent, and kept thirty-five cents out for a haircut, and tucked a dollar in my boot since I usually went dry before the next payday. So the place wasn't one I usually visited. But today I wished to talk to Hubert Sanders, the bank's founder, president, and sole owner, not to mention the most influential man in the county. A word from Sanders was enough to change supervisors' minds, reverse judicial decisions, start a reform, or stop one.

I stepped into its cool quiet, the thick sandstone shielding the lucky fellers inside against the summer sun. There were two teller cages, but Sanders's office was over in a rear corner, where he could discreetly keep an eye on his customers while not being obvious about it.

There was a little wooden gate that kept the hoi polloi like me out of his walnut-walled office, so I approached one of them tellers, whose wife had just gotten bailed out.

"Feller, I'd like to talk to the boss in there," I said.

He reminded me of a glacier ready to calve a new floe, but then headed back to Sanders's lair, only to return a moment later.

"Sorry, he's busy."

"It's a law matter, so I guess I'll just let myself through there," I said.

He looked fit to lose a wisdom tooth, but I unhooked that little walnut gate and headed over to the boss man.

Sanders peered up at me, removed his spectacles, and pouted, without so much as a greeting.

"I got a request. You've got a couple fellows in the loft of your carriage barn I need to talk to. It's a law matter. So I'm looking for your okay on it."

He looked pained, like he was passing a prune pit. "If it wasn't acceptable for you to come in here without my permission, then you can imagine my answer to your intrusion on my house and grounds."

"I thought maybe you could help me solve some crimes around here."

"You're the only crime in sight," he said.

"One of them fellers in your barn, he might be dangerous to you and your wife."

"If your goal is to persuade me of something, bringing up my wife is certainly impolitic."

"I never did hear that word before. It sounds as bad as a kidney stone."

"Out!" He actually waved an arm and pointed a finger, something entirely out of character for him.

"I may have to go in there anyway if I get the goods on the feller. Name's Luke the Butcher, and he's a menace to Mrs. Sanders, and everyone else around here. You don't want him on your place. You don't want that phony lawman, either."

"Out!"

He reached into his desk drawer and produced a small, shiny revolver.

"Shoot the sheriff and you'll swing," I said. "Put that thing away before I get serious."

But he just aimed at my navel. I reached across and slapped his hand to the left, and then just yanked the thing out of his mitt. It was a thirty-two caliber five-shot lady gun.

"You can pick it up from me or Rusty tomorrow," I said.

He looked a little cooked around his gills, so I just left him to stew.

I took the revolver back to my office and handed it to Rusty. "It belongs to Sanders. He's lucky I didn't pinch him. Give it back tomorrow."

Rusty eyed me. "You favoring the rich suddenly?"

That got under my skin. The truth of it was, if

someone in the saloons had pulled a weapon on me, he'd be cooling his heels in my guest cages. But I'd let Sanders go. Maybe it was because I didn't want to rile up the supervisors just now.

"Yes," I said.

Rusty, he was sort of eyeing me crooked-lipped.

I bulled across the town square to the courthouse looking for a supervisor, any supervisor, who was going to listen to me for a moment or two.

Ziggy Camp was sucking Old Orchard from a desk bottle when I barged in.

"I just took Hubert Sanders's revolver from him. He can have it back tomorrow."

"Well, now that ain't politic, right?"

"He was aiming it at the Puma County sheriff. I didn't charge him. So maybe I was politic after all."

"He took offense, did he?"

"He was wishing I'd depart from his altar. I wanted permission to get onto his place. He's harboring Iceberg and the Butcher, and I have some business with the Butcher. Like who and what did he kill? And rob?"

"She's the one harboring them, Pickens. You shouldn't have cut her loose." Ziggy was smirking. "She'll be back at her post this eve, so you can arrest her again."

"If she stops traffic in or out of that opera house, I will. And if that costs me my badge, then it's my tough luck."

Ziggy's eyebrows caterpillared upward and

downward. What he was registering was a change in the Puma County sheriff, from a live-and-let-live lawman to a mean sonofabitch.

"My ma, she always said don't hide in the bull-rushes," I added.

"I think she was referring to Moses."

"I don't know who she was talking about, but if Delphinium breaks the law, she'll get whatever she's got coming."

Camp, he just smiled blandly and lifted his pint and sucked long and hard, and wheezed a couple of times. "Doubtful sure is entertaining," he said. "You gonna pinch Ralston and that showman, Jardine? They've gone naked again. There's a mess of bare-ass ladies prancing around in there, robbing Doubtful of its cash."

"Show me the law, right there on the books, and I will."

"Well, ah, maybe Lawyer Stokes can. He'll sound out the letters for you."

"I already asked him. If there's a law, he ain't told me about it."

Camp sighed. "Your type don't vote. The ones that vote in every election are all like Delphinium Sanders."

"Then let them vote for supervisors who'll pass a law against bare-ass beauties."

Ziggy Camp choked some on that. "Don't be hasty," he said. "We're studying it. I've been over there to that show twice now, studying on it. I'm in no hurry to enact some ill-considered legislation that we'd all regret. It's harder to get a law off the books than on it, and that means we have to act carefully and judiciously. I'm going over there tonight and I'll take notes, and maybe after this Follies leaves town, I'll bring up the ordinance and we'll have at it, carefully and with proper weighty consideration."

"You sure are a bull pecker, Camp."

He smiled at me.

"I've proposed to Ambrosia," I said. "She's the star of the show."

"And?"

"She's not keen on Doubtful."

Camp, he laughed and sucked his Old Orchard, and I got out of there. A feller hardly knew where he stood around Doubtful. One moment I was in hot water, the next moment I wasn't, and the next moment everything had switched around so that them that liked me became them that wanted me out. Well, I had a job to do, which was keep the law and keep the peace, and that's what I would do, no matter what it cost me. I'd enforce laws I didn't like, and treat people I didn't like fair and square, and if it came to that, I'd tell my bosses in the courthouse to cool it if they wasn't following the rules.

"Hey, guy," the redhead said. "You want to talk?"

It was Ambrosia. It took me a moment to recognize her because I was so busy watching the rest of her on stage that I didn't pay no attention to her face. She was wearing a gauzy green dress, neck to toe, but it didn't hide her real hard.

"You talking to me?"

"You could buy a girl a cup of java."

"I thought you were gonna pay me a million dollars."

"Okay, you're cheap. I'll buy you a cup. Take me to your favorite joint."

I could hardly believe it. I sort of polished my star with my fingers to make it shine, and escorted her to the Beanery, where the two of us got into a corner and everyone in there could stare at me and wish they was me. I just nodded and smiled, and she smiled back.

"I hear you want to marry me," she said. "So let's talk."

I spilled the damned coffee. And then I was ready to talk.

Chapter Twenty-four

If I had false teeth I would have swallowed them. But I still have most of my choppers, and the gaps don't bother me none. But there was Ambrosia, sitting right beside me, telling me we should talk about holy matrimony. I could scarcely imagine it. Worse, my ma didn't have no advice on this one.

"So what's the deal?" I asked. That was the most romantic thing I could think of to say.

"I'll make you happy. I know how to make a man real, real happy."

"Right now?" I asked. There was no sense waiting around. "I'll buy you a cup later."

"Pretty quick," she said, and sipped a little. This was going to drive me bonkers.

"Name your deal," I said, patting her arm.

"I just want to know you're real serious," she said. "I wouldn't marry just anyone."

"How serious do I need to get?"

"Why are you patting my arm when you could be patting my knees under the table?"

I sure never had a babe talk to me like that. It was like listening to a red hot horseshoe making water hiss.

I guess I was too addled to think, so I just sat there and waited. She finally figured out that she should tell me the deal.

"I'll marry you for one month," she said. "I want to leave the show. You're my way out. I'm tired of it. That night in the jail sure did it."

"One month?"

"Yessirree, pal, one month, and you can have me every day and night, weekdays and Sundays. After that you divorce me."

"Divorce you?"

"You betcha. You get Judge Rampart to tie the knot, and then get him to sever the knot."

"But that's not marriage."

"Hey, I usually marry for two weeks. After we split, you pay for stagecoach down to the Union Pacific, and for a ticket to Chicago. I got friends there. And I get into a new show."

"I don't think I could swing that. Maybe if I didn't pay Rampart to marry and divorce us."

"What do you think I am? I don't believe in free love."

"You're expensive, all right."

"Is there a druggist here?"

"There's not even a decent doc. You have to go

to Laramie for that stuff. We've got a faith healer though."

"I need some Williams Tooth Balm real bad. Mine got stolen when I was stuffed in your jail."

"What's that?"

"It stops my gums from hurting. It's little pills of cocaine. Take one and my gums are fine. Take two and my elbows don't hurt. Take three and my tits don't hurt either."

"Do they hurt?"

"All the time. They get too much fresh air."

"You'd have to wire Laramie and get the stuff by stage."

"Not me. You. If you want to marry me you got to keep me in pills."

"How much would marrying you for a month cost?"

"Oh, food, tickets, pills, marriage and divorce, maybe three hundred."

"I'm a forty-a-month sheriff, not a bank."

She eyed me. "Most sheriffs make lots more, one way or another."

I sighed. "I can't marry you but I'll give you a free sample."

"You know anyone wants to marry me?"

"My free sample's better than anyone else's."

"I'll pay for your coffee," she said, slapped the cup in the saucer, dropped some change on the table, and hightailed out of the Beanery. People sure were watching.

I felt about two feet tall. My biggest chance for

happiness had flown the coop. I'd never have a chance like that as long as I lived. It was like Ambrosia came down from heaven, and I threw the deal away, and she went back up to heaven again. My pa, he would have said I had nothing between my ears.

I should have married Critter.

Doubtful didn't have any help for the lovelorn, so I decided to get back to work even though my heart was scraping dirt. I had a criminal in town, Luke the Butcher, and he was given sanctuary on the banker's property, and I had to get him out of there and nail him one way or other. He deserved to hang, and not just for cutting Critter's throat. He'd killed a man, too. All I had to do was prove it.

I was fixing to relieve Rusty long enough so he could visit the county outhouse, but as I passed the Wyoming Hotel, I saw a mess of familiar carriages and buggies. And one of them was that ebony buggy that Delphinium Sanders drove around Doubtful. But there were a few more I spotted, the victoria owned by the Wallers, the surrey operated by the Maxwells, and a few more. I knew exactly what was going on in there. Them Watch and Ward gals were planning the next assault on the Ralston Opera House, and sipping tea and eating crumpets. I don't know what crumpets are, but that's what ladies have in hotel dining rooms. I thought maybe to just walk by, but the more I thought about it, the more I thought this was a chance to straighten out a few items.

All I needed was the courage to walk in there and interrupt their meeting for a few minutes. But that ain't easy. Walking into a tea and crumpets meeting of the Watch and Ward ladies is like committing one's self to jumping off a cliff. I began to sweat, and it wasn't the summer heat, neither. It was the terrors. It was the farts. But there was no cure for it. Once I set my feet toward the hotel doors, I was a cooked goose. I'd have to go in there and get it over with.

I got as far as the door, and thought maybe Rusty needed me real bad at the office, but I got my courage together, entered, and sure enough, the dining room door was closed; all them ladies in lavender were in there, and Delphinium was holding court. I broke into a real sweat, and felt it blacken my armpits. I'd rather ride a bronc or lasso a bear than do what I had to do, but I got up my dander and opened up, and stepped in.

The whole Watch and Ward bunch was in there, sipping tea from those little one-finger china cups with saucers under them for the spillover. There was a mess of perfume in there, and it pretty near knocked me flat. I'll put my nose in a rose once in a while, but what hit me was about an acre of lilacs, or something like that. My ma used to say if a woman wears perfume, it's to hide something. Them Watch and Warders was doing a lot of hiding.

All them gals just plain stared my way, like they'd seen two horns and a tail and some feller in red underwear. I looked around there trying to see a crumpet, but I didn't see anything that would answer, so I just cleared my throat five or six times, and finally Delphinium, she says, "Sheriff, this is a private meeting. Good afternoon."

Well, that was more civil than usual, maybe because all them gals was keeping her civil, so I licked my lips a little, and said I'd just like to talk a moment and then I'd vamoose.

"Leave now, Sheriff," she shot back. She sure wasn't going to put up with me.

It was do or die, or both, as a matter of fact.

"I guess you nice ladies are making some plans for the theater tonight," I began. "I'm here to keep the peace, and there's some things that need saying. If Mr. Ralston don't want you on his property, it's his right. So don't trespass. And don't harass them people going in or coming out. That's disturbing the peace. And don't try to block doors. That's not safe, and I'll stop it. Now, you want to shout and wave your signs, that's your right. That's what you're free to do, long as I'm sheriff. You can holler away, and them you holler at can holler back, far as I'm concerned. But if anyone starts hitting on anyone else, that's inviting a trip to my jail, no matter who." I paused. "I guess that does her."

"No, it doesn't do it," Delphinium said. "This society is going to remove that theater from our community, and wipe free the stain upon our virtue and reputation, and there's nothing you can do to stop it."

"Ma'am, you stay within the law, and you'll be fine. You step outside, and you'll be facing a judge."

"Judge Rampart is a friend, and wholly approves, and will free us, just as he freed us before."

"Well, as long as you're taking that sort of view of it, I'll swear in extra deputies, and they'll be on duty at the theater for this performance and the final matinee and evening show tomorrow."

"If there's a theater left, Mr. Pickens."

"What are you talking about?"

"You heard me, sir."

She stared from them deep blue eyes that matched her name, and didn't blink, and I couldn't see into them eyes; there was a wall there that blocked me out, like she was a china doll and not a person, and them china doll eyes were painted on and didn't see a thing.

"Doubtful's pretty much made of wood, ma'am, and that won't change until time passes and the first buildings get rebuilt with stone and brick. The only stone building now is the bank, but that wouldn't survive either, because there's wood on all sides of it. So don't do nothing foolish."

"When one lives in Hades, sir, one struggles to get out, by whatever means. Now, then, are we done with this unpleasantness?"

"You Watch and Ward over this town proper, and

folks will thank you, ma'am. A good watchman, a good warden, those are things we all need."

There was an odd pause, and then the ladies started sipping from those one-finger cups, and I saw that was how it ended, so I left. I guess I didn't make any new friends there.

They'd been warned, but now I had some more warnings to give.

I found both Ralston and Jardine in the little office offstage.

"You got much fire protection around here?" I asked Ralston.

"Not unless Doubtful starts a fire department and buys a fire engine."

"You got some water buckets stashed around?"

"Rain barrels at each corner of the building."

"That's it?"

"Doubtful's a wooden town, Sheriff. A fire two blocks away will turn me to ash."

Jardine peered up at me. "Why?"

I told them about visiting the tea party, and the threat I thought I'd heard.

"We can add a few buckets," Ralston said. "And I'll see about keeping some sharp eyes outside."

"Not during a performance, but at night, or early morning, or something like that," I said.

Ralston shrugged. "I sometimes get the idea that they'd like to lock up the whole company and set fire to us all. Now then, what will you be doing about it? I have ten thousand in this structure."

"I'm going to talk to a few husbands."

Jardine smiled crookedly. "They are helpless against female intransigence. I run a show that's three-quarters female, and am usually in the caboose."

"I don't think they'll want their stores burned down," Ralston said.

"They might simply start a fire elsewhere," I said. "When the town fire bell rings, everyone heads for the flames. Including everyone in the theater."

"Are you certain the ladies were talking about fire?" Ralston asked.

"Nope, but that's what sort of hung there betwixt my two ears."

"What are you going to do?"

"I'm heading for the courthouse and telling the supervisors what's brewing. And if Judge Rampart will see me, I'll give him an earful."

"We'll take some measures here, Sheriff," Ralston said. "But if you don't know what's in the cards, you can't play the aces."

I headed for the courthouse and couldn't find any of the supervisors, and tried Rampart, but he'd gone fishing for the weekend. It was looking like me and Rusty, we'd have to keep Doubtful from boiling over, or burning down, or lynching the whole theater company. And we didn't have much manpower for that.

I headed for the Last Chance Saloon, and

found Sammy Upward busy serving, so I waited a while until we could talk. When he began swirling his bar towel in front of me I asked him to keep an ear peeled, and warned him there could be trouble in Doubtful, big trouble like the town burning down. He nodded. "We're Gomorrah," he said.

CHAPTER TWENTY-FIVE

That was about the biggest bunch of people I ever did see, and they kept coming. The more the Watch and Warders agitated to drive the show away, the more people flooded to Ralston's box office. They were all sorts, not just cowboys off the ranches. Some had come from little places far away, itching to see a real variety show. Others were just curious people, who heard stuff about the show and wanted to see with their own eyes. They kept coming, and I knew Ralston and the Follies would have themselves a sellout again.

I was keeping watch. So far, it was peaceable enough. All them show-goers lined up to buy tickets, and the Watch and Ward ladies stood out of the way, heeding what I told them about disturbing the peace and not trespassing. What's more, the ladies weren't hollering, or taunting customers, or slapping them with signs, or misbehaving. They had their signs, all right, all about keeping Doubtful "clean and pure," and "Motherhood for Decency," and stuff like that.

I kept waiting for something bad to happen, because I couldn't get that hint of trouble in Delphinium's rebuke out of my head. But nothing much happened. The theater had a few extra buckets ready, and had filled the rain barrels. And Rusty was quietly patrolling the back and sides of the theater, as well as the alleys and buildings around there, but no one was setting fire to anything, and no one was even lurking around. I began to think maybe it'd be a quiet night after all, even though I couldn't get my worries out of my head. Before showtime I'd checked with Sammy Upward to see if he'd picked up any rumors, and he hadn't. There wasn't any bar talk about the show.

I'd watched all them showgirls walk in through the stage door, including Ambrosia, and wished I could be inside for the show. I'd never get tired of watching those beautiful gals, or watching the dances or the singing, too. This here Follies was a magic lantern show, and I'd never seen the like. But this time I'd stay outside, keeping an eye on everything while the show went ahead in there. They were all trusting me to keep them safe, and keep the peace, so that's what I intended to do. Ambrosia smiled at me as I stood at the stage door, and I nodded back. I sure wasn't fixed to marry her for a month and pay her way east.

Delphinium, she lowered her sign, which had

a single word on it, DECENCY, and headed my way, so I braced myself for trouble.

"We've followed your directions exactly," she said.

"Yes, you have, and it's been peaceful tonight."

"I can't begin to tell you how deeply this theater offends every honorable woman in Doubtful," she said. "We go to bed weeping for our city."

I hardly knew what to say to that, but I tried. "If it ain't to your liking, ma'am, there's the city council and the county supervisors. They make ordinances and laws. That's how it's supposed to work. They're elected."

"By men," she said. "What chance have we against men?"

She had a point there.

"We'd like our town to be like a beautiful garden planted with roses," she said. "We'd like a town filled with happy homes, good husbands well-employed, good wives and mothers, good sons and daughters, church bells ringing joyously every Sunday. Picnics, pot luck suppers, Fourth of July parties. Safety. No crime. Moral courage, character, grace. We'd like that, but we're powerless to change a thing."

She was speaking earnestly, and the funny thing was that I kind of liked her, talking like that. It really was the first time we'd just talked a little, and not got on each other's nerves.

"You've already got some of that, Mrs. Sanders."

"Very little of it. Women can't vote. And men don't want the town to change."

"You'll have your gardens some day, ma'am."

"Not as long as you're sheriff," she said.

The crowd was pretty much in the opera house now, and the rest of them gals were ready to quit.

"Thanks for your cooperation, ma'am."

She eyed me. "I don't want to know what's going on in there. It's not just the tawdry women who are ruined. It's the fine young men, who'll never look upon womanhood in the same way, and who will never admire virtue again. Good evening, sir."

She and her Watch and Ward crew marched off into the sinking sun, oddly quiet and less militant than before.

"She's a magnificent woman," said a voice all too familiar.

Ike Berg was standing just behind me.

"What are you doing here?" I asked, eying his waist. He was not visibly armed.

"Waiting for you to get yourself fired. I want your job."

"You won't have it."

"You might keep the tin star, Pickens, but I will enforce the law."

"I don't follow you."

"There are higher laws, and there are man-made laws. I'm bound to enforce higher law."

"Such as?"

Berg simply smiled with them dried-up lips, which annoyed me.

"You tell me what higher law, and how you'll enforce it."

"Wait and see," he said.

"Where are you from? You got a family?"

"They're all dead. I am alone."

"You got someone close, a relative or something?"

"Pickens, I am a man without a country, a man who has no safe harbor, no friend, no profession, no religion, no trade, no destination, no future or past. I hear the voice of the universe, the music of the divine, the thunder of Judgment."

"You ain't told me what law you'll enforce."

"Nor will I. It is for you to discover."

He turned away, and I stood there, trying to absorb that entirely unrewarding exchange. If there was one thing to know about Iceberg, was that he was a mystery and intended to stay one. I had no more notion of what he wanted from life, or what he intended to do to Doubtful, Wyoming, or who he was, than before. I watched him vanish into the twilight, which is where he belonged. He didn't belong in night or day, but he lived in some perpetual twilight, a shadow creeping here and there, making the world worse. I didn't think I ever met a feller I understood less than Ike Berg. I could see why he had hooked up with Delphinium Sanders, but not Luke the Butcher. If he intended to enforce his own higher law, why had he tried to be a sheriff, enforcing man-made law? Was he simply mad? It sure made me uneasy, and

I didn't have a clue about what made him tick. But I'd sure keep an eye on him.

I could hear that show cranking up in there. The opera house had a vent in the roof that let the summer heat out, but also the music, which drifted over the empty alleys of Doubtful. The town got real lonesome when that show was running. There was a few old soaks in the saloons, and a few ladies sewing by lamplight in their houses, but no one on the streets. In the twilight I saw not a soul between courthouse square and the far side of town. No one, not even on a soft summer night.

I thought it might be a good idea to rattle doors, so I started down Main Street, checking every door of every dark business. Sometimes a storekeeper forgot to lock up, and then I'd have to fetch him, and also look around the place. But each door was tight this night. I tried the mercantile, the ice cream soda parlor, the milliner, the law office of Attorney Stokes, but they was all tight and clean. That was fine with me.

I headed over to Turk's, and found no one in the livery barn or out back in the pens, or in the loft. I always checked Turk's place because that's where vagrants and cutpurses and drifters would sort of end up, bunking in the hay. They'd pinch a bottle from a saloon and didn't have the sense to get out of Doubtful, but would head for Turk's hayloft to guzzle it down, and I'd let them enjoy a night in my iron-bar hotel for their trouble.

It sure was quiet. I headed back to the opera house in time for the intermission, and saw them cowboys out in the street for a smoke between acts. Ralston was in his box office, doing some arithmetic, so I drifted that way.

"Sellout," he said, "Fifty-five standing room tickets. Biggest night ever here."

"I would've liked to see the show again."

"It's hot in there, even with the vent. The girls are sweating."

"With nothing on?"

Ralston laughed. "Heat got to Jardine, and he's indisposed. He's turned the show over to his substitute, whatever his name is."

"He's a card, that Jardine. Makes the show go right along."

"He stopped here to get the box office take, and then went to his hotel."

"I hope you fellers make some money, after the rough times around here."

Ralston sighed. "We won't even break even."

There was a clanging of a cowbell, sort of, and all them dudes was putting out their coffin nails and drifting back. After watching some of them acts, I'd need a good smoke too.

The music cranked up, and I drifted away, keeping an eye on Doubtful. I thought I'd better check with Rusty, so I headed up toward the courthouse square, and the sheriff's office.

Rusty was in there, reading a Captain Billy Whizbang magazine by the light of a kerosene lamp. That was the sort of magazine that Delphinium Sanders wouldn't want in Doubtful.

"All quiet," he said.

No sooner had he said it then we heard a thump, muffled but plain.

"What's that?" he asked.

"Beats me," I said.

I stepped outside to see if a June storm was coming up, but the night was soft and starry, and I didn't see any flickers of lightning. Just a mess of glitter pasted up there.

"It ain't a thunderstorm," I said. "But I'll go scout."

I headed into the June night, full dark now, and sure didn't see much. The Beanery was black. The bank was black. I eyed it close, and couldn't see any trouble there. I checked around, one business after another.

Maybe it was the bass drum in the opera house booming away for something or other.

I headed back to the bank, for no reason I could explain, and rattled its front door and its rear one. They were tight. But there was something in the air that smelled familiar, like maybe cordite, so I pushed my face against an iron-barred window, but I couldn't see anything in there. I stepped back and studied the windows, and sure enough, a high-up one was cracked and some glass was out of it. I found a few shards on the ground.

I headed back to the sheriff's office and got a reflector lantern.

"Bank's locked but something's wrong," I said.

Rusty and me went across the square and shone the lamp into there. It was murky, like maybe there was something in the air.

"Something got blown," Rusty said. "I get a whiff of powder or something."

"I'll get Sanders," I said. "You stay here and stay armed. Don't know what's in the building or the bushes."

Rusty doused the light and sat on the steps. I had to hike to the north side of town and that big place I was ordered never to enter. The house was dark, even though it was hardly nine. Them two were "early-to-rise and early-to-bed" types. I bet they had separate bedrooms at opposite ends of the house.

I banged away with the brass door knocker, and after a long time Sanders appeared, in a bathrobe and slippers, a lamp in hand, and a dour look on his granite face.

"I need you to come to the bank. Something's haywire."

"Are the doors locked?"

"Tight," I said. "Both doors and the barred windows. I shook every one."

"Then why are you bothering me?"

"There's some broken glass."

"The windows are all barred. You say the doors are locked."

"There's a smell, like something had been set off."

He smiled grimly. "You're full of ill-founded notions. The wicked flee when no man pursueth."

"You want to lend me a door key?"

"Oh, all right. And I'll follow along in a bit."

I took the brass key and hiked back to the bank. Rusty was sitting there on the stoop, a revolver in his hand.

He lit his lamp and I unlocked, and we walked into a wall of acrid air. Something sure wasn't right. I headed for the safe. It wasn't a big one, but about as tall as me and all that was needed in a town like Doubtful. We stepped over a large, tangled tarpaulin lying on the wooden floor. I thought I knew what that was for. Pull it over a charge that's going to go off and it dampens the sound even as it's blown away.

The door of the black-enameled safe hung open.

Chapter Twenty-six

We peered into that safe while Rusty held the lamp close. There was paper stuff on the bottom shelves. But greenbacks and gold were missing.

"Gone!" Sanders said. "All gone! Nothing here but some securities I hold for people."

"What's gone?" I asked.

"Our operating cash. Greenbacks. Our gold."

"How much?"

"I know it to the penny. It's on my desk. I did the ledger only a few hours ago. Of gold there was about five thousand, three thousand in double-eagles, two in eagles and half-eagles. Of bank notes, there were seven thousand and something, in all denominations, singles, twos, fives, tens, twenties, fifties, hundreds. All used. We have little call for currency."

"Wrapped in any fashion?"

"In gum paper packs of ten, mostly. It'd all fit in a canvas postal bag."

"Coins?"

"Locked in cash drawers at the two teller stations. Every penny accounted for."

Rusty threw the lamplight on the drawers and tugged at them. They remained locked.

"I'm ruined. The bank's ruined. Doubtful's ruined. I cannot pay demand against deposits. The town's gone to Hades. I'm a debtor, an outcast. Poor Delphinium, doomed to penury."

"Not yet," I said. "That money's not gotten far. That blast happened just an hour ago. That cash don't fly away. It gets hauled. It gets packed. Gold ain't light. It takes some sweat to carry that load out of town."

"Ruined. I knew the instant you let that theater company into town, it would come to this. Open one door, and all of hell rushes in."

"You think they did it?"

"Who else? No one in Doubtful would even think of doing such a dastardly thing."

"You think someone in the company came here and stole the cash while the show was running? Still is running? That company's still on stage."

Sanders drew himself up and addressed me. "Yes, exactly. Sin begets sin. Evil begets evil. This town turned dark and mean, and it spelled doom for us all."

"Then the loot's still here," I said. "We'll track her down."

"I'm ruined," he said. "Even if you find the money, I'm ruined."

I motioned Rusty to shine the light on that door and the safe. Someone with a good drill had widened the crack where the door fit against the safe, and poured blasting oil in there and then ignited it. I knew a bit about that stuff from the miners around Doubtful. They called it nitro, and most of them were scared of it because it was unstable. They mostly preferred dynamite, which was a type of clay soaked with this nitro for safety. But you couldn't squeeze sticks of dynamite between a safe door and the frame of the safe. Someone who knew a lot about this had been in here and done it.

"Blasting oil," I said. "Poured into that hole. Then it spread down inside there."

"I don't know blasting oil from chewing tobacco," Rusty said.

"See?" Sanders said. "You've always had incompetents in your office. If you don't solve this you'll be out on your ear, and I will celebrate."

"Thanks for helping me out," I said. "Who's got a key? Them doors were locked."

"I have the original. Mrs. Sanders has copy number one. And one of my trusted men, the cashier, Ovid Larousse, has copy number two. It opens both doors."

"Larousse, is he the hairy one?"

"You'd call him that, I suppose. I'd say he has fine muttonchops of a sandy hue."

"Where does he live?"

"He's impeccable, Sheriff, and I'll not have you

harassing an innocent man. He'd guard this bank with his life. He's a missionary, you know."

"That's what I'm worried about. Where does he live?"

"I won't tell you. I'll not have you casting a cloud over his life. I'd even trust him with my wife."

"You mind if I go talk to him?"

"Certainly I do."

"Who might Mrs. Sanders have lent the key to?"

"She might lend it to Sheriff Berg, a man of impeccable stature."

"Did she lend it to him?"

Sanders was getting more and more annoyed. "I'll end this foolish line of inquiry and tell you that you'll not harass my wife, nor shall you speak to her, nor shall you speak to either of our guests, Mr. Berg and his deputy. You will proceed to the opera house, find out who has taken the bank's entire cash and gold assets, and make an arrest. Right now."

"Is there any other way into the bank?"

"Someone picked the locks, obviously."

"Someone, meaning someone in the Grand Luxemburg Follies, picked the lock, entered, blew the safe door loose, took the bills and gold, exited, picked the lock shut after the robbery, and hightailed away."

Sanders lifted himself up again, which gave him height. "Exactly," he said.

"My ma, she always said everyone's got a theory."

"Someone in that company's a demolition expert."

"There's miners around Doubtful that have the knack."

"But the one who blew my door was a safe-cracker."

"What's the difference?"

"That's why you should resign, Pickens. Any competent peace officer would know the difference."

"Well, whoever got the stuff is no more than an hour away. I guess we'd better start local. Rusty, get the blown-up tarpaulin. Maybe it belongs to someone. Mr. Sanders, you got a list of what got took?"

"It won't do you any good. I'm not sure you know how to count."

"You want to name who took it, long as you seem to know?"

"Ralston. I never trusted the man."

"He's sitting in his box office."

"That's what I'm saying. He's got the loot in there."

I didn't see what more could be said to that feller. I was going to start with Ovid Larousse. Someone with a key got in there. Maybe someone borrowed a key. Maybe a lock picker with a couple of wire tools flipped the bank door open and flipped it tight later. That seemed a little far-fetched, but I'd let smarter fellers decide that.

When money's missing, look for it. That's about all I ever knew.

We left the banker to ponder his fate in there. He stood staring at his blown safe, fingering the steel where someone muscular had swiftly cut down to the crack between the door and its frame and pumped some juice in there. Larousse had better have a damned good explanation or I'd be tearing his rooms apart.

"You know where that cashier lives?"

"Yeah, he's got a suite above the Sampling Room. He's a gambling fool. I've seen him lose his shirt to Cronk, the dealer in there. Night after night."

"Now we're getting somewhere."

We passed the opera house. The show was just winding up, and a few people were drifting out ahead of the curtain calls. Ralston wasn't in his box office. Everything at the theater looked normal. The bank had been entered, its safe blown, the loot removed, and the door locked behind the thief, while the popular show was playing and the streets were deserted.

"I sort of admire that feller," I said. "Blowing that safe so fast."

"You think it's Luke the Butcher? He'd have access to Delphinium's bank key."

"He cuts meat, not metal, but who knows? Let's rattle the cashier's cage first."

"Do you think we should tell the county supervisors first? Maybe the county lost some money."

"Don't see how. This was cash and gold."

We turned into Mrs. Gladstone's Sampling Room. That was a mean place. There wasn't no cowboys in there. Another type, mostly rough drifters, they were drinking red-eye neat. This was a place where they'd slip some poor dude a mickey and clean out his purse before he woke up in the back alley. I thought maybe to talk with Cronk, the tinhorn at the green baize table at the rear. He was running a faro game, and pulling cards out of the faro box on his table for two players.

He eyed me coldly.

"You seen Ovid Larousse?" I asked.

"I wouldn't know," he said, pulling the second card.

"He buck the tiger much?"

"Who did you say?"

I saw how that was going, so I lifted his faro box off the table and got fixed to throw it at him.

"Hey!" he yelled, reaching for his pepperbox. Then he saw Rusty's iron aimed at his cheating heart, and settled down.

"He was in here after the bank closed. I haven't seen him since."

"Was he in some kind of mood?"

"He's always in a mood, Sheriff."

"He upstairs?"

"Go to hell," Cronk said.

I set down the faro box, and them gamblers looked like they had swallowed spit.

"I could have won on the jack," Rusty said.

I headed up the stairs at the side of the joint. We knocked, no answer, and busted in. The place wasn't locked. It was dark. We lit a lucifer, and fired up a lamp, but all we saw was Larousse's orderly room, not a feather loose, not anything. Not a razor, not a comb, not a brush. In fact, he'd pulled out. That sure was interesting. Empty armoire, not one dirty sock in a corner.

"Dead," Rusty said.

"Naw, dead people leave smelly socks around," I said. "He packed his underwear."

"Would you say that about me if I disappeared?"

"I'd say your underwear killed you off," I said. "We'd better see what Turk has to say."

If Larousse got a horse or two from Turk's Livery, that might explain a lot. We headed that way, passing the crowds heading for the saloons after a night with the Grand Luxemburg Follies. That bank heist was well timed, if the object was to do the job while much of the population of Doubtful was in the opera house.

I found Turk drunk as a skunk in the stinking office he lived in. He wasn't one to bathe, and usually dipped in a horse watering trough in the middle of the night. But tonight he was clutching a flask of Old Orchard.

"You rent any nags or a wagon tonight?"

"I wouldn't rent you a nag if you begged me," he said.

"That cashier, Larousse, he been around here?"

"Nah, and I wouldn't rent him a nag. I don't think he's ever sat a nag. He arrived by coach."

"Anyone around here tonight?"

"Just the usual rummies," he said.

"Anyone head out with a horse or wagon?"

"What do ya take me for, an idiot?"

I didn't know what was paining him. "You see anything unusual?"

"Caterpillars crawling all over the place. And earthquakes. And tidal waves. I've been slapping horseflies all night."

"And after you sucked on that bottle, everything quieted down, right?"

"How did you know that?"

"Come on, Rusty, let's head for Sanders's place."

"You don't even thank me," Turk said, settling back in his grimy bunk.

We weren't doing real good at finding the thief. But I had a notion he might be up there in Sanders's carriage house, laughing at Hubert and Delphinium and maybe laughing at me. So we headed for the north side of Main Street, where all them comfortable dudes lived, the ones that were always telling me I didn't know my job. My thinking was that Iceberg and Luke the Butcher and maybe the cashier had pulled a heist right there, getting in with Delphinium, getting the bank key, blowing the safe, and then hiding all that cash and gold right there in the safest hiding place in town, the banker's own carriage house.

After a while they'd split up the loot, and get out. The more I thought about it, the more it seemed like that's what happened.

"You think Larousse is up there, too, with all that swag?" Rusty asked.

"I don't know what I think. My ma used to say, quit thinking and start looking, so that's what I'm fixing to do. Maybe we'll nail the crooks right in Sanders's own yard."

CHAPTER TWENTY-SEVEN

It sure was dark. Me and Rusty got over there to where the Sanderses had their big house, and stared into the night. There wasn't no light, not in the house or the carriage house.

"I'm going to wake her up," I said.

"That's not going to get you friends at the courthouse."

"I've been wanting to talk to Delphinium for days. I got a feeling she's the Mama Spider in this web."

"Don't you think we should just go over to the carriage house? Talk with the Butcher, or whoever's there?"

"Women got the say-so," I said. "That's what Ma always said."

"You mind if I go home to bed?"

"You're coming with me. If she shoots, she'll need to hit both of us."

Rusty, he was grinning but it was too dark for

me to enjoy it. We walked through a gate in the picket fence and headed upslope toward that mansion. There was a big veranda on it, and we climbed the stairs to that, and finally reached the front door, made of solid walnut. There was a brass knocker on it, so I banged away. It sure was loud. It sounded like a battle between the Confederates and the Union.

It sure took some banging, but finally there came a hard voice out to us.

"Go away," she said. Her voice was muffled behind that big door.

"Sheriff Pickens, ma'am. We need to talk."

"I'm not available."

"Now's as good a time as any."

"I have a migraine headache."

"I suppose you get one most every night, ma'am. Talkin' with me will make her go away real fast."

"You're an idiot, Pickens. Go back to your pigsty."

"Ma'am, no door's good enough to stop me if I take a notion to break it. And I got that notion. So you go light a lamp and get yourself settled in the parlor real sweet, and we'll talk."

I didn't hear nothing for a bit.

"You are loathsome," she said. "All right. Make it quick. My head is throbbing."

"I hear lot of women get headaches every night, ma'am. But I ain't married, so it's all gossip."

She opened the door, a kerosene lamp in her

hand, and we followed her to the gloomy parlor. She looked haughtier than ever, peering down her white nose at us. She was wearing a huge white tent, which hid her bedroom slippers.

"Where's Hubert?" she asked.

"Cleaning up a mess at the bank, Mrs. Sanders. He'll tell you about it when he returns. There's been some trouble. Now, where's them two fellows out in the carriage house?"

"You are referring to Mr. Berg and Mr. Luke—whatever his surname is. I discharged them this evening. No one is in the carriage barn."

"Discharged?"

"They failed me. I sent them packing. They were no good."

"What did you hire them to do, ma'am?"

"Put you out of office. You're the sole remaining obstacle to scrubbing Doubtful white and pure."

"Put me out of office?"

"I told them by whatever means. Just do it, and make it permanent. They're both incompetent. It ought to be no great task to drive a dunce like you clear out of Puma County, and maybe even Wyoming."

"What did you ask them to do, ma'am?"

"I told you. Drive you out. Get rid of you. Embarrass you. Offend you. I paid them good money for it, and didn't get a return on my investment. You're permitting sin to flourish in Doubtful. People drink spirits. People gamble away their every cent. Evil card sharks ruin good families. And other things."

She was peering at me out of shotgun eyes, two big bores aimed at my heart. You look into her eyes and you don't see sweetness and light; you see two loads of buckshot snugged in there.

"Men! It's entirely the moral failing of men. I wish to spare Hubert further temptation."

"He's tempted?"

"He's the worst sinner. I will cleanse Doubtful of every temptation and then maybe we shall find peace in my household."

"Worst sinner, is he?"

"I am done with you." She stood, and it was like a white pyramid rising out of the floor.

"How'd he sin?"

She slapped me. That sure was interesting. I been shot at a lot, and I've brawled with assorted males a lot, and I've been lassoed and whipped and clubbed and pounded with fists, but I'd never been slapped before. It sort of stung, where her dainty little hands brought up the blood in my cheek. She was a pretty tough slapper, all right.

I'd have to think about it. I imagine I said something that set her off but I sure didn't know what.

"Didn't mean any offense, ma'am," I said.

She was shoving me toward her door. Naw, that's not it, she was kicking me with her dainty feet in their dainty slippers.

"It's been a pleasant visit," I said, bowing, and she clobbered my hat.

The big walnut door slammed behind us.

"She sure got set off by something," I said. "Wish I knew what."

"Never did understand women," Rusty said. "Damndest mystery on the planet."

"I can understand my mother, but I never could understand any of the rest," I said. "Maybe Delphinium'll drop by and explain it to me."

"There's too many women in Doubtful."

"Once they come in, there's no escaping. We're stuck."

"We should keep them out," Rusty said.

"Too late for that."

"You think we should go check her carriage barn?"

I steered that way, and we scouted the stalls and found nothing in the moonlight. I climbed a ladder to the hayloft, expecting a bullet at any moment. A loft door let in more moonlight, and I peered around some. But they'd cleared out. I poked some old hay, and kicked it loose here and there, but it was just hay. No gold or greenbacks as far as I could see. Rusty, he climbed up and joined me, and we pushed a lot of loose hay around and found nothing.

"You think we've covered it?" I asked.

"No banknotes in here," he said.

"And no robbers neither."

We climbed down, and cut across moonlit

lawn, and got out of there without getting slapped again.

"We found out what we need to know, though," Rusty said. "We got two crooks to hunt down; an ex-sheriff and a butcher who's real smart with a toad-stabber."

"I ain't sure we do. Someone smart about using nitro blew that safe."

"Well, you got any other suspects?"

I had to confess I didn't. I wasn't real sure we were chasing the right gents, but tracking them was better than sitting on our butts.

That's when we ran into Hubert, heading back to his house on the hill.

"Well?" Sanders asked.

"We been up talking to your wife," I said.

"She didn't have a headache?"

"She said she fired them two in your carriage barn."

"I didn't know she'd hired them."

"She said she did, all right, to get me out of office."

"Well, Sheriff, you shouldn't take her literally. She was just using figures of speech."

"Well, her figure was hidden under a tent, and she slugged me."

"I am speechless," Sanders said.

"You got the place cleaned up?"

"I'll let my cashier, Larousse, clean up the broken glass. But everything else is done. The bank was robbed of eleven thousand, five hundred ninety-two dollars. But there's more. The safe is ruined, and can be replaced only with great difficulty, from Pittsburgh, and that means I'm out another seven hundred ninety dollars. I've lost twelve thousand dollars, and you're harassing Delphinium."

"She said getting rid of me was to keep you from sin."

"She said that, did she?"

"She said I'm the main obstacle. Get rid of me, and you'll be rescued from all the temptations we got around here. I don't know what you need rescuing from but it sounds pretty bad."

"You understand, Pickens, what it means to have a wife who has a headache every night?"

"I ain't ever been married, sir. But it sure sounds lonely."

He sighed. "Lonely's as good a word as any. Mrs. Sanders has had a migraine every night since our wedding day. 'Good night, sleep tight, don't let the bed bugs bite. But if they do, get a shoe, and hit 'em all over til they're black and blue.'"

He headed up the slope toward his wooden palace.

"He's a pretty nice feller," Rusty said. "I don't think he married real well."

When we got back to the sheriff's office, there was a little feller sitting on the steps.

"I'm glad I found you," said Alphonse de Jardine. "I feared the worst."

"Feared?"

"This town is abuzz, it's aflame, with rumors."

I unlocked and let him in, lifted the smoke coated chimney of the lamp, and struck a lucifer.

"Rusty, how come you ain't cleaned these chimneys?"

"Because I wasn't your deputy until a bit ago," he said.

"Is the Grand Luxemburg Follies safe?" the little fart asked.

"Why do you ask that?"

"There were lamps lit in the bank. One does not see lamps in banks at night."

"What's that got to do with your company?"

"Ralston went over there to make a night deposit of our receipts, and saw Sanders back in there, and disorder. Papers littering the floor. So he brought his deposit back, and now there's no safe place to keep it."

"Safe got blown," I said. "Got cleaned out, too. But we've got some badasses in mind."

"That's truly bad news. When did it happen?"

"Middle of the second act."

"During the show?"

"Wasn't many people from around here on the street. They was all in there watching your vivid tablets."

"*Tableaux vivants*," he said. "Live scenes."

"Whatever. Bare babes, if you ask me. They used blasting oil, nitro, and blew Sanders's safe door open and made off with the loot. It might have been an inside job. Them doors were locked."

"Stolen, ah yes, ripped away from the rightful owners. Including two box office receipts we were euchred out of by that miserable excuse for a judge," he said. "But you have prospects?"

"Yep, the Watch and Ward hired guns."

Jardine cocked his head, tilting his giant stovepipe hat. "I like that. I might invent a scene in the Follies and call it the Watch and Ward Hired Guns. Great box office."

"Well, we'll nail 'em. We got two good suspects. And they ain't going far."

"Will we be safe leaving Doubtful?"

"Safe? Oh, you're closing tomorrow, right?"

"We're pulling out right after the curtain falls. We'll be ten miles toward Casper before we camp. Schedules, you know. You pick up the pieces and keep on going, and open up, and get your show going."

"You'll leave a man behind here," I said.

"Pinky Pearl. Best advance man in the business. Now I have none. I'll need to hire someone to set us up. Someone to book rooms, get cash advances for salary, all of that. I'll be leaving a piece of my heart here in Doubtful, sir. Take good care of that grave."

"I'll do more than that. I've got a good idea who pushed the toad-stabber into your advance man, and pretty quick we'll be bolting together the Puma County gallows."

"Ah, *mon ami*, that brings me to a delicate matter. There is lawlessness here. In the space of a few days there has been murder, theft, a holdup, the most foul destruction of your trusted horse, and more. My poor company will ride without protection into the night after the curtain comes down. Our bags will be in our coaches, the gear in the wagons. And we will be taking our share of the box office, all save for Ralston's portion. How safe will we be? And where can we get help? And what's to stop these outlaws from stopping us, stealing what little we possess?"

"I'll escort you to the Puma County line," I said. "Maybe I can find one of my former deputies to take you the rest of the way. I'm thinking of a fellow named De Graff. I'll talk to one if you want. But they'll want some pay for it."

"Ah, but Sheriff, we have so little. We lost the gross from two showings in court. I can't afford to pay such knights in shining armor. We will be naked to these bandits."

"I guess them gals are used to that," I said.

"Sheriff, you are a card, truly a card," he said. "Maybe the two of clubs, eh?"

CHAPTER TWENTY-EIGHT

The next morning word of the bank heist was all over town. A mess of people were standing around, eyeing the bank, which was closed. There wasn't any way a body could get some cash out of his account or put some in. There wasn't any way a merchant could load up with greenbacks to make change. There wasn't any way a boss man could get a payroll together to give to his workers. No way a rancher could pay his cowboys. No way a woman could get funds to buy groceries. No way Turk, the livery hostler, could buy hay, or get paid for renting a stall and feed for an animal. It was as if Doubtful had sort of croaked. That eleven thousand, that was more money than the town used in a month, and now there was nothing.

Sanders was in there but staying hid. His clerks were in there, too. But the bank was shut tight and no one was saying if it would ever open, and whether a lot of folks were out a lot of money, or if Doubtful itself would survive long without the cash that goes into all buying and selling. I got waylaid by all sorts of people with a mess of questions.

"You gonna get them robbers?"

"I'm sure working on it."

"Is there any cash left in there?"

"No greenbacks that I know of. Some coins, I think."

"Gold go, too?"

"All of it."

"How come you're not chasing the crooks?"

"You tell me who they are and where they're going, and I'll be hot on their tail."

"It's that theater company. We never shoulda let them in here."

"You tell me who, and I'll bring them in."

That slowed them down some, but not much. "You should round up the lot, search everything they got, and then you'd find it."

"Not a bad idea, but I think Judge Rampart might find some fault with it."

"He's not worth spit. You arrest them all, and you'll get it back fast."

There were a mess of conversations like that. But mostly people were plumb scared. Take down the bank, take down Doubtful. But even as the crowds began predicting doom for the whole county, the storekeepers were making other arrangements. People began writing checks and

IOUs. Merchants made change with chits. Bottles of red-eye became a sort of money. A woman might get groceries for some red-eye. A merchant might offer a bottle of rum as change for a twenty. And a few gold coins came out of hiding, and that helped some. But the town was mostly paralyzed, and people were not far from forming a vigilance committee and going after anyone they thought might be carrying that loot.

I thought maybe I could improve on that a little. "I'm fixing to get a posse going, soon as I've got more to work with," I said here and there. Pretty quick I had thirty, forty men ready to ride. I thought that might be an improvement on some lynchings.

My main interest was tracking down Luke the Butcher and Ike Berg. It looked to me like the former sheriff of Medicine Bow County had gone bad, and the pair had pulled off the heist after the old gal had fired them.

I found Turk hiding in his office.

"Did Ike Berg come around here? And was the Butcher with him?"

"He did. He got his nag yesterday. I haven't seen that deputy. He don't own a horse."

"Berg say where he was going?"

"Not a word."

"Did he have bags? A pack horse?"

"No, he saddled up, tied a small bundle behind the cantle, and rode out."

That wasn't very promising. "When was that?"

"Middle of yesterday."

"I'll need a horse tonight. I'm taking the show people as far as the county line."

He studied me a while, not wanting to help me out, but finally he nodded.

"They've paid me, I'll say that for them. They'll be loading wagons before the last show's over."

"That's when I'll want a horse. Back early in the morning."

"We sure didn't have no trouble until that opera house opened up."

That was true. There'd been big trouble in Doubtful from the day the first show arrived.

I discovered advance men pasting up the bills for the next show all over town. They'd brush some sort of flour paste on the back of a showbill, post the bill and then brush it down real good, and it'd stick there for a while. There would be three dark days, and then the next show would roll into Doubtful. It was called the Royal Arabian Nights, and it looked real interesting. There was a mess of fellows in turbans pictured on there, and pretty girls in sort of misty outfits. AN INTIMATE LOOK AT THE HAREM OF SHEIK BARBOUSSE, *with* FOURTEEN WIVES *and* SEVENTEEN CHILDREN *and* TWELVE EUNUCHS. I didn't know what them eunuchs were, but Sammy Upward would know. I sure didn't want any around Doubtful. We had enough trouble without twelve eunuchs on the loose. I studied on the words, wondering what was coming. BELLY DANCERS. SWORD-SWALLOWERS

AND FIRE-EATERS. TWO JUGGLERS. TWO MASKED EXECUTIONERS WILL SHOW A BEHEADING. NOT FOR THE SQUEAMISH.

I sure wanted a front seat for all that. I didn't know if I'd get paid, not that the county's cash got stole, but if I could get in, I wanted to see all that stuff. I never met a cowboy who could do half that stuff.

I headed over to the Last Chance Saloon, looking for Sammy Upward. He was there, all right, with a baseball bat, ready to clobber two cowboys that were starting a ruckus.

"You fellows, you get out of town," I said.

"Try me," one cowboy said. He was pretty well swizzled.

"I'll turn you into a eunuch," I said. I didn't know what one was, but it was worth trying.

That there cowboy turned pale. He nudged the one he was brawling with. "You hear that? The sheriff's gonna do that?"

The other one, a ranny named Rudy, he quit brawling and turned real quiet.

Upward, he laughed like mad. Them two brawlers stared at me, like I had come from the South Pole.

The cowboys both reached for their privates and backed out of there, holding tight to their pants. That was pretty good. I watched them leave and checked to see that they got on their nags, which they did.

"Sammy, what's a eunuch?" I asked.

"Pickens, if you don't know, I ain't gonna tell you."

"Never heard of one. But it sure scared off them two dudes."

"All cowboys are eunuchs," Sammy said. "You get to sitting on a horse all day, every day, that's what you get. A mess of eunuchs. You ever see children on a ranch?"

I was beginning to see the drift of it. "How many days before you get turned into one?"

Sammy leaned over the bar and whispered in my ear. "Sometimes it takes only twenty-four hours."

I reached for mine, but everything was still there, all right. But now I was sweating that trip to the county line this night.

"How do I know?" I asked.

"Cotton, you ask Belle over to your boarding-house. She'll help you figure it out."

"You sure that's proper? Ask her to check my eunuchs?"

"You just ask her," Sammy said.

"I'll do that. Have you seen Luke the Butcher? I want to drag his butt over to my jailhouse and practice some butchering on him."

"Not for a couple of days. I heard he's blown town."

"That's what I'm worried about. I want him. If you get word of him, would you let me know?"

"Did he do the bank heist?"

"I'm going to ask him, and it won't be polite."

"Did that lousy lawman go, too? That's what I heard. Old Lady Sanders kicked his ass out of the county."

Sammy was sure full of rumors. I don't know where they came from, but he had collected his share of them.

By the time I got over to the opera house, the Watch and Ward people were waving their signs again, and the variety company was sliding through the stage door for the final show in Doubtful, Wyoming. I didn't see Delphinium Sanders, and could well understand why. Her husband's bank was broke. I stayed close, determined to prevent trouble, but after a while it became obvious that there would be no trouble. Few people were showing up to buy tickets from Ralston. There was no line.

When there was a break, I asked him about it.

"It's the bank heist," Ralston said. "No one wants to spend a dime. They don't know when they'll see cash. Clerks don't know when they'll get another brown envelope. It's going to be a long, dull night."

I hadn't thought of that. The bank robbery was shutting down all business in town, including that of the Grand Luxemburg Follies. I saw another twenty or thirty people duck into the opera house as the orchestra started up. This time the Watch and Warders simply vanished. Previous evenings they had lingered, ready to embarrass theater-goers during the intermission. But not this final eve. They went home.

Ralston did his books early, and eyed me.

"There's not a hundred dollars here." He sighed. "If this keeps up, I'll fold. I can't run an opera house on thin air."

"What about the next show?"

"Not well-attended. They've had troubles getting booked. They may run into more trouble here."

"I've never seen a sword-swallower."

"He really does it; runs the thing right down his throat."

"There must be easier ways to make a buck," I said. "Like fire-eating."

"How about executioners?" he asked. "There's going to be some beheadings on stage."

"I don't care how many heads roll. What I want is the harem. Lots of girls in the harem?"

"More likely old broads who've got varicose veins. They'll wear a lot of pancake."

"Sounds like a tough life."

Ralston eyed me. "Show business, writing novels, playing music. Those are guaranteed to break your piggy bank. For every one who gets lucky, a thousand starve."

"Why do it?"

"Because we're all bonkers."

I couldn't hardly argue with that. When the show was deep into its final act, I headed over to Turk's Livery Barn to saddle up a horse. I found the company teamsters loading up their wagons and coaches. They would roll as fast as they could break down the sets in the opera house and get the cast into the coaches.

"You got a nag for me?" I asked Turk.

"Saddle him yourself, and if the county don't pay me, I'll come after you."

He sure was grouchy. But everyone in Doubtful was grouchy. And there were people there in the dark, waiting for the show to roll away. I was pretty sure what was going on in the heads of those folks, mostly merchants but also a few cowboys and even a lady or two. They believed that somehow or other the variety show was walking out of town with all their cash.

I thought I better be alert for trouble, knowing how people felt. So I wandered through that bunch, just seeing who wore sidearms and who didn't. There were a few well-armed fellers out there, in spite of a ban on firearms inside city limits. It gave me pause. Should I tell them all to get rid of them now, before I pinched them? I counted a dozen or so openly armed men, and didn't like my options. I was a peace officer and suddenly it looked like there'd be a war right there in front of Turk's Livery.

Maybe a little maneuvering might be better than trying to force the issue.

I approached the head teamster, a feller named Jeff.

"There's trouble brewing here," I said.

"We're used to it."

"I'm hoping you'll get these coaches over to

the opera house and leave town from there just as fast as you load up."

"They follow. They always follow."

"You run into trouble regularly?"

"Sure. They pull their revolvers and hold us up. About when we're ready to roll, they surround Jardine's coach and tell him to toss the money bags."

"Then what?"

"Jardine always has a few real heavy ones, well tied-up and hard to get open, and he pitches them to the ground, and the town people haul them off and we roll away."

"He gives up his money that easily?"

"There's a couple of real greenbacks on top of each bag. And a lot of worthless paper underneath."

I laughed. "You show business fellers can teach us all a trick or two."

"Just let it happen, and there'll be no trouble," Jeff said.

"No, I won't let it happen," I said. "If anyone attempts to rob your company, they'll have to deal with me. And I shoot straight."

CHAPTER TWENTY-NINE

Things were getting ugly fast. I hurried back to the office and collected the double-barreled sawed-off twelve gauge, checked the loads, and hurried back to Turk's barn. There were growing numbers of townspeople collecting there, watching the show wagons and coaches and teams that the teamsters were harnessing.

There weren't any show people yet; the final show was still playing.

I wished Rusty was on hand for backup, but he'd gone to bed. He'd worked double time since I put the badge back on, and I didn't blame him for getting some shut-eye. I'd be alone this time. There wasn't going to be any thefts this night if I could help it, but I wasn't sure how to arrange that. A good shotgun spoke with authority, a lot more than a revolver could, and it was exactly what I might need this hot night.

I plowed into the crowd. Half of them were

good folks I knew well, but they was looking pretty ornery, so I started to talk some. The first feller I found wearing a six-gun was the mayor, George Waller.

"You come to watch the show pull out?" I asked.

"No, I've come to keep the show from pulling out," he said.

"You have a problem?"

"They've got every cent in Doubtful, and are making off with it."

"Why do you say that?"

"Someone busted the bank, and it has to be that outfit."

"You got any evidence of it?"

"You'll see," he said. "They aren't rolling until they dump every cent they got on the ground right there."

"What about money they earned from selling tickets and doing the show?"

"Every cent stays here, and that's how it's going to be. And don't you interfere, because if you do, you're dead meat."

"I suppose you think you're taking back what got took, but them show people might think you're stealing what they earned doing that show."

"They cleaned out this town, and they're not moving until every cent comes back."

"You figure they blew the bank safe last night, middle of their show?"

"They had it done, and that stolen money's in the wagons somewhere, or it's going to be. We're keeping it, and we're putting Doubtful back on its feet."

"So you're going to hold up the theater company, right?"

"You stay out of it, Pickens. It's going to happen, and if you stop it, you'll find a gun stuck in your back faster than you can wonder who's about to blow you off."

"I guess that's all part of your mayor duties, right, Waller? Staging an armed robbery. That'll get you re-elected."

"You stay out of this, Cotton, or you'll be six feet under."

"I see that as a threat to a peace officer. And don't call me Cotton. I got that name hung on me and it makes me mad."

Waller, he just grinned. There were more and more of them town businessmen, town fathers, and all collecting around there, plus a mess of women, and if there would be a fight, a lot of innocent folks would perish or be hurt real hard. I sure didn't know how to slow down this thing, and my thick head wasn't coming up with ideas, neither.

"I'm keeping the peace, Mister Mayor, even if you ain't. And if anyone dies, you'll find yourself in the dock for murder. That's all I'm going to say."

But old George, he just looked real cocky and smiled away at me. It was all I needed to know, actually. The thoughts rattling in his head were inflaming the rest of those people, most of them good folk but now turning into a real tough mob.

"I guess I'll say one more thing, Waller. There's twelve buckshot in each barrel."

He eyed the shotgun, and then shrugged it off. There were thirty or forty armed citizens crowding around the show wagons now, making the draft horses skittish.

"Back away now, these Belgians kick," Jeff said, pushing all them virtuous citizens back from the caravan.

Down the street at the opera house the show was letting out. The first people hit the street and lit up cheroots. Jeff nodded, and the freighters, each team led by a teamster, steered them lumbering wagons that way to load up the sets and all that. The coaches would be next. The Follies ladies would get in, and the show would be on the road. Or so I hoped.

But even as the freighters headed for the stage door, so did the mob. It turned into a big procession, the coaches and wagons, with crowds of armed men on either side. I saw the head freighter, Jeff, cursing and chasing away rascal boys, who were tossing stones at the horses. This here was getting serious.

The coaches arrived, three of them to carry the cast, but those fellers pulled up in front of the theater, not at the stage door in the alley. They were good Concords, hired out of Cheyenne for this tour, driven by some good old boys who could spit a few yards.

Now the crowd shifted away from the stage door, where the teamsters were loading sets and props into the freight wagons. The townspeople, they surged right up to the maroon coaches and waited in the flickering light of a lamp at the box office. It was pretty dark. I knew what they were waiting for, and pretty quick it happened. One by one, those pretty gals, wearing light dresses against the summer heat, climbed into the coaches and settled there, some on the jump seats. The crowd watched them, but didn't do nothing. No one was waving a Watch and Ward sign at them. The gals looked real subdued, and a little afraid, so I made a point of standing between them and that mob.

There was one empty coach up front, with a team of good matched blacks to draw it, and that's where the crowd was drifting now that the gals were all settled. The theater doors were open and I could see lights bobbing in there, and then the maestro appeared. Alphonse de Jardine, wearing that black silk stovepipe, a little feller in the black suit and starched white shirt, he paused, stared at the mob, and then steadily paced toward the coach. He wasn't carrying any satchel. He wasn't carrying a thing. Just a little feller, head of that show, getting ready to roll.

"Hold it right there, Jardine," said Waller.

Jardine stopped at once.

"George, you put that gun away," I said.

But Waller didn't. "You don't leave here alive until you drop the loot," Waller said.

Now there were twenty, thirty revolvers out. If shooting started, a lot of people would get hurt, and it was getting real bad by the second. There were armed men on both sides of the coaches, and a few out in front, so the coaches were surrounded by town merchants with revolvers in their fists. If something set them off, they'd be shooting at one another, and there'd be enough bodies to keep Maxwell's Funeral Parlor profitable for ten years. This here was what they called a circular firing squad.

"Ah, good sir, there's only a trifle. We made little, and it went to paying for the theater. And your hotels."

"You got the bank money," Waller said. "There's gold and greenbacks in there, eleven thousand worth."

"My friend, come search. Take your pick, all the coaches."

"No, Waller, you ain't gonna search," I said. "You ain't gonna rob this company of one nickel, and you're going to lower them revolvers before a lot of innocent people get hurt."

Mayor Waller, he just smiled. He knew who was the boss, with all them ugly six-guns pointing at Jardine, the gals, and me, including at our backs.

I carried my shotgun in the crook of my arm. If I lifted it, my duties as sheriff of Doubtful would come to a bloody halt along with my heart.

"Waller, you come up here," I said.

"He's welcome to search anywhere," Jardine said. "My friends, let this man look wherever he wishes for the gold."

"All right, George, you heard him. You look around in there, and in the boot, and then the next ones, and when you're done, you'll tell this crowd to go home."

Waller, he sensed he had won, which is what I wanted. He headed for Jardine's coach, climbed up to check out the boot, and probed the interior.

"That gold's somewhere," he said.

Waller started for the next two coaches, and them gals all got out, and stood there looking mighty scared. They were so pretty that half those shooters were staring at the gals, which maybe was a good thing.

"These boots are full of luggage," Waller said.

Jardine, he didn't say nothing.

"You ready to let this show leave town?" I asked.

"I want to search every trunk," Waller said.

"You got any evidence these people robbed the bank?"

"Who else?" he said.

"Let them search the trunks," Jardine said. "These are fine, upstanding citizens, and they've welcomed us to Doubtful, and now we welcome them to our underwear and corsets and dainties."

Funny thing was, the town fellers snickered and then laughed. If Waller started pulling out trunks and pawing all the little undies of those showgirls, he'd sure make a spectacle of himself. And he knew it.

"Gold is heavy, Mr. Mayor. Lift those trunks," Jardine said.

Waller did pull out a couple and rattled them and put them back. He was defeated.

Maybe the Grand Luxemburg Follies would leave town in one piece. Maybe the citizens would go home in one piece. Maybe I would, too. But I was ready to turn them all into Swiss cheese if that's what it took.

It's a funny thing how a mob leaks willpower sometimes. This had gone from a murderous mob to a sort of sheepish one. It was still a powderkeg, though, with crazy armed men on both sides of those coaches.

"All right, you people let the company go," I said. "This is over. These people have to head out."

They let it happen. Jardine, he looked around, invited some of them gals to ride with him, and the jehus sitting on the boxes snapped lines over croups and them three coaches slowly rolled into the night, and the freighters followed.

None of it was my doing. Jardine, he'd played the right cards. Maybe he had been in front of an angry mob like that before. Maybe it was just that he was pint-sized, and somehow grown men with revolvers didn't want to gun down a feller hardly four feet tall in his top hat. I didn't know. I'm not much of one to dwell on something. Whatever happened, it worked well enough. That company rolled around the town square and out the road to Laramie, the wagons muffled in the hot night.

I'd promised to escort them as far as the county line, but I'd catch up in a bit. There was nothing slower than a big outfit like that.

"Well, George," I said to the mayor, "you got a law that says it's illegal to wear sidearms in Doubtful. You want to turn yourself in?"

"Go to hell, Sheriff."

"I could pinch the rest of them. I got a list in my head. It's your law. You put her on the books for me to enforce. It's a good law. Pretty near twenty people might have died, and a mess more would be hurt real bad this night. The law's there to prevent that."

"Go to hell, Pickens. I still think the loot's in that company. This town's ruined. There's hardly change enough to keep an ice cream parlor in business."

"You got proof? Some witnesses? You give me proof that they robbed the bank, and I'll go after them. They ain't a mile out of town."

Waller, he got real quiet. "Well, it's good riddance," he said. "We'll close down that opera house and maybe that'll keep our money safe."

I wasn't going to argue with a man whose brain was fried, so I just cut loose.

Turk was waiting for me over at the livery barn with a saddled nag.

"I hope they get robbed," he said. "They cleaned out Doubtful, and we need it back."

I laughed at him. The nag was not particularly obedient, but I'd ridden worse. I steered him into the warm night, and hoped that Doubtful could take care of itself while I was gone.

Chapter Thirty

I rode out into a quiet June night. The variety company was somewhere ahead, lumbering along at the pace of the freight wagons. It would be a long while before they got to the railroad, and they would have to pass through Medicine Bow County, where Ike Berg had been the law, to get there. I wished my badge stretched down to the tracks, but it quit at the county line, and that was where I had to cut loose.

The barn-sour nag wanted to hightail back to Turk's, but I held him steady. I wish I had Critter, who was ornery and sunk his teeth into my hide, but had a good heart when he wasn't trying to kill me. He'd never spent a barn-sour day in his life. It sure was a quiet night, and I enjoyed the peace of the open country. Sometimes I had to get away from a town to let nature work on me a little, and get all the mad out of me. Not just my mad, but the mad of everyone else in a town.

Nature had its way of healing me up when things got mean in town, and now I rode easily through deep dark. In a while there'd be a sliver of moon to help, but for now I was just letting the horse find the road I couldn't see.

I wondered how them teamsters leading the freight wagons, and Jehus on the coaches, figured out the road, but they had been moving the company around for a long while, and seemed to have good night vision.

Then, soft on the June night wind, I heard the thump of a shot, and another, and several more, and I knew that trouble lay ahead, and it was in my Puma County, and that the variety show was in trouble, and that I'd have to kick this barn-sour livery horse into action.

I encouraged the beast with my heels, since I wasn't wearing spurs, and the horse crowhopped and carried on like a spoiled brat, and I whacked him harder, and he took off real good, having met his master at last, and we sailed through the inky dark toward them stray bullets. But the sounds had quit. It wasn't hardly an exchange, and wasn't a war, and it had stopped about as fast as it had started up, with just a flurry.

After a while I did spot a lantern waving ahead, and slowed real careful, not wanting to be mistook. In fact, it was still mighty black, so I just slid off that ornery plug and walked quietly toward the variety company train. They was stopped there. The rear coach was somewhat behind the rest. I studied the scene. There was but a single lamp, and some people milling around near a stagecoach, and something on the ground, and nothing else to see. It was blacker than the inside of an ink bottle.

"Hello, ahead," I yelled.

Those shadowy figures turned.

"This here's the sheriff," I said.

No one responded. I had all the advantage, being in pitch dark, so I edged in, keeping my six-gun handy. But I didn't expect to shoot anyone, since I wouldn't know who I was about to perforate. That livery horse, he liked being led. I knew the type; he hated to carry a burden, but didn't mind being hauled around on a string. I know a lot of folks like that horse. They'd do anything not to work, anything but carry a load.

I studied the crowd ahead, before the lantern light fell on me, and I couldn't see any drawn sidearms.

"All right now, what's the trouble?" I asked.

Now I could get a good look. There was someone stretched out, and even before I could make out the details I knew who it was. Alphonse de Jardine, the proprietor of the Grand Luxemburg Follies was lying there, and most of the rest were the show gals and a few teamsters, and they were staring at me as I edged in.

Jardine was dead. The bleak lantern light

revealed a ruined face where a bullet had ended the little feller's earthly life. The gals, they were real quiet. None was weeping. They looked more than a little scared. The teamsters just stared.

I spotted Ambrosia, star of the Follies, with a shawl wrapped around her.

"Tell me," I said.

"Some men stopped us," she said.

"How many?"

"Just two," a teamster replied. "Both with shot-guns."

"One skinny and one built like a block?"

"And masked," Ambrosia said.

"They knew which coach Mr. Jardine was in and went straight to it and pulled him out," the teamster said. "They simply shot him. Like they were waiting for him."

"Killed him? How?"

"One pulled a revolver and shot him," another teamster said. "Just like that. Nothing said."

"No one even talked? Jardine didn't?"

"Oh, Mr. Jardine, he asked what these gents wanted, and they didn't reply. They just fired on him," the teamster said.

Ambrosia was leaking tears, visible even in the dim light of the bulls-eye lantern. I was feeling real bad, and wish I had been with this outfit from the moment they rolled out of Doubtful.

I gradually got the whole story. Jardine's stage-coach was last in the caravan, and two bandits rode out of a pitch-black night, closed in beside the coach, jammed revolvers through the curtain, and told the jehu to stop. The driver stopped the team. The bandits asked Jardine to step out. The gals with him were terrified. They heard a shot in the dark and the thud of a body. One bandit kept the driver covered while the other one pitched satchels out of the boot, got down to a false bottom in the boot, pulled that out and removed something or other from under it. I got most of this from the driver, who talked in brief bursts. He said he didn't expect to live more than a few more moments. But they let him go, loaded some satchels onto a spare pack animal, and rode into the blackness. The whole robbery was amazing because there was no moon, nothing but a little starlight, and required night vision of a sort that few people possessed.

The rest of the caravan didn't knew what was happening and continued onward for another two or three hundred yards, and then knew something had happened. I needed a description of them two robbers, thinking they were probably Iceberg and Luke the Butcher, but I got as many descriptions as there were witnesses, and I sure couldn't get anyone to say that one was skeleton-thin, and the other was built like a butcher block. They were just a pair of males with black bandanas over their noses and nothing else to identify them. No one could even say what sort of nags the bandits had or how many. One thing was plain. They knew Jardine, and knew he had a hiding place under the false bottom of the boot of the last stagecoach, and knew there was something in it, and knew that if they killed the little maestro of that show, the whole company would fall apart. And that was exactly right.

It probably was Iceberg and his crony, but damned if I could prove it. I didn't have a single reliable witness. Them two rode off into the blackness, direction unknown, and I wouldn't find a track until daylight, and I'd be lucky to find any at all. They could go anywhere on the compass.

Meanwhile, the rest of the company and the teamsters and jehus all collected around that lamp, and eyed the feller who'd created this show.

"I think I've got to get you in this coach to come back to Doubtful with me," I said.

The gals and the driver, they just stared.

"All of you on this coach. I think we'd better go back there. We've got some things to do there, and I'll want to get statements."

"But who'll pay for us?" one asked.

"Jardine's estate," I said.

They stared. There wasn't an estate. These coaches were leased.

Finally one of the teamsters, the one who walked the lead ox team, he asked if they could just go ahead to the railroad.

"We didn't see it, didn't know about it," he said.

"We've got to find a way to get out of here,"
another said.

"You from Laramie?"

"Some of us, and Cheyenne."

We went back and forth with that, and finally
one of them that could read and write, he put
down the names of the outfit and who was in it,
and I got the names of the ones in the company,
and the ones in the stagecoach where Jardine
was riding. They agreed to come on back. We
were only two or three miles from Doubtful.

"I think you people have some burying to do,"
I said.

There were a couple of fellers who were second
in command, and they agreed, and that's how it
worked out. One coach came back with me, and
I let the rest of them poor devils go. Their life had
come to a halt, and they had a tough row to hoe,
figuring out how to get to Chicago or wherever
them shows were put together. But they were all
hardened show people, used to the worst, and I
thought them gals could all get married in twenty-
four hours if they wanted to stick around Wyoming, so maybe it wasn't quite so hard on them.

They lifted poor Jardine gently, and slipped
him across the rear seat and covered him with a
blanket. I borrowed that bulls-eye lamp, a candle
inside of a glass container, and searched the area,
looking for anything them bandits dropped, or
any piece of evidence, but it looked like a clean

haul. They didn't get much. Jardine hadn't made more than a few dollars in Doubtful, between getting fined by Judge Rampart and paying bills and dealing with them Watch and Ward people. So that robbery wasn't worth more than some pocket change. And a man dead for it, too.

There'd be another grave up there in the Doubtful burying ground, next to their advance man, Pinky Pearl. Now I had two murders to solve, and another robbery, and it didn't matter that I knew who done it; I couldn't prove a thing.

I helped the jehu turn the coach around and we headed back to Doubtful, a real slow and sorry procession, death and misery in that coach. I led with that lamp, since it was so dark the driver couldn't see the trail, and we just rattled through a miserable summer night, ignoring mosquitos, not even the crickets chirping, and pretty soon we rolled into Doubtful, which was blacker than I'd ever seen the place. I didn't know the time, but it was late, and the town was slumbering, and hoping that one lawman and one deputy could spare it from trouble. But trouble had come.

I had a lot to do. I had them people wait in the jailhouse while I fetched Rusty out of his slumbers. He sure didn't like my hammering at his door, but pretty quick he was up and I told him to look after those people and get statements from them and put that stuff down in writing. He could do that; I sure would be licking a pencil trying to get it down.

Next was to wake up Maxwell and deliver the body of Alphonse de Jardine. That took more doing than waking up Rusty, and Maxwell refused to get out of bed.

"Leave it on my doorstep," he said.

"You get your carcass over there and take it, or I'll leave you on your doorstep," I said.

"I don't bury theater folk," he said.

"Then I'll bury you," I replied.

He sort of got the message.

I finally got the jehu to drive the coach over to Maxwell's place, where the undertaker took Jardine off the seat, and was pretty ornery about it.

"Shot through the mouth. I suppose that's fitting," Maxwell said. "That's how anyone in that business should check out. Talkers deserve it. Writers should get their hands shot off. Judges should get their privates shot off."

"Empty them pockets," I said, thinking that funeral parlor operators were all too good at it.

Maxwell glared at me, and slowly turned Jardine's pockets out. One of them contained a half-filled blue medicine bottle of something or other. But there wasn't any prescription label. I shook it a little, and the stuff seemed thick. Maybe he had some evil disease. He had some lucifers and an enameled tin with small wad of cotton in it that smelled odd. I collected all that stuff and put it in a flour sack and hauled it away from Maxwell's greedy fingers.

The jehu had put up the coach at Turk's and put the team in the pens, since no one was awake there, either. By the time I got all that taken care of, Rusty had got all them victims settled in the jailhouse and was taking statements about what happened. He sure could write pretty fine. He was sitting them at the desk in the lamplight, and was getting their stories. He was interviewing Ambrosia.

"What's your name?" Rusty asked.

"Margot Parvenue," she said.

"Ain't you Ambrosia?"

"You want my moniker or not, buster?"

Rusty, he shut up and scribbled. He could write longhand, which was going to be a problem for me because I never could figure it out.

Her story was the same as the rest. Them two bandits closed in, stopped the rear coach and let the rest of them go ahead in the night. They pulled Jardine out and killed him, lit a candle-lantern, went into the coach boot, threw out the satchels, and then began tearing at the boot until they got to some hidden part, and took whatever was in there and vanished into the night.

The pair wore dark bandanas; one was skinny, one was thick. They hardly spoke. That's all she could say about it.

All their stories matched up. I asked them to

stick around and bury Jardine, and after that I'd free them to go wherever they were going.

I'd start looking for Iceberg and the Butcher, and see what sort of loot they were carrying. I knew who done it; all I had to do was catch them.

CHAPTER THIRTY-ONE

They was a sorry bunch, sitting there in the light of a lamp while Rusty put down the story. I sure didn't know what to do with them. They might be witnesses if I could ever catch them renegades and get them before a judge. But they were also a long way from anywhere, and wanting to get out of Puma County.

"You want to get married?" I asked Ambrosia. I thought maybe if we got hitched, she'd be around as a witness if I needed one.

"You're an idiot," she said.

I thought maybe there'd be a way to cut these miserable folks loose.

"Tomorrow, you give sworn statements to our county attorney, Stokes is his name, and he'll let you go," I said. "Meanwhile, all we got here is some empty cells."

Them gals and the two fellers stared at me like

I was about to lock them up and throw away the key.

"Or I can try to get you into a boardinghouse. But that'll cost."

They decided on the cells.

"Don't worry about them bedbugs," I said. "They ain't killed anyone yet."

The bedbugs were an asset, I figured. Anyone I tossed in there got bit so bad they could hardly stand it, and got real cooperative real fast. When Judge Rampart sentenced someone to a night in the pokey, it was about as bad as ten nights in one with no bugs. But the Puma County jail had bedbugs big as dimes, or so people believed, and they sure liked a good feast. Of course these show people wouldn't take that kindly, but the door would be open and they could sit on the front stoop if the bugs got to them. The worst of the bugs would get to biting along the inner thigh and drive a body clear into depravity. I sure could get confessions, repentance, promises, and bail money fast because of them bugs. A jail full of bedbugs was better than two or three deputies for keeping order. Criminals arriving in Doubtful soon learned about my pet bedbugs. Over at the Last Chance Saloon, Sammy Upward always told strangers about the bedbug jail around here, and it was a mighty fine way to keep the peace.

But now I had a crime wave, and hardly knew how to put it down.

I didn't get much sleep, and found all them

show folks sitting miserably outside the jail, waiting for me to free them up.

"Time for some java," I said, and walked them over to the Beanery.

"These here are witnesses, and this is on the county," I said to Roscoe, who was on shift.

"Cash up front, Pickens," he said. "You can't get by me so easy."

We haggled awhile, and I finally had to promise to pay from my salary if the county wouldn't.

Those bedraggled gals mostly just swallowed a little oatmeal gruel and sat there miserably.

Maxwell found me there. "Let's get this show on the road," he said.

I motioned to the lovelies and they followed the black delivery wagon to the burial ground outside of Doubtful. Maxwell must have figured that Jardine didn't deserve a hearse, not if the county was paying, but at least he provided a pine box of green wood, still leaking sap, its top hammered down. Usually it was nothing but a canvas shroud if the county was paying.

Maxwell's man had dug a three-foot-deep grave over in the far corner, next to some graves of vagrants and the resting places of three bawds. Three feet was as low as graves got dug in potter's fields.

"Any of you strumpets want to talk? I'll give you a minute or two," Maxwell said.

"Go to hell," Ambrosia said. She had found a dandelion along the way, and gently set it on

Jardine's pine box. The other ladies held hands, and rubbed their eyes. The two gents from the show stared bleakly. They had all pulled deep inside of themselves, as if the whole world was a cruel place they must endure.

"Time's up," Maxwell said.

He and his man slid the small pine box into the rectangle cut in the sod, where it landed with a thump. It remained tilted, and no one straightened it. Then the hired man began dumping the yellow clay on it, which thudded hollowly.

I took my hat off. "You sure were a feller who knew how to make the girls look like heaven," I said. "Good luck to you in the next world. Maybe heaven is like the Grand Luxemburg Follies. I sure hope so, Mr. Jardine."

Dirt kept hammering the box.

Pretty soon we all drifted back to Doubtful, and I told them they were free to go. Their own rented coach would take them to the railroad, and after that, who knew what? Maybe I should have told them that Lawyer Stokes would take sworn statements from them, but I didn't much feel like that. They'd been robbed by bandits, and I just decided to cut them loose. By the time Lawyer Stokes would have finished with them, he'd have turned them all into the perpetrators.

Ambrosia eyed me, and then took my hand. "You're cute," she said.

I been called a mess of things, but that wasn't one of them. I felt about the way a calf does when the branding-iron strikes. My ma, she would have started laughing. That was the worst thing I've been called in my entire life, except for the time I was called a jack-off.

Them show people, they were awful happy to clamber in, and get rolling out of Doubtful. This place had changed their lives forever. I was sorry about it all, but there wasn't much I could do to make life easier for them. I watched that coach roll out of Doubtful, sort of sorry to see it go. They were good company, them theater people.

I discovered Ralston standing there, and was glad of it.

"You mind telling me how much money Jardine was carrying?" I asked. "You'd be the only one to know."

"Nothing," Ralston said. "With all those troubles, Jardine couldn't make expenses. By the time he paid me and the boarding places, he didn't even have enough to pay his company."

"What do you think them robbers took from that hidden compartment?"

"Beats me," Ralston said.

"Did Jardine ever hint at anything?"

"He said it's a lousy business sometimes."

"And now he's dead in a robbery that didn't net anyone anything."

"There may have been something," Ralston said. "Those companies try to keep some emergency reserves on hand."

"A little cash in that boot?"

"Enough to tide them over to the next town."

"Well, it got took."

"Yes, and by bandits who had studied the company, knew where to look, and when to strike."

"I guess I know who," I said. "But catching them's the trick."

Ralston eyed me. "You've got a bank robbery, some holdups, two murders, and assorted thefts. And nothing's being done about any of them."

I got mad, but I tried not to let him see it. He abandoned me there, and headed back to his opera house, leaving me on the street feeling like an old dog turd. I thought I'd have to get up a posse and try to find some tracks and see if I could close in on them two. I'd have to leave Rusty in town, holding down the sheriff duties.

If I had Critter, I'd already be riding, but the thought of riding posse on that livery-barn plug made my belly curdle up and belch. I headed for all them merchants.

"Hey, saddle up your nag. We're going out as a posse," I said to Hubert Sanders.

"Ah, I'll leave that to you fellows," the banker said.

"Maybe Mrs. Sanders?" I asked. "I suppose she's a straight shooter."

"Delphinium has a headache," he said.

I tried a mess of other businessmen, and got the same response. No posse duty; they had stores and offices to attend to. I could have required it, but I knew better than to take a bunch of carping and whining possemen out in the field. So I headed for the saloons, starting with Sammy Upward.

"You want to get me a few posse men? Leave in an hour?"

Sammy grinned. "I'll try, Cotton."

I headed for the Sampling Room and corralled Cronk, who dealt faro there.

"No, sorry, Pickens, I'm out of cigars, and that would keep me from going anywhere," the gambler said. "I live on cigars. I'm epileptic, and without cigars I go into conniptions and they steal money off my table."

I headed for every establishment on Main Street. Harlan Kreutz, the baker, said he was too busy making dough. Magnus Thor, the hardware man, said he needed to fit out a sheep wagon. Conrad Drudger, the harnessmaker, said he was expecting a shipment of cowhide. Marshall Beergarten, the ice and coal dealer, said he'd promised to deliver three tons of bituminous to the assayer, Mike Michaels.

Well, collecting a posse in Doubtful was a lot harder than I would have thought. All them people who were complaining about a crime wave, and death and mayhem, they wanted someone else to go out and get the county cleaned up.

I hunted for my old deputies, De Graff and Burtell, and they'd gone fishing. Maybe that was okay. I'd been wondering what side they were on. And if they were in favor of bass and carp and catfish, that might be better than siding with Delphinium.

So I headed for Turk's Livery Barn, thinking maybe I could put a hobo or vagrant to work, but they were all gone, and Turk was unhappy. "You get that nag shot up, you pay," he said.

"This plug is so rank it deserves to be shot up and eaten by magpies," I replied.

He didn't like that none. One thing about Turk. If you insulted any nag of his, or complained about any squeak-wheeled wagon of his, he would get huffy. And now I'd insulted his nag.

"You deserve your fate," was all he said to me. "This here nag is a miracle horse. He's ready with a miracle any time you ask."

"What's his name?" I asked.

"His name is Jesus Mary Joseph," Turk said. "I didn't name him. The feller that sold him to me named him."

So I took Jesus Mary Joseph, a yellow sucker with missing teeth, and led him back to my office to load him up and tell Rusty he'd be acting sheriff for a while.

Rusty was in there at my desk, studying that stuff I took out of Jardine's pockets. The flask of something thick and the enameled tin with some cottony stuff in it.

"Ace was in," Rusty said. "He was looking at this stuff here, what we got off Jardine, and he turned white."

"Ace Grundy, the mining supply man?"

"Himself."

Ace had a yard outside of Doubtful where he kept mining equipment, and had a bunker full of explosives.

"He says this stuff in the bottle is nitroglycerin, or blasting oil. It's a bit touchy. Dynamite is this stuff mixed with clay to stabilize it. And the stuff in the enameled tin is guncotton. He says if the bullet that killed Jardine had hit him in the chest, where this stuff was stored in his breast pockets, it would have blown the whole wagon train to kingdom come."

Guncotton? I'd heard a little bit about that. If you sneezed the wrong direction, it would go off. And nitro wasn't far behind. So there was the head of a variety show carrying enough explosive to level Doubtful. It sure was a puzzle.

"You got any idea why Jardine had turned himself into a walking bomb?"

"Ace said it's actually safer to carry it like that than to let it ride in a wagon and get jolted."

"But why? What would a little French showman want with stuff like that? And why would he endanger his entire company?"

"Ace said it'd be pretty handy cracking safes," Rusty said. "What's needed is a set of safe-cracking tools, drills, pry bars, wedges, whatever it takes to get some nitro between the door and the frame. But sometimes it's easier with guncotton, carefully packed into whatever little space you've worked up to take the charge."

"Alphonse de Jardine?" I said. "Him with the stovepipe hat?"

Rusty, he was grinning at me.

"Don't set them items off," I said. "Don't even wave your hand near there. Don't get up to go to the outhouse. Don't move. Don't talk. Don't spit. Don't blink an eye. Don't think evil thoughts."

I thought of that rotten horse tied out there and hoped he wouldn't blow up.

The Doom of Doubtful sat on my desk. I thought maybe to give them items to Reggie Thimble or Ziggy Camp as a little token of my esteem, but I thought they might not appreciate it. Maybe I'd give the stuff to Judge Rampart to help him move his bowels.

CHAPTER THIRTY-TWO

It looked like I was going to be a posse of one. Somewhere, them two renegades, an ex-lawman and a thug, was living high on other people's money. I didn't have much real evidence, but it was enough for me to go after them. They'd robbed that show company only a few miles out of Doubtful.

"Rusty, I'm not figuring you'll survive for long, not with that stuff on the desk and you enjoying it. You'll blow your ass to bits. But I've got to head out of town and bring in those two, and that means you'll be doing the sheriffing around here until I get back. If you blow yourself to bits, it's your own fault."

"Who would you want me to blow up, Cotton?"

"You can start with them supervisors and throw a judge or two into the bonfire."

Rusty yawned. That's how he treated me, yawning away.

I collected the sawed-off scatter-gun and a few cartridges of buckshot. That was the weapon for real male lawmen, while six-guns were for the tooty-fruity. Ike Berg had a six-gun and was dangerous, but not half as dangerous as a sheriff with a shotgun. I headed across the square to the Beanery, and had them give me a half-dozen porterhouse steaks. I could eat good steaks for breakfast, lunch, and supper, two days running, and bill the county. Long as I was saving them posse salary, I figured I could cook some steaks on Puma County.

I added a blanket and I was ready to roll.

I eyed that yellow nag, who was standing lop-eared, one leg cocked, and I thought he must be my blood brother. He stood real quiet while I tied down my blanket and stuffed the steaks and spare shotgun shells in my saddlebag.

But when I untied him, took hold of the reins and stepped into the saddle, he erupted, pitching me up and letting me crash two, three times. I was lucky I didn't harm my private parts on the saddlehorn or I would have to quit dreaming about Ambrosia. That's what happens to cowboys and why they never marry. They got no tools to marry with, after a while on horses.

Well, that livery stable nag of Turk's, he just kept crow-hopping, bucking, whirling, and trying to bite my leg, and it was getting to the point where I'd either bail off of him or he'd kill me.

"Jesus Mary Joseph!" I yelled.

Now that was the dangdest thing. That miracle nag, he quit all his hightailing and settled right down, real quiet. I can't explain it. All I done was shout his name. It was sort of prayerful, though. Maybe he answered my prayer. Whatever it was, Jesus Mary Joseph turned quiet and was ready to go.

I glared at Rusty, who was watching from the door of the jailhouse.

"Go get blown up," I said, and rode off in a huff. It didn't take long for me to figure out that Jesus Mary Joseph was the smoothest and most eager and most friendly nag I'd ever sat upon. He was even an improvement on Critter. The thought made me feel guilty, and also sent a pang through me. But maybe I'd catch Critter's killer this time.

I got out there to the holdup place in a bit. This time I had daylight to help me, and not some lousy candle-lamp. Everything looked different, wide open. It wasn't flat at all. The road curled around a slope, with a gulch on one side and hillside on the other. There wasn't any hiding place. Them two renegades just had to wait until it got real dark, and then sit their horses until the show company rolled by. I found where they'd waited, back a hundred yards so the wagon oxen and coach teams wouldn't pay them heed. They'd known to go for the rear coach, where Jardine kept the company cash. I found the place where they'd shot him. Brown blood caked the clay.

They'd put a bullet into his face just like that, no reason for it. It was sheer luck that his guncotton didn't blow when he hit the ground.

Down in the gulch off to one side there were satchels and trunks around, untouched. They belonged to them showgirls and guys. I'd have to send someone out to pick them up. It was odd; the robbers didn't even touch them. The satchels got tossed into the gulch. Them holdup men went after whatever lay in the bottom of the boot. I got off the yellow nag and tied him up, not trusting him. He'd probably trot clear back to Turk's if I let him loose. He eyed me like he was seeing what his molars could chew on, but I ignored that.

I sprung open the first of them satchels to see what was in there. Some lady's undies mostly, plus a robe and some stuff to paint her face. But wrapped in oilcloth was a big lump of something that was pretty firm, so I got it out and unrolled it, and found myself staring at a heap of greenbacks, some of them real big, twenties and fifties. Holy cats. I put that aside and dug into the next item, a leather trunk. Some feller owned it. There was a straight-edge and a mug in there, a brush, some gray longjohns, and some moccasins. And another of them oilcloth packets, and that one was all loaded with greenbacks too, but mostly fives and singles. This was a heap of cash.

I looked around hard, not wanting anyone to show up just then, and decided maybe to move this stuff over to my nag. The best bet was to unroll my blanket and roll up the cash in it and tie it down. So I lifted all that cash with sweaty paws, and lined it all up in my gray blanket.

Two of the other satchels revealed the same oil-cloth packets, and by the time I'd checked the rest, I figured I'd gotten all the bank's paper money back, or most of it. That sure made the owners of them bags and trunks look real guilty, but I thought I'd better not rush into any notions until I got things anchored down. Maybe they didn't know what was in the oilcloth.

I hunted around, checking that luggage, but there wasn't any more. I thought maybe I had the greenbacks from the bank, but the gold was still missing. Maybe that's what them two crooks got. The gold would be heavy, and make all them satchels too heavy, but it could be hidden down in that boot with a cover sewn over it, and a robber would hardly know the difference. But somehow Iceberg and the Butcher knew where to go.

I got all that cash rolled into my blanket and tied down real good, and just in the nick. Coming at me was a mess of cowboys, probably off the Anchor Ranch, heading for a good time in Doubtful. If they knew what I'd just hid in my bedroll, they could retire for life out in Arizona or some godforsaken place like that, with nothing but cactus and thirst for company.

Sure enough, it was some rannies I knew all

too well, Big Nose George, Alvin Ream, Smiley
Thistlethwaite, and Spitting Sam.

"Howdy-do," I said.

They was peering around at them satchels
down the hillside.

"Coach got robbed last night. Them poor souls
got themselves held up. I come out for a look-see.
Say, fellers, you could help me. I got to get these
bags back to town. They belong to the people
that got held up. You mind piling them into your
laps and taking them in?"

Spitting Sam, he rode over to one satchel and
peered in.

"Undies? You want us to carry undies?"

"Belonged to them showgirls from the Grand
Luxemburg Follies."

"That's what they wore? This here is Follies
stuff?"

"They didn't wear much of anything. But if
you fellers could help me, you'd be looked upon
with special favor next time I have to lock you up
on a drunk and disorderly."

Spitting Sam eyed Big Nose George. "You want
to carry ladies undies to Doubtful?"

"Maybe we should help the sheriff," Ream said.

"I'll take some undies," Smiley said. "You peck-
erheads can take the ones with the razors and
shaving mugs."

"I'm not going to take them," Big Nose said.
"Give me corsets and nighties."

They sure got to arguing about it, and I finally

said I'd load them two trunks on my nag and walk him to town.

"That's some horse, Sheriff." Thistlethwaite said.

"None of your lip," I said.

I collected the two leather trunks and managed to tie them so they hung to either side of my saddle, and started walking, while them rannies accompanied me. The horse behaved himself, mostly because I was leading him. I hated to think what might have happened if them cowboys watched me mount that miserable nag. The gossip would never quit. It was a regular parade back to Doubtful, with the Anchor Ranch rannies each carrying a satchel or two, and me walking that Turk nag. Little did they know what I was carrying.

We got back to the sheriff's office, and the rannies loaded the stuff inside. Rusty was sitting in there, smoking cigars and knocking the ash onto the enameled tin box that held the guncotton, which made me turn green.

The cowboys grinned and retreated. They didn't much care for local lockups, where they had spent more than a few hours.

"I thought you were out pretending to be a posse," Rusty said.

"I went to the site and found them bags," I said. "Had to bring 'em in."

"Why? Those show people are gone."

"Them bags are evidence," I said. "I'm thinking maybe the entire Grand Luxemburg Follies is a gang of thieves. Maybe even Ambrosia. Maybe those are her undies."

Rusty, he thought I was crackbrained.

"The stagecoach robbers missed some loot, because it was scattered through all those bags wrapped in oilcloth."

Rusty knocked more ash on that enameled box.

"Dammit, Rusty, you carry that box and that flask to the last cell and put them on the bunk. And leave your cigar right here."

Rusty yawned, carried them two bombs to the rear of the jailhouse, and resumed chomping on his stogie. He tapped ash onto my desk, and settled into my chair, looking smirky.

I went out to Jesus Mary Joseph and untied the bedroll behind the cantle and carried it in. I weighed an extra twenty or thirty pounds with all that paper wrapped in there.

I undid all the ties on my bedroll while he watched lazily, deliberately yawning to let me know what he thought of his boss.

I stretched the bedroll on the grimy floor and slowly unrolled it until there were five oilcloth-covered lumps of something or other, and then I undid these. Rusty, he quit puffing and started staring. The first of them oilcloth caches revealed a stack of fifties and twenties, crisp green and brand new. The second doubled that. The third revealed a mess of tens and fives. The fourth a bunch of singles and twos.

"Where are the three-dollar bills?" he asked.

"Smartass," I said.

"We could retire," he said.

"I sure hate to give them to Sanders," I confessed. "But I guess I have to."

"Delphinium will kiss you."

"Rusty, you're fired. You can't say something like that to me and expect to keep your miserable job. Get a pad and a pencil. You're going to count these."

"You can count it yourself," he said.

"I only got ten fingers."

We set to work. By Rusty's count there was seven thousand, four hundred and fifty-two dollars in there.

"You've rescued Doubtful," Rusty said. "But couldn't we spend a little over at Rosie's palace of a thousand delights?"

"Maybe Delphinium and Hubert will give us a reward."

"Am I fired yet?"

"Go fetch Sanders. I'm gonna sit here and guard these with my life."

"You could get them out of sight, you know."

That was a good idea. I emptied the undies out of a satchel and loaded up all them bills and took them back to the rear cell and set them down beside the black enameled case with the guncotton, and the flask of blasting oil, and then locked the cell door.

It must have took some doing to get Hubert Sanders to come in, but eventually he showed up with Rusty. He sure looked haggard, and had great hollows under his eyes.

"He was playing with his revolver and aiming it at his ear," Rusty said.

"What's the meaning of this?" Sanders said.

"The metropolis is rescued," Rusty said.

I steered the angry banker to the rear cell and unlocked it and retrieved the satchel and carried it to the front office and handed it to him.

"What on earth is this? I've never seen this satchel in my life."

I sure get tired of bankers now and then. I unbuckled the thing and shoved it at him. He dipped his fingers in there like he was expecting them to get burned, and pulled out some fifties.

He studied them, and studied the satchel, and poked around in there, and stared.

"Where's the gold?" he asked.

That's what I admire about bankers.

"We're working on it," I said.

"Why didn't you get this to me sooner? What's it doing here? Why didn't you bring it to the bank? Is this all of it?"

I showed him Rusty's accounting.

"Yes, that's the currency, but where's the gold? You didn't do your job. Where did you get this?"

"It was in the undies."

He jerked his hand from the bag.

"Go give Delphinium a kiss," I said.

He stared at me like I was some kind of worm, which I am. Rusty relit his stogie and smiled.

CHAPTER THIRTY-THREE

It didn't take but a few minutes before a mess of them officials trooped in. Hubert Sanders was leading the pack, and right behind him were Puma County's virtuous politicians, Reggie Thimble and Ziggy Camp, along with Mayor George Waller, and Lawyer Stokes.

It was the attorney who started the grilling.

"Where'd you get this?"

"In the undies," I said.

"Where's the gold?"

"I haven't the faintest notion, but I think I know who got it."

"Who got it?"

"Your former employees Ike Berg and Luke the Butcher."

"Why haven't you arrested them?"

"Well, it's on my mind."

"You don't have a mind. Go get them."

"Wait!" said Sanders. "I need him here to guard

this cash. I have no safe. Its door won't shut. These bills are naked to the world."

"You could store it in a jail cell until you get a new safe," Rusty said.

"I don't want bedbugs eating the new fifties," Sanders said.

"You just give it all to Delphinium," I said. "She can tuck it down her dress and no one will ever get it."

"Thimble, fire that man," Sanders said.

"Actually, that's a good idea, Hubert. You just give the bills to Mrs. Sanders and they'll be safe as Gibraltar," Reggie Thimble said.

"That's the first intelligent thing ever to issue from Pickens's mouth," Ziggy Camp said.

"My ma used to say that nothing could ever get into a whalebone corset," I said. "Of course she was talking about men."

"You've insulted my wife," Sanders said.

"Well, she'll keep all them fifties warm," I said. "Nothing like hot money."

The banker knew we had a case, but Stokes had another idea. "We'll give it to the postmaster. Alphonse Smythe has a small lockbox."

"You could keep it in the rear cell, next to the guncotton," Rusty said.

"Guncotton!"

"Yep, guncotton and blasting oil, taken off of the late Jardine. If he'd been shot ten inches lower, it would've blown up the robbers."

"Why isn't it three miles out of town?" Stokes asked, real lawyerly.

"Maybe some drunk will polish it off," Rusty said. "He'll think it's Old Crabapple. Schnapps. He could blast himself to smithereens if he lights up a cheroot."

"Guncotton? Doesn't that stuff blow if someone looks at it cross-eyed?" Camp asked.

"I'll show you," I said, heading toward the cells.

"I'm getting outta here," Thimble said.

"So am I," I said. "I have to find them two and get the gold."

"Oh no, you don't. I've got no place to keep it secure. You wait until they deliver a new safe to my bank," Sanders said.

"You don't want me to fetch Iceberg and the Butcher in?"

All them politicians, they just stared at each other.

"You don't want me to arrest them? Get the gold they took?"

"Of course we do," Camp said. "Arrest those crooks and get the gold back."

"You should have done it already," Thimble said. "You've done a half-assed job. That's been the whole trouble with you all along. If you'd done it right, you would have come back with all the loot, not just part of it."

"You want to join my posse?" I asked.

"I'm sure you can manage, Pickens."

"I'd like you and Lawyer Stokes on my posse," I said. "Politicians make the best posse of all."

"What for?" asked Lawyer Stokes.

"So you can talk Iceberg and the Butcher into giving up."

"Yes, I'd be excellent at that," the attorney said. "But I have a lame knee and can't ride more than a few minutes."

"I've got bursitis of my elbows," Ziggy Camp said. "Doc Harrison tells me not to board a horse for the next three years."

"I'm subject to seizures on horseback," Reggie Thimble said. "It's the saddest thing. I get onto a nag and get all seized up. Doc Harrison says it's congenital."

"I need to keep Doubtful prosperous and moral," said Mayor Waller. "What would Doubtful do without me?"

With that, them pols quit me and headed into the bright day.

Rusty, he was smirking at me.

"Guess I'm still a one-man posse," I said.

"Before you go, you got any notion of how all this worked?" Rusty asked. "We got greenbacks, a blown safe, undies, and guncotton."

"I don't know yet. It looks like Jardine slid out of a show when most of the town was in the opera house, and cracked the safe, and hid the cash in those satchels of undies, and the gold in the false bottom of the boot."

"You think that whole company was crooked?"

I got up and pulled gray undies out of them bags. "These are just rags or spares. I don't think these belonged to anyone at all except Jardine," I said.

"Are you an expert on undies?"

Rusty had me there, but I seen a bunch of my ma's, and they were cleaner because she washed them regular.

"These here are grimy," I said.

"Showgirls are grimy," Rusty said.

"No, not Ambrosia. She was clean. I think showgirls aren't grimy. Too many people would see the dirt. You can't expose acres of grimy flesh."

"You got me there," Rusty said.

"I think Jardine owned all of these satchels and trunks, and he told people they were all for spare clothing for his show, but he really wanted them to hide his loot."

"Didn't work this time. He's dead. Iceberg figured out where he kept the gold and they got it and didn't hardly look for the greenbacks."

"Iceberg's real smart," I said. "He got ahead of me on Jardine. I thought the little twerp was up and up."

"Yeah, and you thought Iceberg was up and up."

"I never laid claim to smart," I said, feeling tetchy.

"You going out now? Get the gold?"

"I'm the posse. It's not the gold that gets to me. It's two murders, killing my horse Critter, which is pretty near a third murder, and robbing me and the stagecoach and all. If I get the gold, that's fine. But whoever killed Critter, he's going to swing."

That reminded me that Turk's miracle horse was still tied to the hitch rail.

"I'll see you around," I said.

"I've got to watch this," Rusty said.

"No, you don't. You go play with the guncotton. Get yourself blown to bits."

I stepped out and eyed that yeller broken-tooth nag, and looked him over real good. He stared back and yawned. I anchored my bedroll behind the cantle, and decided I was as ready as I'd ever get. So I untied the reins and stepped aboard, and he took off, crow-hopping, whirling, bucking, lifting me straight out of the saddle and letting me crash down just when he was coming up again. I was hurting, and thought I'd get pitched half up the office stairs. I was getting a little put out.

"Jesus Mary Joseph!" I hollered.

The miracle horse quieted right down. The nag rotated his ears back, checking to hear any further instruction. Rusty, he just shook his head and went back inside to flirt with the nitro.

Turk's nag swung his head around and gave me the eye, and then we trotted smartly out of town.

I took him out that same road and when we got to the robbery site, I began running circles, looking for hoofprints leading in and out of there. It was pretty dry and hot, and I didn't scare up much at first, but I kept spiraling outward and finally did connect with some faint tracks out of the north, maybe up around Douglas or Casper or somewhere over there. There sure was a mess of open country around there, and looking for them two bastards would be like hunting mosquitos.

But then the tracks began to curve west, and finally southwest toward Medicine Bow County, where Sheriff Ike Berg once was the law. There appeared to be three sets of prints, one with narrow hooves, probably a pack mule. So Berg was heading for home turf. I wondered if he was still sheriff down there. I hadn't heard a thing.

That sure was a lonely ride. I was working toward a gold sunset through a vast land, with distant mountain ranges and arid flats sliced by washes where anyone could hide. A feller who wasn't watchful could get into trouble fast. In fact, a watchful feller could, too. In that country, human beings were ants crawling over a giant land.

I lost the trail now and then, when cattle stomped it out, but I knew where them two was heading. Medicine City, Ike Berg's old haunt, where he was sheriff for years. Maybe he'd got his job back after trying for mine. That was a horrifying thought. Ike Berg had gone bad, and he never had been good. I kept on going, heading for Medicine City now, and not worrying about hunting down hoofprints. I crossed the line somewhere in there, and now my Puma County badge was no good so I pocketed it. If Berg was wearing a star, he'd have the law on his side, such as it was. In Medicine Bow County, he was about the only law around, so he always did what he felt like doing.

It was a long, lonely ride, and I wished I was back in Doubtful and enjoying a nice day at the jail. I rode straight over a long hogback and descended into the broad valley where Medicine City slumbered. It mostly catered to ranch owners. It was just about the deadest place in Wyoming. It was half desert and half jackrabbit. The people there all tried suicide after a few months, and some succeeded. Thanks to Berg, there wasn't even a saloon, and the only restaurant in town opened for lunch and then quit so the owner could go home for supper. There wasn't even a church because no one felt the need. Someone in Medicine City had an alkali spring and bottled the water as a tonic. That's how the town got its name. It was supposed to improve the bowels and bring a little color to the flesh. The population of Medicine City was growing a bit because word got around that it cured melancholia. All them that felt blue gravitated there, hoping to improve, but once they got there they discovered they was no different than anyone else. It'd been ten years since anyone happy had lived in Medicine City.

I rode in there to the sound of silence. Even the June breeze kept its mouth shut. There wasn't a mutt around, but maybe I could find a black widow spider. Medicine City had no small children, so it had no schools. Women were scarce. I rode straight down the main drag, since there wasn't hardly no side streets. Medicine City was just a single stretch of false-front whitewashed wooden structures, plus the town cemetery that was mostly empty and full of weeds. Half them structures had nothing in them but packrats. But down at the far end was the log courthouse of Medicine Bow County, and a stuccoed-up jailhouse that was where Ike Berg sheriffed, or used to. He might be in there, so I looked around real sharp before I steered that livery stable nag over to the hitch rail.

If he was in there, I was going to arrest him and ditto for the Butcher, and it didn't matter that my star was no good here. I didn't know how I'd get them back to Puma County, but I would. I tied up that nag and eased toward a barred window and peered in real quick. There was some fat fellow sitting in there, his boots on the desk, his spurs dug into the top. It wasn't anyone I was looking for, but maybe that was good. I saw a square badge on him, the kind mostly wore by deputies. That was good, too.

So I meandered in there and took the measure of the man, who eyed me like I was a tarantula.

"I'm looking for Ike Berg," I said.

"Not here."

"Where is he?"

"Took a leave."

"He the sheriff?"

"Imagine so; he ain't said otherwise."

"You seen a blocky fellow known as Luke the Butcher?"

"He ain't around either."

"What's your name?"

"Ernest Howitzer."

"I'm, ah, Cotton Pickens. Sheriff over in Puma County."

"No, you ain't. You're a horse thief."

"What are you talking about?"

"That there horse. That's the best known horse in Wyoming."

"That's a Turk's Livery Barn nag."

"No, that's Jesus Mary Joseph, and you've took him. You're under arrest."

"Took him! Turk rented him to me."

"You stole the most famous horse in history."

He had a six-gun out and aimed at my bellybutton almost before I could get a handle on what was happening.

"Get in there," he said, nodding me toward the single iron-barred cell.

This wasn't the way I thought it'd play out.

CHAPTER THIRTY-FOUR

I gave that feller the evil eye. My ma used to give me the evil eye, and it reduced me to butter every time. So I stared at him without a blink, fixing my glare right on his fat carcass.

"You know who I am? I'm the sheriff of Puma County. And if you discharge that piece in my direction, you'll swing."

He wavered a moment.

"I'm going to reach real slow inside my shirt pocket. And I'm going to pull out a star. And I'm going to pin the star on my shirt."

I did so, wondering if the beebee-brain would shoot. But he didn't. And pretty quick he saw the star that said Sheriff Puma County Wyoming on it, and slowly lowered his piece.

"How come you got that horse? There's a reward for that horse," he said.

"That's news to me," I said.

"I've always wanted to ride that horse. I've heard about it for three years. That horse has started more bar fights and saloon brawls than any horse alive."

"You want to ride him? Let's go out and you can ride him."

Howitzer looked hesitant. "He sort of kills, don't he?"

"Yep."

"He sort of bites, don't he?"

"Yep."

"When you land on the saddlehorn your privates are done for, ain't they?"

"That's the horse, all right."

Howitzer sighed. "I'm a fool," he said.

He arose from his chair and we headed out to the clay road, and I undid the reins from the hitching post and handed them to him. He looked a little green, but he was game.

He stepped aboard, and that nag erupted like nothing I'd ever seen before, crow-hopping, whirling, knocking Howitzer upward, and meeting him coming down, just one bad crash after another.

"Jesus Mary Joseph!" Howitzer yelled, and that miracle nag, it quit right there, midair, and a couple seconds later that horse was the gentlest piece of horseflesh in Medicine Bow County. Howitzer rode him up and down and around, and the horse responded instantly, just as sweet as it gets. Finally, Howitzer rode him back to the rail and got off and tied the reins to the hitching post, shaking his head.

"I've been waiting all my life for that," he said. "Now I got a story to tell. But no one will believe it. That's the trouble with this town. No one believes anything."

He headed back inside where it was cooler, and we settled down.

"You want some java? I could make some."

"It gives me the fits except early in the morning," I said.

"Sends me to the outhouse," Howitzer said.

"You the law here now?" I asked.

"Yep. Until Sheriff Berg gets back, but there's some wondering if he will. He put me in charge and took off and said he was taking a break for a few weeks, and that's the last anyone's seen of him. So I'm it. I've got the whole county and I don't even have a deputy of my own. So I keep office ten hours a day and there's no law the other fourteen."

"That's the way law should be," I said. "My theory is that criminals should all do their stuff by daylight so everyone can sleep at night."

Howitzer sighed. "No one's even woke me up since I've been filling this chair."

"Well, maybe Medicine Bow County's got no criminals in it."

"That's an entertaining idea," he said.

"I'm looking for a gent named Luke the Butcher. I've got a score to settle with him."

"Oh, him. He was in that cell there, and one day Ike Berg let him loose. I've never seen him since."

"What was he in for?"

Howitzer laughed. "You name it, you got it."

"And Berg let him out?"

Howitzer just sighed. "In one day, out the next."

"Was he actually a butcher?"

"That's his trade. But he got to carving on a lot more than beef. He cut the ears off some rancher he didn't like, and killed a few cows."

"Rustler?"

"Oh, sort of. Mostly he wanted supper and if one wasn't on a plate in front of him, he went off and butchered his supper."

"Did Berg ever say why he sprung him?"

"Nary a word, Pickens. Ike Berg, he just kept his mouth shut. He never spoke more than two words to anyone. He just ghosted around the county, and maybe still is. He's my boss. He could take my badge back."

"Did he say where he was going when he left?"

"Nope. He was the quietest man around."

"If them two show up here, would you mind putting them in that cell?"

"You got warrants?"

"Nope, but I got a grudge or two. And if I rattle the Butcher hard enough, I'll shake a couple of murders out of him. Over in my county."

"Why do I believe you?" Howitzer asked.

"He butchered my horse. So I'm looking to butcher him."

"What am I gonna do about that horse out there? There's a five-hundred-dollar reward for him. Down to Laramie, that's where the owner is." He showed me a reward sheet with a description of the miracle horse in large print. That was the horse, all right.

The bad thing was, I wanted to keep him. He was my kind of horse. Except for Critter, I never had a better one. But if the nag was stolen, I plain couldn't keep him.

"You got a horse for me? One I can give to the livery-barn man in Doubtful?"

"What are you looking at?"

"You give me a real good horse, you take this one and get him back to the owner and collect your five hundred. You buy yourself a new horse."

"You mean you won't ride him down there yourself?"

"I got things to do," I said. "The horse you give me's got to be as good as that one out there. It's going to the livery man who rented that one to me. And I want that dodger so I can show him it was a stolen horse he couldn't keep."

Howitzer stared outside, stared at the nag, stared at me. "All right, dammit," he said.

"And you write it up good," I added. "And I'd better like the one you're going to give me or it's no deal."

He wrote out a bill of sale for a three-year-old gelding, in that curvy longhand.

"You mind reading that to me?" I asked. "My eyesight is a bit weak."

"I, Ernest Howitzer, sell a three-year-old red roan gelding with a slash-Q brand on left thigh to Sheriff Cotton Pickens," he read.

"Let's go see your nag."

We hiked over to a place with a weathered sign that said HORSES BOUGHT AND SOLD, BOARDED AND RENTED, RAMBO MCCOY, *Prop.*

There wasn't hardly anyone in there, and not many nags either. Medicine City was giving me the willies. Howitzer headed for a stall with a strawberry roan in it, bridled him, and backed him out. It was a decent-looking nag except for a roman nose. The deputy saddled him up and handed the reins to me.

I looked at the hooves first, and the hocks. An unsound horse wasn't worth beans to anyone. This one was well-shod, had no hoof cracks, no splints, no trouble that I could see. I got onto him, and rode him away from the stable, and the nag didn't fight me. I rode him up that desolate main drag, and the horse moved along, shifting gaits when I put heel to flank, and at the edge of town I settled him into a lope for a while. He wasn't smooth, and bounced me some, but he'd do. So I took him back and shook hands with the deputy. We switched saddles, and I was fixing to ride out of that cussed town when I saw a nag in the pen in the back that plain shook me. I swore I was studying Critter. I walked out to the pen and eyed that beast. He was younger, maybe a three-year-old. He sure stabbed at something in my heart.

"You know anything about him?"

"He's mine. Greenbroke, just started."

"He looks like one of mine, got killed a while ago."

"Klled?"

"Throat cut by Luke the Butcher."

"You know that for sure?"

He had me there. I didn't know it for sure. "Nope," I said.

"You want that one?"

"I can't afford a horse now. I got robbed in Doubtful and I might not have a job for long."

"He's yours if you want him."

I started to shake my head, but Howitzer pressed on. "Take him. I'm collecting the five hundred reward, and that's enough to buy me two good horses and have half left over."

I stared at that young critter, feeling real strange. It was like maybe I'd betray the real Critter if I took this one.

"Ride him if you want," Howitzer said.

We saddled him up, and he was sort of dumb, but I didn't mind. I pulled and hauled him around for ten minutes. He didn't pitch. He was eager. Next I knew, I had another bill of sale in hand and a horse that might turn into a new

Critter if I was lucky. That new one wouldn't replace Critter; nothing could. Critter was one of a kind. But we have to get past what we've lost and get on with life, and this new one might work out.

I got another bill of sale out of Howitzer, and he threw in a halter and a lead rope, and I was ready to ditch that place. I wouldn't recommend Medicine City to anyone except maybe Hubert Sanders. In fact, I thought I'd tell him to move his bank over there.

"Deputy, if you see Luke the Butcher around here, would you send for me?"

"If you want him, I'll make sure you get him."

"I do," I said. "Real bad."

We shook on it.

I eyed that yellow miracle horse, which was still tied at the hitch rail.

"You're not worth five hundred," I said.

Jesus Mary Joseph yawned.

I rode out of Medicine City leading the horse, wondering if I should call him Critter. I decided I'd wait. The real Critter was real ornery, and if this one wasn't I sure wasn't going to give him the same name.

I didn't find my quarry around there, but I'd keep looking. Somewhere around there was a crooked sheriff and a common criminal. I kept a sharp eye out, but knew my chances were pretty slim. The strawberry roan was a good horse, and Turk would be pleased to get a trade for the stolen nag. It would be two days of hard riding to get back to Doubtful, and I'd have to find a meal somewhere or ride on a real empty belly. I got into the rhythm of it, eating up the miles. Wyoming was a big and good land, with great arid flats and forested mountains. I got as far as the Puma County line that day, camped at an alkali spring that would clean out my innards, and spent a hungry night while the horses grazed on thin, short grass around the spring. The next dawn I got off fast, knowing it would be a hot day and Wyoming could turn into a frying pan fast. Them days I'd just as soon move to Canada.

So I took off at first light and we covered ground fast until mid-morning, when it got heated up and the horizons shimmered and the horses began to drag. I kept going at a real slow pace, and made it to Doubtful early afternoon, while it was so hot that not even a dog was out.

Rusty, he was sleeping in my chair, and woke up with a start as I came in.

"How'd the posse go?" he asked.

"It didn't," I said. "What's new here?"

"The new show, Royal Arabian Nights, came in. And Ambrosia's in it. She said she hired on as a harem wife."

"She's gonna be wearing something this time?"

"Not much. They open tonight and we can find out."

I remembered the playbills plastered all over Puma County, announcing Sheik Barbousse, his fourteen wives and twelve eunuchs, belly dancers, sword-swallowers, fire-eaters, jugglers, and the Masked Executioner. There wasn't anything like that ever come to Doubtful before. I mostly wanted to know how all them wives shared one sheik. It must have wore the fellow out.

I sucked up some fresh water and led them nags over to Turk's Livery Barn. He saw me coming and stared at one nag and then the other.

"Jesus Mary Joseph was a stolen horse," I said, "but I got you another."

It took some explaining and I showed him the flyer. He eyed the strawberry roan, rode him a little, accepted the bill of sale, and nodded. That was as much of a thanks as I'd ever get out of Turk. He'd done real good. I arranged to board the colt.

"He looks like Critter, all right," Turk allowed.

"I ain't named him yet. If he's as ornery as Critter, I might call him Critter. If he ain't, I'll name him Apples. Making apples is all he's good for."

"You catch any criminals?" Turk asked.

"They're still loose," I said.

"Maybe the new show's full of 'em," he said.

"I'm going to fetch a nap and then find out," I said.

Turk, he was smiling real evil.

CHAPTER THIRTY-FIVE

Soon as I got back to Belle's boardinghouse she was after me for back rent.

"I'll pay you as fast as the county pays me," I said. "I got them greenbacks to the bank, and they'll soon go into pay envelopes."

"Yeah, and what about the gold? You let that slide through your fingers."

"I haven't seen a double eagle yet, but when I fetch the gold, you'll know about it."

"Yeah? When you get that gold, I'll eat my shirt."

"If I don't get it, I'll eat my underdrawers."

"Is that a promise?"

I thought I'd better back out. "They ain't fit for eating," I said. "They don't get washed but once a month. But I'll eat one square inch."

She smiled and patted me on the cheek. That was Belle for you.

I hardly got rested before it was showtime at

the opera house, so I dragged myself out of my bunk, spruced up, and headed toward Ralston's place. Sure enough, the Watch and Ward Society was back, trying to shut down the new show. And there was Delphinium Sanders leading the charge, waving a big hand-lettered sign. And she had all her biddies and a few male biddies with her, too. But the ticket line was full. Them cowboys didn't pay much heed to her, and they were stepping right up to the ticket window and buying. I guess Sanders had got the greenbacks out around town fast, because there was some cash showing now, after the town pretty near starved for a few days.

Delphinium Sanders spotted me near the box office and whacked me over the head with her sign.

"Take me! Arrest me!" she said.

"I think you should be in the harem scene," I said.

She assaulted me again with her sheet of pasteboard, while the people in line were elbowing one another and enjoying the show.

"Take me away from this vice! This town is a cesspool," she said.

"I'd like to see the bellydancers," I said.

She whacked me again. She was getting real serious about getting hauled off.

"You wouldn't want to sit in a cell with bedbugs and guncotton and nitro in it," I said.

"What's that?"

"You could blow yourself up, and half the town."

"If that's what it takes— Arrest me."

"You'd like to see all them eunuchs in there," I said.

"What are they?"

"Beats me. Maybe they're lacking a few parts."

"Well, so are you. Namely, brains."

She was trying real hard to get hauled off, but I just ignored her. I headed in, and found the opera house mostly filled up and ready to go. Just because I was sheriff, I headed through a door at the side which would take me backstage and watched for a while, enjoying them harem wives and belly dancers, and some feller dressed up as Sheik Barbousse. What I wanted to see was the Masked Executioner, but he didn't show up. I supposed he was down in his dressing room sharpening his scimitar. But I got a look at the fire-eater and the sword-swallower. They sure were peculiar. Oh, them harem girls were pretty, with big gauzy white pantaloons and little vests with a mess of gold braid and not much under them except pure girl. They wore real colorful stuff, too, oranges and reds and golds you hardly ever saw on the street. One feller had a green pillbox on his head. I wanted to see them eunuchs, but so far they were all hiding. Maybe they were the orchestra. I peered out of the curtain a little, and saw a few fellers in red fezzes tuning up a bunch of stringed instruments that I'd never seen before, along with a drummer and a rattle-shaker. I figured musicians could all be eunuchs easily enough, and I'd probably see them again in the big harem scenes.

They were all ignoring me. But then some feller in a robe of Araby, or whatever they wore, he lit all the footlamps, until the reflectors were tossing light onto the stage, and then the orchestra whined away. That's the only word I could think of. Them players were whining out Arabian music. Whenever one came backstage, I planned to ask him what a eunuch is. Maybe they were men with horns. Who could say?

Just then I stared at a harem girl and she stared back.

"Ambrosia!" I said.

"I'm not Ambrosia any more. I'm Zelda Zanadu."

"How come?"

"We ran into this company in Laramie. They wanted girls, so I hired on."

"You're in the harem scene?"

"Lissen, Sheriff, I need to talk to you. There's trouble around here and I'm scared."

"Well, fire away," I said.

She peered around fearfully and motioned me to the stage door leading to the alley, and we stepped outside into the summer twilight.

"You know when we were robbed? When Jardine was killed? I got a good look at one even if it was only by lantern light. He had a way of walking. He was sort of square, and muscular, and heaved the bags off the coach, and was sort of taking orders from the thin one with the reedy voice."

"The Butcher," I said.

"He's hired on, too. He's the Masked Executioner."

"Here? In the show?"

"Yes, and I'm the virgin tonight."

"You couldn't be."

"The girl who refuses to marry the sheik and gets beheaded."

"Beheaded?"

"It's a stage trick. The head is papier-mâché with a wig on. He brings his sword down and then picks up the head. Only he has to be real careful, you know? I mean, he has to do it just right. And he knows I know who he is. The robber of Jardine's coach. He's been staring at me ever since we both joined. And . . ." She started shaking. "I'm afraid. It'll look like a horrible accident."

"Listen. I'm staying right here. When he comes out, I'll collar him even before the scene. Maybe it'll mess up the show, but I'm going to lay my hands on him and drag him out of here before you lose your head and he's calling it an accident."

There were tears in her eyes.

"I'll do my best. But if there's trouble, head into the audience, don't stay backstage. Get out where it's safe. Right there with the cowboys."

"You're not sure?"

"I'd like some help but there ain't any. He's a tough little thug."

She thought about that, and then we slipped back into the theater. The curtain had gone up on a line of harem girls and the juggler, who was tossing three balls all over the place. It sure was different, watching from backstage. I could see them gals and the juggler, and the band was sawing away, and then there was a dance done by the harem girls and then a belly dancer came out. She sure had a lot of belly showing, I never seen so much belly, and them skirts riding her hips, and a lot of bare upwards from there too, and then she was rotating around and behaving like someone about to lose her dinner, but that changed into something never did see before, a woman sort of, well, I can't find the words for it, but she shouldn't be doing it on a stage in front of a mess of cowboys. It wasn't a bit proper. She was doing stuff with her belly that made me think Delphinium Sanders was dead right.

Not that the cowboys could do anything about it. Cowboys all have ruint themselves on horses, which is why they never get married. A woman in with a mess of cowboys is safer than anywhere else on earth. Cowboys have no children. You ever heard of a son or a daughter of a cowboy? It's not known.

Then came the sword-swallower, and I swear that little freak pumped about a foot of steel blade down his gullet, and looked like he'd spill blood all over the planks, but somehow he got it out safe, and no one clapped. Not one cowboy liked sword-swallowers. I didn't much care for the act myself. But then came the fire-eater, and how that feller, dressed up in gold braid, could blow flame out of his mouth like that I'd never know. He just lowered that flame down in there and sent a plume of it at the audience. Danged if I could figure it out. I'd have burnt myself to ash, cooked my tongue, and cracked my molars doing what he did. How could anyone eat fire, anyway? He must have been hot-tempered. My ma told me to blow out the candles on my birthday cake, not swallow them.

I just stayed there backstage, watching everything, and no one seemed to mind. Once in a while I could see all them cowboys, but it was pretty dark. This show wasn't as well lit as the Follies. Next was the big harem scene, and I crowded close as I could to get a good gander at all them ladies. They were sprawled out there on big pillows and divans, wearing gauzy pantaloons and little vests with a lot of themselves showing. They were mostly just lying around awaiting the sheik, but there were some fellers dressed in big diapers and turbans waving fans at the gals. That was a good idea because it was hot, and the fellers in diapers were stirring the air real good.

I finally figured out those gents were the eunuchs, though no one told me what one of them was or how he got that way. But they mostly waved their fans and pretended not to be interested in the ladies, and I thought maybe I was missing something, and I'd have to ask what one was. Maybe Lawyer Stokes would tell me if I asked him. Meanwhile, the musicians were sawing away on the string instruments, until at last Sheik Barbousse came trotting out. He was a fierce customer, all right, with a lot of black hair, and gold pantaloons and bare arms and a white vest sort of like the ones worn by the ladies. But now he circled around, eyeing them women, who were all seeking his attention. Man, he was a lucky feller, and I thought maybe I'd like to be a sheik. Some of them got up and began pawing him, and smiling, and showing a lot of teeth, and the music gets bigger and bigger until finally there's a clear winner, a babe with long brown hair, real curvy, and the shiek smiles, grabs her by her topknot and hauls her away.

That got a mess of applause, but I wanted to know what the sheik and that lady were doing, but when I got over there they had parted. I thought maybe the way they'd gotten steamed up they would retire somewhere, but it was nothing but show, and that's why show business is nothing but a big fraud.

Then there was a clash of tambourines and drums, and some feller with a turban was saying that this maiden had refused the sheik's hand in marriage for a thousand days, and now she would be taken to the wooden block on stage and beheaded for resisting the sheik. Well, that was pretty entertaining, and the audience got real quiet, and then Ambrosia stepped out, looking real scared, dragged by two of them big eunuchs. I shouldn't call her Ambrosia because she was Zelda Zanadu now, but anyway they pushed her down on the chopping block so her neck and head's over the edge, and out comes the Masked Executioner, and he's got a great big scimitar, one of them steel blades with funny lines to it, and he's swinging that thing around real bad. And I took a close look, and it's Luke the Butcher behind that mask, and maybe he's gonna kill the witness who figured out who shot Jardine, so I went after him. I grabbed one of them ostrich-feather fans and headed toward him, and the whole audience rose up and cheered as I moved in on the Masked Executioner. He sure was slinging his big blade around. It whipped past me, back and forth, clipping ostrich feathers, and he was driving me back offstage, and I was circling around looking for my chance. That blade was mean, and it was real, and its sharpened edge glinted in the footlights. And the Butcher knew how to use it, too, as he drove me backward. Everyone out there recognized Sheriff Pickens, and they were howling. This was the best entertainment they'd ever seen. But I didn't have time for any bows because the Butcher was trying to separate me from my head, and his blade slashed real close to my neck.

There was a lot of hubbub backstage too but no one came out to help me. That glinting blade swung back and forth and I edged back. He had me. Then two things happened. I tripped on something, and Zelda Zanadu grabbed the Butcher by the leg and twisted, putting him off balance. He staggered, his blade ran wide, and I rolled up and into him, and grabbed that arm waving the scimitar around, and now it was me fighting for my life. There's nothing like a swinging broadsword to inspire a man, and I just boiled into a frenzy and pretty soon I got the blade out of his paw and was pounding on him real hard, and all them cowboys were cheering, and Zelda Zanadu was on her knees biting the leg of the Masked Executioner.

He didn't give up easy and landed a kidney punch on me, but I pressed a forearm into his neck until he gagged, and finally it was over. I got him. Out there the audience was standing and clapping and cheering, and they thought I was the star of the show, and the best act at Ralston's opera house.

I hauled that bastard to his feet. I'd got the killer of Critter, the killer of Jardine, the killer of the advance man Pinky Pearl, the feller that mugged me, and one of the fellers that robbed the stagecoach.

"Get on with the show," I said to all them eunuchs. "The beheading's over."

CHAPTER THIRTY-SIX

Backstage, I patted down that piece of wormy beef, and found two more toad-stabbers on him, and then hauled him to his feet.

There sure was a lot of hubbub around me but I paid it no heed. "Get on with the show," I said.

The audience was tearing up the place, standing and hooting, but then Ralston went out on stage and them cowboys quieted a little.

"That was the best act we've ever seen," he said, "and it starred our own sheriff. And now we'll go to the next, the juggler."

Ralston caught me as I dragged that lout through the stage door, and he simply patted me on the back. I nodded. There were a lot of unspoken things being said between us.

I hauled that chunk of rotten meat to the jailhouse, with a fistful of shirt holding him up, and he staggered along. Rusty wasn't around, but I didn't need him. I tossed Luke the Butcher into the chair in front of my desk.

"Talk," I said.

He eyed me, getting a little cocky as he studied me.

"Where's Iceberg? Where's the gold? Who'd you kill? Who put you onto it?"

The Butcher yawned, smiled, and settled down for the fun.

"Why'd you kill that advance man, Pinky Pearl?"

The Butcher had started to sweat, and his slimy shirt was getting soaked. He just stared, not showing me his gap-toothed mouth.

"Why'd you kill my horse?"

The Butcher smiled.

"Why'd you rob me on the street?"

The Butcher started cleaning his fingernails.

"Why'd you kill Jardine? Who put you up to it?"

The Butcher's face began to drip, and sweat was running down his cheeks.

"Where's Iceberg? Where's the gold?"

He began to smell real bad. He didn't ever smell right, but now he started to stink like a rotten carcass.

"That gal was a witness. She knew you'd killed Jardine. So you was going to cut her head off right there on stage and vamoose."

The Butcher, he laughed a little.

I could see this was going nowhere, and I was feeling a little impatient. So I grabbed him by the shirt again, wary of him now because he was halfway recovered, and I dragged him back to the second cell and tossed him in and locked the door.

"Now talk," I said.

He sat down on the bunk and yawned.

"See that over in the next cell? That's Jardine's guncotton and blasting oil. I took it outta his suitcoat. If you'd shot him a little lower, we'd have picked up your pieces and planted them."

That caught his attention. Sure enough, there in the next cell was a small flask of the nitro, and the tin of guncotton, sitting real quiet.

"Safest place in town to keep that stuff," I said. "But I tell you what. I'm going to put a bullet into that guncotton, and it'll blow that nitro, and you'll be chipped beef."

"You wouldn't."

"Try me."

"But you'd kill yourself."

"Try me."

I lifted my six-gun and shot at the wall a few feet left of the nitro. If I blew myself to kingdom come, I didn't much care. The shot racketed loud and chipped some rock off the wall. The Butcher covered his ears and closed his eyes, and when he discovered he was still alive, he started shaking.

"All right, start yapping or I'll blow the place up."

The wormy beef was oozing out his lard.

"Why'd you mug me?"

"Iceberg put me up to it. He wanted a crime wave."

"He wanted to be sheriff here?"

"That banker's wife, Delphinium, she wanted to get rid of you."

"She put him up to it?"

"She told him to employ any means but don't tell her about it."

"Why'd you kill that advance man for the Follies?"

"To make a crime wave."

"Make a crime wave? You'd kill a man for that?"

The punk didn't say nothing.

"You killed my horse."

"Yeah, that was easy! Got your goat, didn't it?"

I fired another round, this time missing his head. The racket scared the crap out of him.

"You killed Jardine."

"He was really a safecracker. He blew the bank safe in the middle of his show."

"Where's the gold?"

"Iceberg double-crossed me. He's gone."

"Where's the gold, dammit?"

I pointed my revolver straight at the flask of nitro in the next cell.

"Don't!" he said. "I don't have it. Iceberg don't have it, either. The bank's got it back. Delphinium's got it."

"You telling me that Sanders got that gold?"

"You messed everything up, and Iceberg's on the lam."

I wasn't making a whole lot of sense of it, but it didn't matter much. "Where's Iceberg?"

"He and Delphinium are going to take off with the gold. She can't stand Doubtful and she can't stand her old man."

"Say that again, dammit."

"She and Iceberg, they're in love. They're going to ditch Doubtful and live somewhere nice like Cicero, Illinois."

"Where's he right now?"

"How should I know?" The Butcher was getting annoyed, now that I hadn't blown him to smithereens.

"What does that woman see in that man?"

Luke the Butcher smiled this time. "They hate mating. They hate lust, and they want to spend their life together hating lust and attacking evil."

"Does her husband have the gold?"

"Naw, she's got it, and Iceberg's got it. He took it out of the boot."

"And missed the bills."

"He didn't care. He got what he wanted."

"Delphinium."

"Some people got bad taste," the Butcher said.

That was all I needed from that buzzard. I left him in the cell, where he could contemplate his own death, and I headed into the night. They'd be building a gallows for that one soon enough. I locked the front door of the jailhouse tight, just in case Iceberg was floating around. I didn't know where to find him, but I had a notion the bank gold was out in that carriage house on Sanders's place on the north edge of town.

Delphinium was sure entertaining. She'd set in motion mayhem and murder, and for what? To put me out of office and clamp Doubtful in her own moralistic vise. If that twice-stolen gold was there, I'd be putting her in the other cell, which would probably terrify the Butcher even more than nitroglycerin. Delphinium was sure a strange lady.

The place was dark. I rattled the front door, waited, and rattled it again. No one showed up. I circled around the building in moonlight, and hollered a few times. The windows upstairs were open to the July breeze, but no one answered my call. I thought maybe something was very wrong, and decided it wasn't smart to stand around in moonlight, so I headed for the carriage house and peered in. The buggy was gone. And so was the dray. I studied the shadows, not seeing anyone. I began checking everything, the loft, the servant quarters, the stalls, quietly poking around for gold. Harness in the harness room was gone. I lit a lamp and did a thorough search, and after an hour or so I gave up and returned to the house.

I tried again to raise someone, but no one answered, and I finally pushed inside, lit a lantern, and began a search. I didn't have far to look. Hubert Sanders, in his bathrobe, lay on the parlor floor, a bullet hole through his mouth. I tried to pump life into him, but he was dead. The last person to die from a bullet in the mouth was Jardine. So Iceberg had been here, and Mrs. Sanders, the buggy, the dray, and harness were all gone.

I lit more lamps in that dreary house. It belonged to the most prominent couple in Doubtful, and look what it had come to. Gold was only part of it. Mrs. Sanders was determined to spread her misery from one end of the earth to the other, and she'd found a willing ally in Iceberg, another of those persons who resented anyone who was cheerful or happy. Hubert shared some of that too, but he wasn't at the heart of this, and now he lay dead from a single shot through the mouth—like Jardine.

I turned Sanders over a little, and sure enough there was an exit wound. There'd be a bullet buried in a wall somewhere, and I'd find it, and maybe it would match the caliber of Ike Berg's revolver. I didn't see the bullet hole offhand, but lamplight isn't much good for finding things like that. I felt sorry for the man, mostly because he'd been stuck all his good and faithful life to a terrible mate, who never knew what love was or what good companionship could be.

The Royal Arabian Nights was just letting out. I could hear the crowds faintly on the summer breeze. Maybe Maxwell was still up. I needed Rusty, but he'd no doubt gone to bed. There's only so much two men can do when they have a whole sheriff's office to run.

I peered around there, wondering if I'd missed something, and it turned out that I had. The revolver on the parlor carpet gleamed dully. I picked it up. It had one shot fired from it, and it was real clean, left there by someone who liked to keep a weapon in prime shape. Like the sheriff of Medicine Bow County. I tucked it into my belt and hiked down into town, and found a lamp stil! lit at Maxwell's Funeral Parlor. I knocked real hard, and he opened the door, eyed me, and grouched, as I knew he would.

"Pick up Hubert Sanders. He's dead in his parlor. Delphinium's gone."

"Heart attack?"

"Murder."

That took the undertaker back. "No, not Hubert."

"He's dead, and a bullet did it. This is the weapon," I said. "You ever see it before?"

He looked a little pale. "Could be anyone's," he said.

"A thirty-eight caliber Smith and Wesson," I said. "With a short barrel."

The funny thing is that I didn't remember ever seeing Ike Berg wearing a sidearm.

"I'll get the hearse," he said. "He's king of Doubtful. It'll take a while."

"Get him with a one-horse wagon. I don't have time," I said.

"And who's paying?"

"Delphinium, when I catch her, and before she hangs."

"I heard there was a commotion at the opera house."

"You heard right."

He was waiting for more, but I wasn't of a mind to feed his lust for gossip.

"Well, this is a sad night," he said. "Another immoral show at Ralston's Opera House."

"Yeah, it really's a black eye on this moral town," I said.

I left him there, chewing on the evil that had come upon Doubtful. I had things to do.

First was to fetch Rusty from his slumbers and second was to go after the criminals in that buggy. That wouldn't be easy, but nothing ever was easy.

Rusty simply wouldn't wake up. He'd been on duty for days, and now he just yawned and muttered. I didn't know what to do; I couldn't leave Doubtful without a lawman, especially with a fresh murder. But then I realized that night riding wouldn't get me anywhere; I'd have to go after Iceberg and Delphinium by daylight.

I found Ralston in his dim-lit office. The theater had emptied. The troupe had gone to bed.

He reached for a small revolver as he entered, and then relaxed. "Glad you're here," he said. "You were the star of the show."

I told him that I'd nailed the Butcher and got

a confession out of him, too. And then I told him the rest. The banker dead in his parlor, Delphinium missing, the Sanders buggy and dray with her. Probably heading for the railroad.

"If I had a wire, I'd send a bulletin and every train in both directions would be searched. But I don't," I said. "Nearest telegraph's fifty miles away. The problem is, I don't know what direction they went. In the morning I might find iron tire-tracks heading north toward Montana."

Ralston stared, processing all that. "Hubert dead? I'm sorry. He didn't like my theater, but he was a good man, and his bank held this town together. Now Doubtful's in trouble. No bank. Its gold is gone. Maybe the bank's directors could keep it afloat, but not with half its assets heading out of town." He eyed me levelly. "Doubtful's doomed. My opera house is doomed. Without a solvent bank, not one business here is going to survive."

"I was going to get some sleep, but you just changed my mind for me," I said. "I'm heading out tonight."

CHAPTER THIRTY-SEVEN

I headed for Turk's, lit a lamp, and eyed that greenbroke beast in the stall, the one that might earn himself the name of Critter. This was going to be an entertainment. I eased into the stall, avoided a hoof aimed at my groin, pushed his head back when he tried to bite, and finally got a bridle over him and stuffed the bit into his miserable mouth.

He sawed his head up and down trying to spit it out.

Greenbroke was not exactly accurate. He wasn't hardly broke at all. But I got a saddle blanket on him and managed to avoid getting killed when he reared up and planned to pound me into the straw. But he was acting like a Critter all right, so I just saddled him up and drew the girth strap tight and led him out into the aisle to look him over. He clacked his big teeth at me.

"You're getting there," I said.

I led him into the yard, blew out the light, and stepped aboard. He stood real still. I nudged him with my boots. He refused to move. I slapped his croup, and he took one step.

"You ain't gonna ever be Critter if you quit before you start," I said. "You got a lot to live up to, and if you don't live up to your name, then you'll be stuck with Skunk. I'll name you Skunk, and you'll regret it the rest of your miserable life."

He turned his head clear back and eyed me, and sniffed, and then took a few tentative steps. We sawed around a little, but he was going the direction I aimed. I tried the brakes, and they worked. Maybe he was greenbroke after all. I'd see. Maybe he'd end up named Critter after all.

I was pretty tense. I headed for the lockup, loaded the double-barreled short scatter-gun into my saddle-sheath, checked on the Butcher, who was staring at me, and headed out. Rusty would feed him in the morning. I was a posse of one again.

I rode into a burst of moonlight. Behind me the wounded town of Doubtful slumbered. A light was lit at Maxwell's and the rest of the town was bleak and quiet—and dying. I didn't feel up to the task of rescuing a whole town, but sometimes we are given tasks that are bigger than we know how to do, and we've got to try.

I rode over to Sanders's place first, hoping to get a glimpse of the buggy tracks, but I couldn't make any sense of anything even with some moonlight. The only thing I had going for me was a hunch or two. Heading for the railroad was too easy. Iceberg wouldn't risk it. Getting on a train was too easy. Once telegrams got shuffled around, he and his partner in crime would get caught, somewhere, somehow. Where, then?

I turned Skunk north, and he didn't get the message and was inclined to head for Turk's, so I warned him again. "You better behave or you're Skunk, not Critter."

He rotated an ear back to catch all that, and then stepped smartly toward the north, where I wished to go. Maybe him and me would get along. I started thinking what a feller like Iceberg and a gal like Delphinium would do. I thought maybe they'd go wreck Casper. I could never figure out why Casper existed, and what anyone saw in the town, but there it was in all its plainness, finding some excuse to grow. Yes, that's where they would go. They'd set up shop in Casper and wreck it real good. Or maybe Douglas. That was a little better place than Casper, but you couldn't pay me enough to live in either one. Them two, Iceberg and Delphinium, they'd like a miserable town to ruin, and both fit the bill.

It proved to be a real nice July night, with lots of stars and a half-moon. I couldn't hardly get lost, and the night was so pleasant I didn't even feel real tired. Once in a while I stopped Skunk—he didn't want to stop but I have my ways—and climbed down and looked for iron tire-tracks. I couldn't see any, but that didn't mean much. There had been a fair amount of traffic on that dirt road, and there were hoofprints, wagon tracks, footprints, and a lot of cowpies too.

This whole thing was probably futile, but at least I felt like I was accomplishing something. Sometimes you got to start a trip without knowing where it will end. My ma, she called that faith. She was usually right about things. Me, I was inclincd to call it a wild-goose chase.

Skunk was settling into the trip, walking real pleasant. I think maybe he was liking this. It beat chewing creosoted posts in Turk's rear left-hand stall. Once I saw something bound across the road, and it looked like a wolf or a coyote, but it was gone in an instant. There was a whole life lived at night in the animal world, lots of critters that got their dinner while the moon was shining. After a couple of hours I was getting lonely, and unhappy because I hadn't packed anything to eat, and Casper was a long ways away. I was getting to the north end of Puma County, and soon enough my badge wouldn't be worth a damn, but that wasn't going to stop me. It might not have been hot pursuit, but it was pursuit, and I'd lasso that pair if I could.

A creek blocked the way, so I dismounted and added a little to the flow, while Skunk took a drink, and then we forded it and kept on riding north by west. That there creek flowed into the

North Platte. So we were moving along toward Casper.

The moon was clear over to the east by the time I got to the abandoned ranch on Little Gopher Creek. I knew about that place. It was a little north of the Puma County line. Bayer, its owner, tried raising crossbred cattle there in what looked to be a splendid grassy range, but it was loaded with jimson weed and the cattle kept sickening and aborting and failing to grow, and nothing he could do helped much. He finally quit the place, but only after he'd built a substantial log home and barn and pens. Even now, travelers sometimes made themselves comfortable there, but there was no glass in the windows and pack rats pretty much owned it all.

I headed up that road, thinking to rest a bit myself. I'd been awake for pretty much a full day, and needed a little shut-eye. It didn't take long for the old log buildings to rise up in the moonlight. July night wind eddied the air around, and that's when Skunk rotated his ears and shivered. I was real glad he kept quiet. I stopped him at once, and stood there, looking at the slumbering and silent old place, trying to get a sense of what had alerted the horse. Then I saw a horse in the pens. It was staring my way and might whinny at any moment. I slowly turned Skunk around and retreated into a cottonwood grove, and tied Skunk up. For good measure I collected the scatter-gun and edged toward the Bayer homestead. It sure was one of the pleasantest nights of the summer, with soft air and a deep peace pervading the whole country.

Sanders's ebony buggy gleamed in the moonlight. I'd seen it often enough.

A breeze made the leaves dance, dappling the ground with dancing shadows. It was all too peaceful there. I circled around, choosing a blind kitchen side of the old house to make my approach. The other sides had a wide veranda and a porch deep in moon shadow. That dray stared at me, but didn't whicker, and I thought I'd be all right. I began to figure out ways to make the pinch. I had one wrist manacle, and that was about it. But nothing is ever easy. I edged around real careful, testing boards that might creak, and studying on everything. It sure had been a nice place once. I could live there in the white moonlight.

I finally got around to the west side, and edged toward an open window. Moonlight streamed into the room and there they were, asleep. He'd made a bed of straw with a blanket over it. She had undone her hair, and now it fell loose over her white shoulders. The moonlight seemed to erase years from her body, making her smooth and young and maidenly. He lay beside her in the white light, looking younger himself. Her arm fell loosely over his back.

Their clothes were stacked off to one side, and his holster lay nearby, but not within easy reach. Now all this was the most astonishing thing I ever did see in all my life, and I wasn't ready for it. These two were a thousand miles from where they were before, and in a different world from the one they had inhabited. They looked so young, like they were in their twenties, and newly wed. In their sleep, they seemed utterly at peace.

Instead of enjoying this capture of a pair of killers I found myself dreading it. I stood there stupidly, wondering what to do next. Them two and the Butcher had done a world of harm to Doubtful, and the town would die most likely because of it. But there they were. I never dreamed that Delphinium Sanders could be beautiful, but in that soft, ethereal light she was prettier than any woman I'd ever seen, even more than Ambrosia.

The thought of her, and how she'd almost lost her head just to keep her silent, finally galvanized me. I slipped back from the window and worked around to the door frame, which now lacked a door. I readied my scatter-gun and then raced into that room. I'd get there before Iceberg could get himself together and reach for the holster.

And it was easier than that. They had awakened, but neither had moved.

They saw me, saw my scatter-gun.

"I knew it would come to this," Iceberg said.

She didn't say anything. Neither did she try to cover up. She just lay there looking up at me, from eyes that had seen a whole new world.

"I've got to take you in," I said. I reached over and collected his holster and the revolver in it.

That sure was an awkward moment. They were my prisoners. so I couldn't give them privacy, but they didn't seem to mind. They slowly got up and dressed, even as the eastern heavens began to lighten. It was just before dawn. Then, after she had laced her shoes and stood, he kissed her, and they turned to face me.

"It was worth it," she said. "Whatever happens to me, it was worth it for this one night of joy."

What was likely to happen to her was a hanging, but I didn't say so. It might depend on who shot her husband, and whether she had been a part of it. That would be for the court to sort out.

I motioned them outside and into a serene dawn, one of those summer dawns when the whole world is hushed and waiting to leap into splendor. We headed out to the buggy.

"Harness the dray," I said.

Iceberg nodded. He eyed my shotgun briefly, knew I was well aware of possibilities, and set to work. I eyed the buggy briefly. As I expected, there were some canvas sacks in the box behind the seat. I lifted one and found it heavy, and peered in. A mess of gold coins glinted up at me.

Iceberg slid a bridle onto the draft horse, and then a collar, and then he tightened a surcingle and ran the lines back. It took a few minutes for him to finish the task and back the horse to the buggy and hook him up. Delphinium watched quietly. I wished she had pinned her hair up, but she let it flow loosely about her shoulders, and that unnerved me. I wanted her to return to her old ways, but she had no intention of it.

Iceberg finished and awaited instructions. I thought maybe to manacle his right wrist to her left one, but I saw no need. If they tried anything at all, I'd do it.

"Get in and drive to Doubtful," I said. "I'll be following along.

There were a bunch of birds trilling their hymns to the newborn day. A red-winged blackbird cheered. A dove cooed. Iceberg snapped the lines over the croup of the dray, and it started obediently, picking up a brisk pace while I rode beside. I didn't expect trouble. This pair, which had imposed their own sullen hurt upon the world around them, even to the point of death and mayhem, had been transformed. Yesterday Iceberg would have tried to kill me. Today Ike Berg was resigned to his fate, and oddly at peace. Whatever had happened, it was too late to save them. There would be a reckoning back in Doubtful. They knew that, and somehow accepted it, or at least were resigned to it.

I was tired and that was a long, long drive, but we kept on going. We watered at creeks, but I had no food for any of us, and except to rest the horses we kept right on, past the county line, through basins and ranges, around lonely highlands, past a few two-rut ranch roads, like ants crawling across the universe.

They didn't talk much, but sometimes they held hands, and I had nothing to say to them. I had all three now: Butcher, who'd killed two people and my horse and robbed me; Iceberg, who'd wanted to be sheriff and strangle Doubtful to death the way he'd strangled other towns; and Delphinium, who'd set it all in motion with her loathing of what she secretly yearned for. When I thought about what they'd done I quit feeling a little tender toward them.

That was just about the longest ride I'd ever had. I felt Skunk grow real weary under me, but he kept on going, like Critter. The dray pulling the buggy was wearing out, too, partly because that buggy was loaded with a lot of gold.

"Skunk," I said, "you've passed the test. From now on, you're Critter."

The horse didn't object. In fact he just continued to be annoyed by all the work I was putting him to, and dropped a few apples.

We got into Doubtful late in the afternoon, and I steered them toward my sheriff office. Rusty, he saw us coming and rushed outside.

"Get them explosives out of the other cell, and if you blow yourself up do a good job of it," I said.

He rushed in, and I watched while Berg helped Delphinium out and helped her walk into my lair. I put down a carriage weight and hefted some gold and brought that in. Rusty, he had parked the guncotton and nitro on my desk, and was taking them two prisoners down to the other cell, while the Butcher watched, amazed. I watched Rusty lock up the lovers and then he helped me haul all that back-busting gold inside.

"What's the story?" he asked me.

"They discovered life too late; that's all there is to it," I said.

CHAPTER THIRTY-EIGHT

Well, I still have a job. And they even raised my pay by five dollars. The whole town was real glad to see the gold back in the bank along with the greenbacks. And glad to see the three in jail that started all the trouble.

The directors named our Mayor, George Waller, president of the bank, and he got the doors open real fast, and it was business as usual. There's money in Doubtful. They buried Hubert Sanders real good, with lots of wreaths and speeches, and the bank paid the freight.

Rusty, he is no longer a deputy. I appointed him undersheriff, with a two-dollar raise, and he's happy as can be. I'm looking around for a couple of deputies now, not my old ones who aren't worth spit.

The trial's coming up and I don't know who'll swing and who won't. There's some feeling about Delphinium. She set the trouble in motion, but didn't really know what sort of kindling she'd touched a match to. It was Iceberg's gun that killed Sanders. I'd guess the jury will spare her, but give her some time in the pen at Rawlins where she can think about undoing all the trouble she started.

Ralston's opera house is doing just fine. That Royal Arabian Nights show packed them in, especially after I starred in the beheading act. Ralston told me that was the first show that made some money for him. When it left town, it traveled safely up to Casper, and that's the last I heard of it. I never did see Ambrosia again, or Zelda Zanadu, when she hired on to that show, but that's how it is with show people. You can make friends with them for a few days, and away they go and you never see them again.

The next show rolled in on schedule, and I'll see it one of these days. It's called Joe Gibson's Flora Dora Girls, and it's mostly comic sketches and a lot of dancing by ladies with big hips and skinny waists. I might fall for one or two of them ladies, too, but I'll know it will be real temporary.

Ralston's opera house sure changed Doubtful. All sorts of interesting people started coming to town and entertaining us. We all heard new music, heard good jokes, listened to pretty interesting orchestras, watched some new dance steps, and got taken on little trips whenever a scene was set somewhere like New York, or Paris, or Tahiti. There was a regular circuit for these shows, and

there were comedians like Eddy Foy who went
from town to town making people laugh, or
singers like Jenny Lind who warbled away, and
got every randy male in the audience dreaming
of a cottage with lilacs and children.

So I have to thank Ralston for all that. Instead
of a town full of bored cowboys looking for trouble on Saturday nights, we have become a town
brimming with entertainments. In fact, because
of Ralston's opera house, Doubtful is booming.
There's people moving here just so they can enjoy
all the troupes that come rolling through town.

I think he's doing all right, too. His problem is
not getting customers, but getting shows to come
to a small town like Doubtful, and sometimes he
has to guarantee them a minimum gate, and if he
doesn't make the minimum he has to fork over
some of his profit.

The bank got the new safe installed real fast,
and could store the money again. Me, I'm still at
Belle's boardinghouse, and on my dresser are
them explosives we took off of Jardine. That
guncotton is still in its enameled box, and the
blasting oil is still in the flask. Maybe some day
I'll have cause to use that stuff.

GREAT BOOKS, GREAT SAVINGS!

When You Visit Our Website:
www.kensingtonbooks.com
You Can Save Money Off The Retail Price
Of Any Book You Purchase!

- All Your Favorite Kensington Authors
- New Releases & Timeless Classics
- Overnight Shipping Available
- eBooks Available For Many Titles
- All Major Credit Cards Accepted

Visit Us Today To Start Saving!
www.kensingtonbooks.com

All Orders Are Subject To Availability.
Shipping and Handling Charges Apply.
Offers and Prices Subject To Change Without Notice.